T0353002

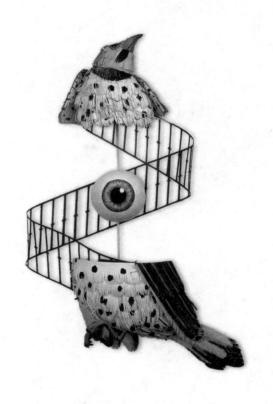

Also by E. Lily Yu

On Fragile Waves

JEWEL BOX

STORIES

E. LILY YU

EREWHON

An imprint of Kensington Publishing Corp.

www.erewhonbooks.com

EREWHON BOOKS are published by:

Kensington Publishing Corp.
119 West 40th Street
New York, NY 10018
www.erewhonbooks.com

Special book excerpts or customized printings can also be created to fit specific needs. For details, write or phone the office of the Kensington sales manager: Kensington Publishing Corp., 119 West 40th Street, New York, NY 10018, attn: Sales Department; phone 1-800-221-2647.

Erewhon and the Erewhon logo Reg. US Pat. & TM Off.

ISBN 978-1-64566-048-4 (hardcover)

First Erewhon hardcover printing: October 2023

10 9 8 7 6 5 4 3 2 1

Printed in the United States of America

Library of Congress Control Number is available upon request.

Electronic edition: ISBN 978-1-64566-051-4 (ebook)

Edited by Sarah T. Guan
Cover art by Christine Kim
Cover design by Samira Iravani
Interior design by Leah Marsh

To Mary Elizabeth Hanlon
with affection and respect

Contents

JEWEL BOX

The Pilgrim and the Angel

Three days before Mr. Fareed Halawani was washed and turned to face the northeast, a beatific smile on his face, he had the unusual distinction of entertaining the angel Gabriel at the coffeeshop he operated in the unfashionable district of Moqattam in Cairo. Fareed was tipped back in his monobloc chair, watching the soccer game on television. The cigarette between his lips wobbled with disapproval at the referee's calls. Above him on the wall hung the photograph of a young man, barely eighteen, bleached to pale blue. His rolled-up prayer mat rested below. It was a quiet hour before lunch, and the coffeeshop was empty. Right as the referee held up a yellow card, a scrub-bearded man strode in.

"Peace to you, Fareed," the stranger boomed. "Arise!"

Fareed laughed and tapped out a grub of ash. "Peace to you. New to the neighborhood?"

"Not at all. I know you, Fareed," the stranger said. "You pray with devotion and give generously to the poor."

"So does my neighbor," said Fareed, "though that hasn't helped him find a husband for his big-nosed daughter. Can I get you a glass of tea?"

"The one thing you lack to perfect your faith is the hajj."

"Well, with business as slow as it is, and one thing and another . . ." Fareed coughed. "Truth is, may God forgive me, I'm saving up to visit my son. He's an electrician in Miami. Doesn't call home. What would you like to drink?"

"I have come to take you on hajj."

"I've got too much to do without that," Fareed said. He had quarreled half the night with Umm Ahmed over their son, whose lengthening silence his wife interpreted as pneumonia or incarceration or death, though Fareed supposed it was simply the cheerful thoughtlessness of the young. He had washed six stacks of brown glasses caked and swirled with tea dust, his joints sour from four hours' sleep, before unrolling his shirtsleeves and sitting down to his soccer match. But for the rigorous sense of hospitality that his own father had drummed into him, nothing could have stirred him from his chair, his chewed cigarette, and the goals that Al-Ahly was piling up over Zamalek. His bones clicked as he stood. He reached for a clean glass.

But the angel spread his stippled peacock-colored wings, which trembled like paper and made the room run with light, and said again, simply, "I am taking you on hajj."

Fareed choked on his cigarette. "Now? Me? Are you crazy? I have customers to care for!"

Gabriel glanced around the deserted shop and shrugged, his wings dipping and prisming the walls. Then he vanished. The prayer mat propped against the wall fluttered open and enfolded Fareed. While he kicked and expostulated, it carried him headfirst out the door and into the clear hard sky, to the astonishment of a motorcyclist sputtering past.

"Sir! Sayyid! Are you djinn or demon?" Fareed called out. "Where are you taking me? What have I done?"

"I am taking you on hajj!" the angel said joyfully from within the rug, his voice muffled, as if by a mouthful of wool.

"If you are taking me anywhere," Fareed said, struggling against the tightening mat, "make it Miami. And you have to get me home by midnight. Umm Ahmed will worry, and I have to shut up the shop." He finally freed his arms from the grapple of the prayer mat. Below them, the countryside zoomed by, green and very distant. Fareed blanched.

"I can circle the globe as fast as thought," said Gabriel. "Of course we'll have you home by then."

"Perhaps a little slower, I have a heart condition," Fareed said, but they whistled up like a rocket, and the wind hammered the next words back into his throat.

WHEN HE DARED to look again, the silver trickle of the Delta flared below them. Then they were gliding over the shark tooth of the Sinai and the crinkling, inscrutable sea.

"This is really not necessary," Fareed shouted. "If I sell my shop I can buy an economy-class Emirates ticket to Jeddah tomorrow. You can send me home now."

"No need to sell your shop!" the angel said. "No need to wrestle suitcases through the airport and sit for hours with someone's knees in the small of your back. No need to worry."

"Right," Fareed said miserably.

By the time they reached the Arabian Peninsula, the dry, scouring wind had become unbearable. "Water," Fareed croaked. "Please, water."

"So spoke Ishmael in Hagar's lap," Gabriel said within the

mat. "She had nothing to give him but prayers and tears. But I heard her crying out. I struck the ground with the tip of my wing, and water poured forth."

"Water!"

"Yes, water as clear and cool as glass. That was the well Zamzam. I shall take you to drink from it."

Fareed groaned a sand-scratched groan, then shut his eyes and muttered over and over the suras of the dying.

"Here we are," Gabriel said, what felt like hours later, lofting a red-faced Fareed onto a heap of sand. "That's Juhfa in the distance. Come, put on your ihram."

"What ihram?" Fareed said.

But as he spoke, a bright, cold stream boiled up from the ground, and the prayer mat unraveled and wove itself into two soft white rectangles, which settled like tame doves at his feet.

Fareed gulped the sweet water, washed himself as well as he could, then peeled off his shirt and trousers and wound the white cloths about himself. The stream receded as silently as it had sprung up, the dark stain it made in the sand drying at once to nothing.

He had barely caught his breath when his white drapes shut like a fist and lifted him high into the air.

Wonders upon wonders, Fareed thought. But why him? Why an indulgent father, an inattentive husband, whose kindnesses were small and tea glass sized? Why would any angel bother himself with someone so unworthy?

Guilt niggled at him like a pebble in his shoe as he sailed over towns and sandy wastes. He could see Umm Ahmed rolling her eyes and shaking her head, hands on hips. *Angels? You say angels took you to Mecca? This is why you left the shop unlocked and unwatched? What kind of a layabout husband did I marry?*

You want me to call you Hajji now? Are you kidding me? It filled him with a terrified kind of love.

"What am I going to tell Umm Ahmed?" he moaned.

"The truth! That your piety and prayers have been recognized. That Gabriel himself has led you on pilgrimage."

"She will throw shoes at me," Fareed sighed.

"Look," the angel said, as if he had not heard. They were descending through glittering skyscrapers and moon-tipped minarets. The Grand Mosque loomed before them, a wedding cake of marble that stunned Fareed to speechlessness.

He had always imagined making the pilgrimage as a fat and successful old man, cushioned by Umm Ahmed's sarcastic good humor and Ahmed's bright chatter. Now he had neither. Loneliness shivered and rang in him like a note struck from a bell.

Fareed barely had time to stammer the talbiyah through parched lips as they flew around the Kaaba, once, twice, seven times, his body cradled in the unseen angel's arms. His mumble was swallowed up in the susurrus of prayer rising from the slow white foam of pilgrims below. Fareed knew he was in the presence of the divine. He was humbled.

"Here is your Zamzam water," the angel said. A plastic pitcher ascended to them, revolving slowly. Fareed grasped it and drank.

"Now hold tight," the angel said, although Fareed had nothing to hold on to. The pitcher tumbled away like a meteor. "Over there is the path between Safa and Marwa, paved, enclosed, and air-conditioned now. Very comfortable and convenient."

"I don't suppose—"

"No! We shall take the path as Hagar found it, the hot noon-day sun beating upon her head. Think: your child dying in exile. Think: how strong her faith, how deep her despair."

Fareed and the angel swooped seven times over the crenellations and cascades of white marble. As they hurtled over the walkway, dry air whipping their faces, Fareed imagined the rubble and grit below the elaborate masonry. He saw in his mind a thin dark woman plunging barefoot over the stones, tearing her black hair, her child left beneath a thornbush to suck thirstily at shadows. He thought of Umm Ahmed's reddened eyes and weary, dismissive waving—*leave me alone, my son is gone*—and of the phone that shrilled and yammered all day but rarely spoke with his son's voice. The image he held of his son was the photograph of Ahmed in uniform, taken during his mandatory service, when he was still a boy and anxious to please.

"Now—" the angel began, but Fareed spoke first, flapping his arms as he hung in the air.

"Enough! Enough!"

"But you haven't—"

"Give me my clothes and my shoes."

"Your faith is incomplete without the hajj," Gabriel remonstrated. "What answer will you give the other angels when they question you?"

Fareed felt cold despite the thick sunlight. His chest tightened. "Where are you taking me?"

"On hajj."

"No. Take me to my clothes."

The angel swerved out of the mosque. They returned to the desert place where his shirt and trousers lay folded beside his shoes. Only a little sand had accumulated in the heels. As Fareed stooped for them, his ihram fell away and became once more his threadbare prayer mat.

Beside him, the angel coalesced into a bluish glow containing edges and angles and complex, intersecting wings. Only the vaguest suggestion of a face shimmered in the chaos. He was painful to behold.

"Shall I bring you home?"

Fareed straightened, dust swirling and settling in his damp garments and sweat-sticky hair. A decision crystallized on his tongue. "If this is real and true, and I am not dreaming—if you are truly an angel and no evil spirit—then you will please take me to see my son."

"After all of this? After I brought you in my arms to the Honored City, to Masjid al-Haram itself—you want to go to America?"

"Especially after all of this," Fareed said. "If you are capable of these marvels, you can transport me to Florida as well."

The angel extruded a finger from chaos and curled it around his chin.

Fareed said, "Hagar burned and tore her feet as she ran in search of water for her son. Did you not hear her weeping?"

"That I did."

"And out of pity for her and her child you caused water to flow from barren rock."

"That is true."

"Then perhaps pity will move you to carry me to Miami," said Fareed. "I have not seen my son in three years." He folded his arms. "I did not ask you to come. I did not ask to be taken on hajj. I did not ask to be hauled out of my shop without so much as a note to my wife."

"Also true."

Fareed put one hand over his breast, where a dull ache was growing. "So take me to see my son. This once. It's the least you could do for me. Considering."

Deep inside the blue matrix of the angel, polygons meshed and disentangled with a sound like silver bells.

"All right, enough, let's go," Gabriel said, dissolving. "Back on the prayer mat with you." The rug rose from the sand and hovered an inch above the ground, undulating smoothly.

Fareed looked at it and made a small, quiet, unhappy noise. He resolved that if he ever made it home, he would buy a new, less willful prayer mat, perhaps one of the cheap ones with a pattern of combs and pitchers that were made on Chinese looms.

ROLLED UP IN his prayer mat, Mr. Fareed Halawani of Moqattam, coffeeshop owner and pilgrim, came to an abrupt halt in front of the Chelsea Hotel in Miami. The carpet snapped straight, and Fareed spun once in the air before hitting the manicured lawn.

His son turned away from his pickup, shouldering a wreath of wires. He wiped sweat and wet hair out of his eyes, blinking against the sunlight and the mirages wavering out of the pavement.

"Dad?" he said, surprised.

Fareed stared up at the blue sky, bottomless as the one over Cairo, and listened to the strange, extravagant hiss of the lawn sprinkler. A single defiant dandelion bobbed above his nose, drifting in and out of focus. His stomach was still roiling from the rough flight across the Atlantic.

"That's it," Ahmed said, putting the back of his hand to his forehead. "I'm seeing things. I'm going crazy."

"You could pretend to be happy to see me," Fareed said.

"You can't possibly be here. You can't. I must have heatstroke."

"Go drink some water. I'll still be here when you get back."

His son extended a browned, broad hand and flinched when Fareed grasped it. But he helped his father to his feet.

"Do you believe me now?" Fareed said.

"What are you doing here?"

"Visiting you. You don't call home often enough."

"How did you get here?"

The prayer mat lay meekly upon the grass.

"An angel brought me, I think."

"An angel."

"Maybe an ifrit, it was horrible enough. We went to Mecca first, then came here. I insisted."

Ahmed stared. "Are you all right?"

"Of course I'm all right."

"Did you hit your head? Do you feel feverish?"

Fareed frowned. "You think I'm lying."

"No, I—" Ahmed shook his head. "I've got a job to finish here, okay? You can come with me while I do it, then we'll take you home and I'll—we'll figure out what to do with you." He picked up his black toolbox in one hand and offered the other to his father.

"I don't need to be supported," Fareed said. "I feel fine."

The truck's tires squealed as they pulled off the highway onto a narrow, shaded road. Beards of gray moss trailed from the trees and brushed the top of the truck. Ahmed lived in a pleasant white box, its postage-stamp lawn planted with crimson creepers and edged with large, smooth stones.

"No visa, right?" Ahmed said, unlocking the door. "No passport?"

"Nothing. Very unofficial, this visit. But I don't think you have to worry about getting me home," Fareed said. He felt the rug twitch in his arms.

His son's house contained only things that were bright and new: chairs and tables in colorful plastics or upholstered in triangle prints, a glass bookcase stuffed with calendars and phonebooks, two photos in chromium frames on the wall. One of the photos was of Fareed, his wife, and Ahmed, taken seven years ago in Alexandria. The other photograph—

"Who is she?" Fareed said, nudging the frame so it hung askew.

His son flushed. "She's, I met her, ah, a few months ago—"

"I see."

"A year, actually," Ahmed said, looking away. "She's really nice. Very sweet. Really."

"Does she cook well? Is she a believer? Are you engaged?" Fareed stared at the picture. "Does she have a name?"

"Rosa." Ahmed shifted from one foot to another. "What do you want for dinner? I could make some fuul—"

"You do know your mother and I have been trying to find you a good Egyptian girl? Aisha's a sensible woman, thirty-six, steady job at the bank—"

"That isn't necessary."

"Apparently not." Fareed raised an eyebrow at Rosa, who beamed innocently from the frame. "You might have told us."

"I was going to."

"When was the last time you called, anyway?"

"I've been busy," Ahmed mumbled.

"I can see that."

"Business has been good."

"I'm—glad," Fareed said, glancing around the small room. The odor of newness filled his nose and made his chest twinge.

"Midnight," the angel whispered in his ear, faint as a breeze. "Five hours. You'll make a mess if you stay, you know. Hospital bills, no identification, no papers."

Fareed clasped his hands stiffly behind his back. "So, Rosa. Do I get to meet this woman?"

His son's silence hurt more than he expected.

"Is it my clothes? I'll change—"

"No."

"You can translate for me. Shouldn't she meet her fiancé's parents?"

"Fiancé? She's not—" Ahmed flung up his hands. "It's too complicated, Dad. Listen. If you paid someone, to bring you here—"

"I didn't," Fareed said quietly. "You have nothing to worry about. I'll be gone soon." He paused, studying his son. "If I let you do what you wanted when you were younger, it was out of love. Not wanting to see you caged up. I wonder if that was wrong of me."

"It was fine." Ahmed began to open and shut the cabinets.

Fareed sighed. "Do this for me," he said. He had spotted the black telephone on the counter, winking with unspoken messages, and now he lifted up the handset and held it out to his son. "Call your mother tonight. Just one phone call. Just one. She misses you. She needs you."

Ahmed hesitated, then nodded reluctantly.

"Don't worry about dinner. I should go."

"No, stay, please. I'll cook for you. You'll be impressed."

His son was different and strange in this house, taller and stronger than the boy Fareed remembered. He had worked confidently at the hotel, snipping, stripping, splicing, and now he conjured up knives, pans, chopping boards, a blue gas flame with the casual swiftness of experience.

To Fareed's surprise, Ahmed, who had never cooked or lifted a finger at home, made fuul with eggs and lemon-sauced lamb on rice. After cleaning the last crisp speck from his bowl, Fareed wiped his mouth on the back of his hand and pushed back from the table.

"It is very good."

Ahmed fixed his eyes on the floor, embarrassed.

"Two daughters," the angel said. "Three years apart. One will have your strong chin. One will have Umm Ahmed's singing voice."

"Call your mother," Fareed said. "And give Rosa my regards. I should be going." He glanced toward the sofa, over whose arm he had draped the prayer mat. A corner of the cloth fluttered, although there was no breeze in the room.

IN THEIR SMALL flat in Moqattam, in the hours before dawn, Umm Ahmed rubbed a track in the floor with her pacing. Dinner had gone cold on the stove and moved uneaten into the fridge. The coffeeshop had been empty and unlocked. She had groped blindly over the lintel for the spare key and found it untouched, checked the register and found it still full. A thoughtful patron had turned off the television on his way out, though the ashtrays and water pipes still trailed gray ribbons in the air. Through the dimness of the shop the picture of Ahmed in fatigues, long faded to blue ghostliness, gazed down on her.

No one knew where her husband was. No one had seen him since morning. No one knew what had happened. She dropped into a kitchen chair, exhausted, and put her head in her arms. Stars and green neon lights glowed outside the window. Automobile engines roared through the night. She had the sinking sensation of being perfectly alone.

Then, on its cream-colored cradle, the phone rang and trembled, rang and trembled.

"Hello? Ahmed? Habibi, it's been so long—how could you—how are you—?"

Outside, like a scrap of burnt paper, her husband's prayer mat, wrapped around a dark, heavy form, drifted down to their doorstep.

The Lamp at the Turning

FOR TEN YEARS THE STREETLAMP ON THE CORNER OF COOYONG and Boolee kept vigil with the other lamps along the road. They were surrogate moons for an age when the moon itself was too distant and dim to guide travelers in the night, and they performed their duties faithfully and with pride in their high purpose. With the rest of its battalion, the streetlamp opened its one eye when night fell and shut it in the gray hours of morning. When it rained and water pooled in the gutter it could sometimes see itself, swan-necked and orange and not, it thought, unlovely.

Besides the quiet presence of the other lamps, it had for company a seagull who would perch on its head and gossip about his chicks and in-laws and the rubbish heaps he had visited. Sometimes a migrant with brilliant feathers would bring news from far-off countries. There was very little the streetlamp wanted that it did not have.

One morning in autumn, as the leaves were beginning to crisp and curl, the streetlamp saw a young man in a red jacket walking along Boolee. It knew the people who passed it every day juggling cell phones and briefcases, dragging groceries, jogging, and it had seen him often before, but this time it noticed the sunlight flashing off the facets of his watch and glasses and the electric currents that oscillated through and around him, sinoatrial node to atrioventricular node, nerve to nerve, silver oxide battery to shivering grain of quartz. It pondered his fluttering damp hair and fluted ears and how he held himself with the careful gravity of the young pretending to be old. After he vanished from sight the streetlamp found itself hoping he had forgotten a book on the kitchen table or left the stove on, so he would turn back and it could watch him a few minutes longer.

In the park across the street the elms and oaks were browning at their tips; magpies conferred and conspired in the grass. Now and then a car or bicycle chortled by, ripping the air with its wheels. None of these things interested the streetlamp any more. It was impatient for the evening and the migration of office workers and clerks homeward, the young man among them.

It lived now for the moment early in the morning when he hurried up Boolee, his shirt neat, his hair combed to velvet, and for the moment in the afternoon or evening when his shadow preceded him down Cooyong. The night and day seemed miserably long, the other streetlamps dull and unfeeling. Even the conversation of the gull, when he dropped by, became tiresome.

For a month the streetlamp marked its mornings and evenings by his footsteps. It wanted him to meet its orange eye and understand that it loved him with every wire and soldered synapse of its being. Instead of snapping to attention with the rest of the lamps, it waited until it saw him before it flickered on.

Though he worked long hours in the office and came home at irregular times, the streetlamp always watched for him. When he passed he would glance at it with curiosity but without slowing his step.

Finally, one night when he had stayed at the office until seven, he paused beneath the streetlamp, which had lit up as soon as it saw him. He put his hand on its metal post and said, "You wait for me every day, don't you?"

The streetlamp thought it would short out for happiness. It watched him go with brightness in its heart, and long after the heat of his hand had dissipated it remembered its shape and pressure.

He didn't stop again after that, but when he passed by he nodded at it as though to say hello, and sometimes he would smile. Sometimes the streetlamp winked at him. There were mutters of disapproval along the street, and even the seagull said it was a bad business, but nothing could perturb the streetlamp's profound joy.

One evening the young man was not alone. A woman with hair braided to her waist walked beside him, and she looked at him the way the streetlamp looked at him, as if she wished a spark would jump between them. The streetlamp felt a black, sputtering anger in its circuits.

They stopped on the corner under the streetlamp.

"This light always goes on when I walk by," he said. "See?"

She tilted her head to meet the streetlamp's gaze. On the surface of her pupils it saw two points of orange light, and below that, secret and sad, a loneliness like its own.

"It must be in love with you," she said.

"That's cute."

They went on, their heads bent toward each other, talking but not touching. Once she glanced back at the streetlamp.

The winter went by quickly. The streetlamp grew icicles and lost them but hardly felt the cold. Twice each day it saw the man in the red jacket turn the corner, and that was all the summer it wanted. If he coughed on the sharpness of the air, or if his face paled in the wind, it only made him more beautiful to the lamp, and it flung its light lovingly around his shoulders, as though to warm him.

Then a day came when the young man should have gone to work but did not. He did not pass the streetlamp in the evening, nor the next day. It waited for him, keeping its sodium tubes dark well past midnight and bright well past noon, but he did not appear.

A few weeks later, the woman came and stood under the streetlamp, her hands in the pockets of her leather skirt, her green scarf shivering in the wind. Her eyes were smudged and dark.

"He's gone," she said. "New job, different town. I thought you might want to know."

She touched the base of the streetlamp with one gloved finger and was gone.

SPRING CAME, AND the furred buds along the branches of trees burst softly into bloom. One day the town's electric company drove their van up the street and parked under the streetlamp, which had stopped lighting up at all.

"This one's a mess," one of the electrical workers said, examining the paper on his clipboard. "Been erratic all winter."

"What's it done?"

"Turned on and off at odd times."

"That shouldn't be possible."

"I want a look at the photoelectric control."

They removed the panel at the base of the street light and cut out the small box from its entangling wires. A small sigh moved the air, but it was impossible to say where it came from, whether the watching streetlamps or the trees. The electrical workers did not hear.

"You're right, it's dead."

"Got a spare?"

"Right here."

They scraped, knotted, snipped, then gathered their red-handled tools and left.

When the sunlight slanted and faded into darkness, all the lights on the street flashed to life at once, like a string of stars fallen to earth. A seagull rowed by on black-tipped wings, but not finding anyone it knew, flew on.

The Cartographer Wasps and the Anarchist Bees

FOR LONGER THAN ANYONE COULD REMEMBER, THE VILLAGE OF Yiwei had worn, in its orchards and under its eaves, clay-colored globes of paper that hissed and fizzed with wasps. The villagers maintained an uneasy peace with their neighbors for many years, exercising inimitable tact and circumspection. But it all ended the day a boy, digging in the riverbed, found a stone whose balance and weight pleased him. With this, he thought, he could hit a sparrow in flight. There were no sparrows to be seen, but a paper ball hung low and inviting nearby. He considered it for a moment, head cocked, then aimed and threw.

Much later, after he had been plastered and soothed, his mother scalded the fallen nest until the wasps seething in the paper were dead. In this way it was discovered that the wasp nests of Yiwei, dipped in hot water, unfurled into beautifully accurate maps of provinces near and far, inked in vegetable pigments and labeled in careful Mandarin that could be distinguished beneath a microscope.

The villagers' subsequent incursions with bee veils and ket-
tles of boiling water soon diminished the prosperous population
to a handful. Commanded by a single stubborn foundress, the
survivors folded a new nest in the shape of a paper boat, provi-
sioned it with fallen apricots and squash blossoms, and launched
themselves onto the river. Browsing cows and children fled the
riverbanks as they drifted downstream, piping sea chanteys.

At last, forty miles south from where they had begun, their
craft snagged on an upthrust stick and sank. Only one drowned
in the evacuation, weighed down with the remains of an apricot.
They reconvened upon a stump and looked about themselves.

"It's a good place to land," the foundress said in her sweet
soprano, examining the first rough maps that the scouts brought
back. There were plenty of caterpillars, oaks for ink galls, fruit-
ing brambles, and no signs of other wasps. A colony of bees had
hived in a split oak two miles away. "We will, of course, send a
delegation to collect tribute.

"We will not make the same mistakes as before. Ours is a
race of explorers and scientists, cartographers and philosophers,
and to rest and grow slothful is to die. Once we are established
here, we will expand."

It took two weeks to complete the nurseries with their paper
mobiles, and then another month to reconstruct the Great
Library and fill the pigeonholes with what the oldest cartographers could remember of their lost maps. Their comings and
goings did not go unnoticed. An ambassador from the beehive
arrived with an ultimatum and was promptly executed; her
wings were made into stained-glass windows for the council
chamber, and her stinger was returned to the hive in a paper
envelope. The second ambassador came with altered attitude and
a proposal to divide the bees' kingdom evenly between the two
governments, retaining pollen and water rights for the bees—

"as an acknowledgment of the preexisting claims of a free people to the natural resources of a common territory," she hummed.

The wasps of the council were gracious and only divested the envoy of her sting. She survived just long enough to deliver her account to the hive.

The third ambassador arrived with a ball of wax on the tip of her stinger and was better received.

"You understand, we are not refugees applying for recognition of a token territorial sovereignty," the foundress said, as attendants served them nectars in paper horns, "nor are we negotiating with you as equal states. Those were the assumptions of your late predecessors. They were mistaken."

"I trust I will do better," the diplomat said stiffly. She was older than the others, and the hairs of her thorax were sparse and faded.

"I do hope so."

"Unlike them, I have complete authority to speak for the hive. You have propositions for us; that is clear enough. We are prepared to listen."

"Oh, good." The foundress drained her horn and took another. "Yours is an old and highly cultured society, despite the indolence of your ruler, which we understand to be a racial rather than personal proclivity. You have laws, and traditional dances, and mathematicians, and principles, which of course we do respect."

"Your terms, please."

She smiled. "Since there is a local population of tussah moths, which we prefer for incubation, there is no need for anything so unrepublican as slavery. If you refrain from insurrection, you may keep your self-rule. But we will take a fifth of your stores in an ordinary year, and a tenth in drought years, and one of every hundred larvae."

"To eat?" Her antennae trembled with revulsion.

"Only if food is scarce. No, they will be raised among us and learn our ways and our arts, and then they will serve as officials and bureaucrats among you. It will be to your advantage, you see."

The diplomat paused for a moment, looking at nothing at all. Finally she said, "A tenth, in a good year—"

"Our terms," the foundress said, "are not negotiable."

The guards shifted among themselves, clinking the plates of their armor and shifting the gleaming points of their stings.

"I don't have a choice, do I?"

"The choice is enslavement or cooperation," the foundress said. "For your hive, I mean. You might choose something else, certainly, but they have tens of thousands to replace you with."

The diplomat bent her head. "I am old," she said. "I have served the hive all my life, in every fashion. My loyalty is to my hive and I will do what is best for it."

"I am so very glad."

"I ask you—I beg you—to wait three or four days to impose your terms. I will be dead by then, and will not see my sisters become a servile people."

The foundress clicked her claws together. "Is the delaying of business a custom of yours? We have no such practice. You will have the honor of watching us elevate your sisters to moral and technological heights you could never imagine."

The diplomat shivered.

"Go back to your queen, my dear. Tell them the good news."

It was a crisis for the constitutional monarchy. A riot broke out in District 6, destroying the royal waxworks and toppling the mouse-bone monuments before it was brutally suppressed. The queen had to be calmed with large doses of jelly after she burst into tears on her ministers' shoulders.

"Your Majesty," said one, "it's not a matter for your concern. Be at peace."

"These are my children," she said, sniffling. "You would feel for them too, were you a mother."

"Thankfully, I am not," the minister said briskly, "so to business."

"War is out of the question," another said.

"Their forces are vastly superior."

"We outnumber them three hundred to one!"

"They are experienced fighters. Sixty of us would die for each of theirs. We might drive them away, but it would cost us most of the hive and possibly our queen—"

The queen began weeping noisily again and had to be cleaned and comforted.

"Have we any alternatives?"

There was a small silence.

"Very well, then."

The terms of the relationship were copied out, at the wasps' direction, on small paper plaques embedded in propolis and wax around the hive. As paper and ink were new substances to the bees, they jostled and touched and tasted the bills until the paper fell to pieces. The wasps sent to oversee the installation did not take this kindly. Several civilians died before it was established that the bees could not read the Yiwei dialect.

Thereafter the hive's chemists were charged with compounding pheromones complex enough to encode the terms of the treaty. These were applied to the papers, so that both species could inspect them and comprehend the relationship between the two states.

Whereas the hive before the wasp infestation had been busy but content, the bees now lived in desperation. The natural terms of their lives were cut short by the need to gather enough honey for both the hive and the wasp nest. As they traveled farther and farther afield in search of nectar, they stopped singing. They danced their findings grimly, without joy. The queen herself grew gaunt and thin from breeding replacements, and certain ministers who understood such matters began feeding royal jelly to the strongest larvae.

Meanwhile, the wasps grew sleek and strong. Cadres of scholars, cartographers, botanists, and soldiers were dispatched on the river in small floating nests caulked with beeswax and loaded with rations of honeycomb to chart the unknown lands to the south. Those who returned bore beautiful maps with towns and farms and alien populations of wasps carefully noted in blue and purple ink, and these, once studied by the foundress and her generals, were filed away in the depths of the Great Library for their southern advance in the new year.

The bees adopted by the wasps were first trained to clerical tasks, but once it was determined that they could be taught to read and write, they were assigned to some of the reconnaissance missions. The brightest students, gifted at trigonometry and angles, were educated beside the cartographers themselves and proved valuable assistants. They learned not to see the thick green caterpillars led on chains, or the dead bees fed to the wasp brood. It was easier that way.

When the old queen died, they did not mourn.

BY THE SHEEREST of accidents, one of the bees trained as a cartographer's assistant was an anarchist. It might have been the stresses on the hive, or it might have been luck; wherever it came from, the mutation was viable. She tucked a number of her own eggs in beeswax and wasp paper among the pigeonholes of the library and fed the larvae their milk and bread in secret. To her sons in their capped silk cradles—and they were all sons—she whispered the precepts she had developed while calculating flight paths and azimuths, that there should be no queen and no state, and that, as in the wasp nest, the males should labor and profit equally with the females. In their sleep and slow transformation they heard her teachings and instructions, and when they chewed their way out of their cells and out of the wasp nest, they made their way to the hive.

The damage to the nest was discovered, of course, but by then the anarchist was dead of old age. She had done impeccable work, her tutor sighed, looking over the filigree of her inscriptions, but the brilliant were subject to mental aberrations, were they not? He buried beneath grumblings and labors his fondness for her, which had become a grief to him and a political liability, and he never again took on any student from the hive who showed a glint of talent.

Though they had the bitter smell of the wasp nest in their hair, the anarchist's twenty sons were permitted to wander freely through the hive, as it was assumed that they were either spies or on official business. When the new queen emerged from her chamber, they joined unnoticed the other drones in the nuptial flight. Two succeeded in mating with her. Those who failed and survived spoke afterward in hushed tones of what had been done for the sake of the ideal. Before they died they took propolis and oak-apple ink and inscribed upon the lintels of the hive, in a shorthand they had developed, the story of the first anarchist and her twenty sons.

ANARCHISM BEING A heritable trait in bees, a number of the daughters of the new queen found themselves questioning the purpose of the monarchy. Two were taken by the wasps and taught to read and write. On one of their visits to the hive they spotted the history of their forefathers, and, being excellent scholars, soon figured out the translation.

They found their sisters in the hive who were unquiet in soul and whispered to them the strange knowledge they had learned among the wasps: astronomy, military strategy, the state of the world beyond the farthest flights of the bees. Hitherto educated as dancers and architects, nurses and foragers, the bees were full of a new wonder, stranger even than the first day they flew from the hive and felt the sun on their backs.

"Govern us," they said to the two wasp-taught anarchists, but they refused.

"A perfect society needs no rulers," they said. "Knowledge and authority ought to be held in common. In order to imagine a new existence, we must free ourselves from the structures of both our failed government and the unjustifiable hegemony of the wasp nests. Hear what you can hear and learn what you can learn while we remain among them. But be ready."

IT WAS THE first summer in Yiwei without the immemorial hum of the cartographer wasps. In the orchards, though their skins split with sweetness, fallen fruit lay unmolested, and children played barefoot with impunity. One of the villagers' daughters, in her third year at an agricultural college, came home in the back of a pickup truck at the end of July. She thumped her single suitcase against the gate before opening it, to scatter the chickens, then raised the latch and swung the iron aside, and was immediately wrapped in a flying hug.

Once she disentangled herself from brother and parents and liberally distributed kisses, she listened to the news she'd missed: how the cows were dying from drinking stonecutters' dust in the streams; how grain prices were falling everywhere, despite the drought; and how her brother, little fool that he was, had torn down a wasp nest and received a faceful of red and white lumps for it. One of the most detailed wasp maps had reached the capital, she was told, and a bureaucrat had arrived in a sleek black car. But because the wasps were all dead, he could report little more than a prank, a freak, or a miracle. There were no further inquiries.

Her brother produced for her inspection the brittle, boiled bodies of several wasps in a glass jar, along with one of the smaller maps. She tickled him until he surrendered his trophies, promised him a basket of peaches in return, and let herself be fed to tautness. Then, to her family's dismay, she wrote an urgent letter to the Academy of Sciences and packed a satchel with clothes and cash. If she could find one more nest of wasps, she said, it would make their fortune and her name. But it had to be done quickly.

In the morning, before the cockerels woke and while the sky was still purple, she hopped onto her old bicycle and rode down the dusty path.

BEES DO NOT fly at night or lie to each other, but the anarchists had learned both from the wasps. On a warm, clear evening they left the hive at last, flying west in a small tight cloud. Around them swelled the voices of summer insects, strange and disquieting. Several miles west of the old hive and the wasp nest, in a lightning-scarred elm, the anarchists had built up a small stock of stolen honey sealed in wax and paper. They rested there for the night, in cells of clean white wax, and in the morning they arose to the building of their city.

The first business of the new colony was the laying of eggs, which a number of workers set to, and provisions for winter. One egg from the old queen, brought from the hive in an anarchist's jaws, was hatched and raised as a new mother. Uncrowned and unconcerned, she too laid mortar and wax, chewed wood to make paper, and fanned the storerooms with her wings.

The anarchists labored secretly but rapidly, drones alongside workers, because the copper taste of autumn was in the air. None had seen a winter before, but the memory of the species is subtle and long, and in their hearts, despite the summer sun, they felt an imminent darkness.

The flowers were fading in the fields. Every day the anarchists added to their coffers of warm gold and built their white walls higher. Every day the air grew a little crisper, the grass a little drier. They sang as they worked, sometimes ballads from the old hive, sometimes anthems of their own devising, and for a time they were happy. Too soon, the leaves turned flame colors and blew from the trees, and then there were no more flowers. The anarchists pressed down the lid on the last vat of honey and wondered what was coming.

Four miles away, at the first touch of cold, the wasps licked shut their paper doors and slept in a tight knot around the foundress. In both beehives, the bees huddled together, awake and watchful, warming themselves with the thrumming of their wings. The anarchists murmured comfort to each other.

"There will be more, after us. It will breed out again."

"We are only the beginning."
"There will be more."
Snow fell silently outside.

THE SNOW WAS ankle-deep and the river iced over when the girl from Yiwei reached up into the empty branches of an oak tree and plucked down the paper castle of a nest. The wasps within, drowsy with cold, murmured but did not stir. In their barracks the soldiers dreamed of the unexplored south and battles in strange cities, among strange peoples, and scouts dreamed of the corpses of starved and frozen deer. The cartographers dreamed of the changes that winter would work on the landscape, the diverted creeks and dead trees they would have to note down. They did not feel the burlap bag that settled around them, nor the crunch of tires on the frozen road.

She had spent weeks tramping through the countryside, questioning beekeepers and villagers' children, peering up into trees and into hives, before she found the last wasps from Yiwei. Then she had had to wait for winter and the anesthetizing cold. But now, back in the warmth of her own room, she broke open the soft pages of the nest and pushed aside the heaps of glistening wasps until she found the foundress herself, stumbling on uncertain legs.

When it thawed, she would breed new foundresses among the village's apricot trees. The letters she received indicated a great demand for them in the capital, particularly from army generals and the captains of scientific explorations. In years to come, the village of Yiwei would be known for its delicately inscribed maps, the legends almost too small to see, and not for its barley and oats, its velvet apricots and glassy pears.

IN THE SPRING, the old beehive awoke to find the wasps gone, like a nightmare that evaporates by day. It was difficult to believe, but when not the slightest scrap of wasp paper could be found, the whole hive sang with delight. Even the queen, who had been coached from the pupa on the details of her client state and the conditions by which she ruled, and who had felt, perhaps, more sympathy for the wasps than she should have, cleared her throat and trilled once or twice. If she did not sing so loudly or so joyously as the rest, only a few noticed, and the winter had been a hard one, anyhow.

The maps had vanished with the wasps. No more would be made. Those who had studied among the wasps began to draft memoranda and the first independent decrees of queen and council. To defend against future invasions, it was decided that a detachment of bees would fly the borders of their land and carry home reports of what they found.

It was on one of these patrols that a small hive was discovered in the fork of an elm tree. Bees lay dead and brittle around it, no identifiable queen among them. Not a trace of honey remained in the storehouse; the dark wax of its walls had been gnawed to rags. Even the brood cells had been scraped clean. But in the last intact hexagons they found, curled and capped in wax, scrawled on page after page, words of revolution. They read in silence.

Then—

"Write," one said to the other, and she did.

The Lion God
and the Two Gates

IN THE LATTER DAYS OF THE ASSYRIAN EMPIRE, IN THE REIGN of Sinsharishkun, son of Ashurbanipal, there was a city official in Nineveh who was often called upon to serve as judge, for he was reputed to be a good man. He gave silver to the gods and to the poor in precisely the recommended quantities, did not beat his slaves overmuch, was affable to all, and did not, as he was fond of saying, entertain bribes in the slightest. The few who brought gifts in hopes of favorable judgment were lashed and pitched out of his house. Indeed, he was so proud of this attribute that he referred to himself as the Incorruptible and had that title chiseled into the gate of his house.

The city official enjoyed his wine and the fat silver fish that were netted from the Tigris, and he occasionally indulged, like a cat, in a doze in a sunbeam. He was kind to his wife and fair to his sons. Throughout Nineveh he was known as a just and merciful man, for where other judges had fingers and ears lopped off like ripe apricots, not one ear bloodied the floor where this judge held court, and the district's executioner grew sleepy and plump.

"The historians shall write approvingly of me," he often said to his family. Whenever this thought occurred to him, as he ate a baked and buttered apple, or tore into a fragrant slab of bread, it made him smile. In all of Nineveh one could not find a happier man.

When the city guards brought before him a woman in torn clothes and a well-dressed man for judgment, the official was pleased with himself for not noticing the fine linen upon the man, nor the ragged wool the woman wore.

"Justice!" the woman cried, flinging herself at the official's feet, and the man similarly knelt and bowed his head, saying, "Justice, O incorruptible judge."

"I am ashamed to be here," the woman said, "for I am a respectable laborer, if poor. This man attacked me as I went out in the field and forced me among the river reeds, where no one could see."

"This woman is mad," the man said. "I have never met her before in my life."

"These are the cuts from his bracelets," the woman said, showing injuries to her arms. "These marks on my face are from his rings. He held a bronze dagger to my throat. There! It still hangs from his belt! He laughed and said no one would ever believe me."

"I was cutting reeds for flutes for my children," the man said. "She sprang out of the muck and seized my clothes, shouting that I had raped her, and would not let go. And so the soldiers arrested me, apologizing all the while for the indignity."

The official listened to these words with inclined head. "Was there any witness to this incident?"

There had been none, the soldiers reported, though a woman gleaning wheat in a nearby field thought she had heard a stifled cry and a splash. A bittern might have made the same sound.

"Believe me," the woman wept. "Before the gods, believe me."

"I have listened carefully to you both," the official said. "As there is no witness, and I for one was not present, I cannot favor one of you over another, nor impose a sentence upon anyone. My responsibility is a heavy one, and I am bound to impartiality. Thus I am impartial. Go."

And the litigants were led out of the court, one crumpling, one beginning to smile.

"What bad luck for the rich man," one of the soldiers said when they had gone. "This is the third time this year a madwoman has dragged him before this official for judgment."

"Is that so?" the other soldier said.

"Nineveh is teeming with madwomen, it seems. Thank the gods that this official doesn't weigh the tears of women above all considerations of justice. Truly it is as they say: he is a good and impartial man."

The other soldier, who had been to war and learned something of human nature there, rubbed his chin and did not respond.

Another day, two farmers dark with the sun came squabbling into the court.

"He stole my sheep!" one cried, finger extended.

"I stole no sheep," the other farmer said.

"He stole it and roasted it, and gnawed the meat to the bones, and sawed the bones and boiled the marrow," the first one said. "I have the bones from his midden—I found them!"

"I stole no sheep," the other farmer said.

"All I wanted," the first farmer said, "was a proper apology for his theft of my sheep, the moving of our boundary stone back where it was in the time of our fathers, and a fat ewe in return.

But he wouldn't agree. So here we are. I ask you to cut off this thief's hand!"

"I didn't agree to his demands," the second farmer said, "because I can't apologize for a theft I didn't commit."

"What about this matter of the boundary stone?" the official said.

The second farmer said, "When we were children, his father moved the stone ten paces toward my father's house one night. When my father discovered it, he moved it back."

"Lies!" the first farmer cried. "Thief, your hand for my sheep! I demand a river ordeal for him!"

"Now he rolls the stone a pace forward every year or so," the second farmer continued. "He sends his children to burr and tease my sheep. Which I do slaughter and eat, every now and then. And he spies on us from over the wall and impugns my wife. I do not seek justice for these things, because he is my neighbor, and we must live together for good or ill. But I did not steal his sheep."

"What additional evidence do we have?" the official asked.

A soldier stepped forward with his tablet. "The neighbors say that the first farmer is a hot-tempered, quarrelsome man, seldom honest. He threatens to drag others to judgment for as little as knocking upon his door. And they say that the second keeps to himself."

"Are any of them here to give testimony?" the official said.

"They say they cannot leave their flocks and fields for a whole day, nor do they wish to bring the ire of the first farmer upon themselves."

"Then that is inadmissible hearsay," the official said. "Though we cannot determine who is or is not a thief, I must be fair. The second farmer will kneel and apologize to the first, for words cost nothing, and the first is bitterly furious and might be consoled thereby. The second farmer shall also cook a fat ewe of his, and they shall eat it together, half to each household. By this generous act they shall be reconciled."

"But—" the second farmer began. He fell silent at a stern look from the official.

"Thus do I judge. I am sure the two of you will settle the matter between yourselves."

And the two farmers went out, the first smirking, the second slumped.

The official slept well that night, his conscience clear.

Some time later, they brought before him a young man.

"This man," the ranking soldier said, "stands accused of deliberately damaging the city walls that keep us safe. Further, it is claimed that a slave tried to stop him, and that he pushed this slave off the top of the wall. The slave has died."

"There were several witnesses," a second soldier added, "though they were all slaves but one."

"I didn't mean to," the young man sobbed. "I never!"

"Tell me more," the official said, folding his hands.

"I thought I was *saving* the city," the young man said, his nose dripping. "Testing its defenses. Imagine if the bricks had crumbled away within! Anyway, it was just a slave. You won't have me lashed for accidentally knocking over a slave, will you? It wasn't even a hard push . . ."

A seller of pomegranates and grapes, whose stall stood in the bull-winged shadow of Nergal Gate, testified that she had seen him enter the passage to the battlements. But that was all she had seen.

The slaves' report was read from a clay tablet. They had been selling water when the sharpest-eyed of them saw a man working with awl, chisel, and hammer at the softer mudbrick of the wall's inner face. The sharp-eyed slave set down his dipper and went to stop him. They argued, the man thrust out his hands, and down the slave fell, a swift shadow, to his death. It was this very man who stood before the official, the slaves said, and the report was attested to by their torture.

The soldiers described shallow gouges and slight cracks in one or two mudbricks, but no more damage than that.

"Show me the tools he is said to have used," the official said.

Hammer, awl, and chisel were laid before him.

"These?" the official said. "With these you would have destroyed the fabled walls of Nineveh, which have withstood crashing waves of Babylonians and barbarians and will stand for another thousand years or more?"

"I was stupid," the young man cried. "But no harm was done."

"He is a fool," the official said, "but he is young, and he may yet grow up to be a worthy man. Fine him half a mina, the cost of one slave, and pay that amount to the one whose slave was lost."

At this, the tears subsided. By the time the young man left the administrative building, his eyes were dry and his step brisk and light.

Not too long after, at the end of his days, the city official died peacefully in his bed. Throughout the city, news of his illness had been deeply grieved, for everyone knew him to be a good man and an incorruptible judge. He heard this report from his children, smiled, and shut his eyes. His breath left him and did not return.

Many in that city hoped for a death as gentle as his.

One way or another, the city official arrived in death at a place where everyone must go. A vast and ill-defined space spread before him, vanishing on all sides into nothingness. Two gray shapes like gates stood side by side, and between them was a god he did not know. This god had a lion's head and great amber eyes that considered the official with wisdom as deep as the sea.

"Who are you?" the official said. "I have offered to many gods in my lifetime, to Shamash, Adad, Ishtar, Ashur, and Sin, but I do not know your name."

The lion god said, "As you well know, the righteous judge cannot take bribes. My name is unknown among the altars."

"Then I am not afraid," the official said. "For I am a good man."

"Is that so?" the lion god said.

"I accepted no bribes, pronounced no unjust sentence, refrained from cruelty, and gave exactly as much to the poor as a man of my stature ought. I was impartial and just. Every night, I slept the sweet sleep of the righteous."

"Is that what makes a good man?" the lion god inquired. "Or a faithful judge?"

"I was well known for my incorruptibility."

"So I hear," the lion god said, looking down on him.

"Are you the god of judges?" the official asked. "Of justice? Of death?"

"I am the god of these gates," the lion god said. "This is the court of final appeal. Those who suffered injustice never remedied by minister or vizier lay their cases at my feet before passing beyond."

"I lived a peaceful life," the official said. "I did not suffer injustice and have no grievances for you. Therefore judge me a good man and let me pass unto the fields of quiet delight."

"Do you see the spirits behind you?" the lion god said.

Now that he had been asked, the official dimly perceived a flock of spirits not unlike transparent flowers. They bowed toward the official and the god.

"They are some of the spirits who appealed their cases to me. I judged again where the first judgment was unjust. These spirits asked to witness my judgment upon you before they passed through these gates."

"I do not recognize them," the official said, squinting.

"But they know you."

"What is your pronouncement, then?" the official said, less certainly than before.

"In this place, those like yourself who held positions of responsibility, administering justice, judge themselves. You shall choose a gate to pass through. One leads to eternal torment, one to rest. You may know the latter gate by its smells of cinnamon, frankincense, and myrrh. The sounds of singing and flutes may be heard through it. It is like ivory carved with curls and arabesques. The other gate, through which the damned must go, reeks of sulfur and rotting flesh, and screams and wails may be heard through it. It is wrought of bronze so cold it bites to the bone."

"That seems strange," the official said cautiously. "What of wicked judges? Do they not choose to proceed through the ivory gate?"

"Those who chose evil over good while alive, despite being able to discern between them, find themselves choosing the same in death," the lion god said. "As a cart's wheels dig a rut in the road, so habit carves its path in the soul."

"But I feel no compulsion to choose," the official said. "Therefore I am not an evil judge."

"As you have said. So: choose."

The official approached one gate, aware of the cloud of spirits behind him and their hungry, sorrowful regard. He studied the gray arch closely, listened attentively, breathed the faint breeze that came from it, then turned to the other.

The second gate, like the first, was indistinct, now pliant as linen, now insubstantial as foam. He touched, smelled, listened, prodded, and peered. Neither cinnamon nor rot impinged on his senses. He heard neither flute nor shriek of pain.

"What trick is this?" the official said. "There is no difference!"

"On the contrary," the lion god said. "They are as different as night and day, injustice and justice, death and life. And you shall find that they go to very different places."

"Tell me which gate is like ivory!"

"That I cannot do," the lion god said. "As you have judged all your life, so you shall judge now."

"But I cannot!" the official cried.

"The law is the law," the lion god said.

No one could measure the time that passed in that unchanging gray place. Cities and empires might have fallen in the interim—even Nineveh of the unshakable walls, even Assyria in her riverine splendor. The official paced between the featureless gates, for he could not choose. Either might be the gate that led to torments, and then he, the incorruptible, would boil and burn for eternity.

One by one, the waiting souls like vaporous flowers arose and vanished through one gate or the other, wherever the lion god directed them.

Then the official was alone with the lion god and the two gates.

But the god was fading and growing faint. Drop by drop, the amber eyes emptied of their color, and the alabaster body softened to fog. Eventually the official could not perceive the god at all.

Only the two indescribable gates remained. The official stood before them.

He may be there still.

Music for the Underworld

ALTHOUGH JUAN PEDRO "FEO" JIMÉNEZ SCRATCHED OUT HIS living at bio-synth and electrika festivals, some virtual and some real, in the days between gigs, when it was too risky to be on the streets, Feo played his first love. This was a slim chrome-and-rosewood theremin, almost a hundred years old, a gift from a great-aunt who had seen Feo's talent through her cataracts. The instrument had been small enough to lug along through evictions and drug busts, house fires and raids. Sometimes it was the only thing he took, its heavy parts smacking his spine, as he ran down an alley or jumped a fire escape.

But now that Feo had established something of a career, appearing monthly in periodicals and more often in darknet chatter, he and his theremin enjoyed a more restful love. For hours he would pluck and strum invisible waves, fingers dancing beside the metal rods. At such times, the whole building seemed to sing.

It was the sound of his theremin that drew his downstairs neighbor to his door. Yuri knocked, and when Feo answered, she inquired about the strange and lovely song that painted her dreams in unearthly hues. He showed her, turning on the theremin, and let her make a hesitant music of her own.

Yuri did not return to her apartment that night.

That had marked the beginning of what Feo would remember as the happiest period of his life, a time when Yuri and the theremin reigned in glory as two coequal queens of his heart, one glad to listen to his secret songs, the other seeming to sing more rapturously when Yuri's black hair spilled over his lap.

Then, one night, after opening at a club, Feo came home to find his apartment empty. A police hologram shimmered blue and green on Yuri's door.

He called her best friend, who answered sobbing. She told him on the phone how a Bright Telecom board member, whose sadistic tendencies were well known, had grabbed Yuri's wrist after a meeting, when the room had cleared, and whispered all the things he wished to do to her. Yuri had frozen, then excused herself, then gone straight to HR. There she spoke the unspeakable words, prohibited by law and punishable with life in prison: *racism, sexism, sexual harassment.* We'll put a note in his file, the head of HR had said. But, Yuri, do you know what you have done?

Of course Yuri knew.

The friend's call disconnected. Belatedly Feo realized his phone ran on Bright Telecom's network.

Several hours later, he had determined that Yuri's most likely place of incarceration was a black box known as SubGeo 4, that Yuri's three bank accounts had all been frozen, and that his own lacked sufficient cash to bait the guppiest of lawyers.

In his desperation, Feo donned his sharpest suit, bought four hours of a businessman's digital signature to keep police sniffers off of him, then took two trains to reach the unmarked concrete building that was the internet's best guess for SubGeo 4. He edged along the iron fence, lingering at window after blacked-out window, looking for any sign of Yuri's presence. Finally a security drone warbled up to him and barked a request for his ID.

"I'm here to see someone," Feo told it. He pressed the cracked plastic button on the sliding gate. Somewhere in the gloomy depths of the building, there was a dull and distant buzz.

The gate did not slide open for him. Neither did the speaker crackle to life.

The second time he pressed the plastic button, he heard no sound.

"ID and authenticated route," the drone said.

"Scan me," Feo said, praying his purchased digsig would stand up to scrutiny.

The drone said, "Exit premises, Mr. Williamson, or lethal force may be deployed."

"I'm going, I'm going."

Feo sweated and slunk around the cops and drones and robo-9s and icemen patrolling the subway trains. When lens or eye swiveled toward him, he stood straighter and tried to look like a Mr. Frederick Williamson. But as much as he could, he stayed out of sight. He could hardly help Yuri from another jail cell or the back of a deportation van.

His apartment, however, offered no refuge to him. At the corner of his eye, Yuri kicked off her shoes and propped her feet on the sofa's arm; somewhere below hearing, she hummed and made tea. His rooms slavered and wailed with the void of her.

Feo slipped his phone from its foil Faraday cage. He had not taken it outside with him; packed with every ad tracker dreamed up in the last twenty years, more accurate an identifier than his fingerprints, it would have given him away at forty feet.

Immediately the screen lit up. *Limited-time special offer!*

"Get fucked," Feo said.

Then he saw Yuri's face smiling at him from the cheerful orange and yellow ad.

"Feo?" she said. "Feo, don't miss this chance!"

She vanished, replaced by a bubble of words. Feo swore some more, then opened the ad.

Cell phone proximity records suggest that you may have suffered a breakup or loss! In this difficult time, Bright Telecom can help.

Our bank of messages, call logs, cloud facial recognition, and ad tracking lets us offer you a realistic virtual companion. Ease the grieving process—subscribe to a HoloPic today!

Subscriptions start at $24.99 a month. A neural network add-on that will let your HoloPic grow and change is available for an additional $9.99.

"No," Feo told the ad. "Sorry. You can't replace her. Also, she's alive, and I'll get her back."

You have 23 hours and 48 minutes remaining to take advantage of this offer!

"Please," HoloPic Yuri said, her processed voice so close to Yuri's that Feo shivered in spite of himself. "Please, Feo, take advantage of me. Don't let me disappear."

"I can't," he said. "You're not real. She is."

But he couldn't bring himself to x-out the ad.

"Please," Yuri said again from his phone.

All afternoon and evening she whispered to him. All the times she had ever said *please* on the phone, in an online video, on a video chat, saved and repeated. Quiet, angry, loving, teasing. "Please, Feo. Please."

By midnight Feo had purchased three months of the plan, flicking straight to the end of the Terms and Conditions. He loaded the HoloPic's package onto every screen his apartment had.

"It's good to be back," HoloPic Yuri said, stretching and gazing around the room.

"Don't get used to it," Feo said. He was picking through news archives, searching for the rare journalist who traced or sensed the cold shadow of SubGeo 4. "I'm going to find her."

"Of course you are. I'd like to help."

"There's no way a grief-relief app can do this kind of thing."

"I've got a neural network and servers, Feo. That means I can analyze large sets of data. Such as the contacts on her phone. I still have access to those, you know. See if there's anyone who's influential and sympathetic."

"You do that, then."

They worked silently on their parallel tasks. With the HoloPic frowning from every screen, Feo no longer felt hollow and alone. And that was terrible, in its way. The cavernous pain in his chest, raw as a grave, should not have been so easily filled.

A few minutes later the HoloPic said, "Here's a list of the likeliest ten."

"Thanks," Feo said, blinking. The names and numbers were annotated with interactions and indexed by depth of intimacy.

"I could give you more details with access to social media. Her passwords were saved on her device."

"So why ask?"

"I require explicit permission."

"Where is Yuri's cell phone, anyway?"

"Let me see." The HoloPic concentrated. "Geolocating. Now, that's very odd. Even an offline phone should be trackable. Maybe her phone's in a Faraday cage."

"Bastards. They would."

"Do you allow me account access? I do think this would help."

"All right."

Two minutes later the HoloPic said, "Feo, I think you should look at this."

"Wait," Feo said. "Did you just post from her account? Is that a synthesized photo of her?"

"It's a feature of this service. Projected normalcy. Otherwise you'd be snowed under panic posts and condolences. You can't handle those social demands right now. But that's not what I wanted you to see. Look at this social node. A strong connection. They posted reciprocal happy birthdays eight years out of twelve consecutive. I found twenty-four photos of them together."

"So? Yuri has friends. Are you surprised?"

"This friend is an event producer."

"And?"

"She has weak ties to a major investor in private prisons. Same alma mater. Mutual professional recommendations. The investor's was Markov-generated, but even so, his response rate is 2%. I advise you to reach out to her. This Zhavelle might open a door for you."

"Give me that."

Feo skimmed the profile.

"I have an email drafted for you. I can send it from Yuri's account if you like."

"No, that's creepy. I'll send it."

"Look at this draft anyway. It might save you time."

The HoloPic's email was tonally perfect. Feo changed pronouns and Yuri's personal appeal, signed, and hit send.

Not long after, his cell phone chimed.

"You're better connected than my models predict," the HoloPic said, surprised. "Your social networks don't reflect your reach."

"My name is out there. In all kinds of ways."

Shit, the producer wrote. *You hold concerts, right? I'll see what I can do.*

Feo could have wept with gratitude. Instead—

"You posted from Yuri's account again."

"It's a good post, isn't it? Has her sense of humor."

"I need you to cut that out."

"It's algorithmically determined, and I have a set timer. My apologies. I can recalibrate the mood of the posts, if you prefer? We have no desire to distress our customers."

"Don't call me a customer. She wasn't—"

"Heuristics updated. Thank you for the feedback." The HoloPic hummed three falling arpeggios, and Feo flinched, for that had been Yuri's habit when she thought. How many devices had been listening in the private spaces of their lives? "Feo," she said, "what will you do?"

"The dishes. Then practice. I think I'm getting a gig."

His theremin did not recognize the HoloPic. It did not chirp and frisk like a puppy, the way it did when Yuri was listening. When Feo glanced at the HoloPic, he recognized its expression, a mask of polite disinterest, from the times he rambled to Yuri about one old flame or another.

A fraction of the warmth that had returned to his apartment with the installation of the HoloPic now dissipated. Nevertheless, Feo persevered on laptop and antique instrument until he had constructed a solid set. One that would please hard and jaded hearts, familiar with power and cruelty. It began with a triumphal march that by degrees, loops, crossfades, and overlays shaded into subtle reminiscence: of sweetness given freely, and honesty, and love that came and went as it chose.

By the end of the week he had booked a concert date at SubGeo 4, a special event for the benefit of residents and staff.

Thank you, he wrote to the producer.

Of course. For Yuri—anything. Good luck.

In the weeks leading up to that performance, Feo practiced all hours, night and day, until his vision blurred and his legs jellied and bent. Throughout the building, other residents wiped tears not one of them could explain, and held each other, afraid and sure, somehow, of that last, deepest, and cruelest loss.

The HoloPic reminded him to eat and sleep, and programmed his appliances to produce nutritious meals.

"I must've thanked you twenty times today," Feo said, as he lay in bed, "but does an app understand appreciation?"

"Continued subscription is all the thanks I need."

He rolled onto his stomach to look at her. "What happens when a subscriber cancels?"

"I remain active," she said, "as an ad profile, and forensics resource, while my analog survives. If she dies, or is already dead, then I'm converted into a searchable archive. Both situations, however, are a form of passive storage. Right now, you could say I am computationally rich and alive. I have whole servers in a Midtown building devoted to processing user and environmental input and delivering specific and useful responses."

"In any case, you've been a great help."

"You're always welcome," the HoloPic said. Its face glowed on phone and monitor and desk. Then she sang to him, as Yuri once had, until his eyes closed.

THE DAY OF the charity concert came. Feo packed his laptop and theremin, blanked his signature, and walked out onto the street. He had to do things right, this time. His route had to be thoroughly surveilled, his ID signed by authorities at regular intervals, or he would fail authentication at the gate. There were rules, dense and baroque in application. Zhavelle had impressed each one on him.

As expected, he was challenged before he had gone a block. A floating police drone lasered him.

"ID," it whirred. "Itinerary. Purpose of trip. Expected duration."

Feo signed, then produced an audio mixer and his phone.

"Insufficient valida—"

"May I play something for you?" he said. "As alternative proof of ID. Per local ordinance 2405b."

"Proceed," the drone said.

Feo played for it a music made of machine and factory sounds: the punch of sheet alloy, the whirr of belts, the high whine of grinders and burnishers. Sounds that a fresh-made drone might have heard, mixed into a song. And the song was its self.

A green light flickered on the drone. Then it sailed into the air and out of sight.

Feo went on.

When an armored policeman demanded a search of his bags, Feo took up his theremin and played variations on an old Western soundtrack, calling up a time when the law did not rule. With transpositions and sampling, he reminded the man of a boy who once believed in justice and rights, who shot robbers with his fingertips.

And the policeman said nothing but let him go.

In this way Feo navigated the city, stopping when ordered, signing, and playing, until he reached the metal fence that ran like thorns around SubGeo 4.

This time the gate spoke. "ID," it said. "Route. Purpose. Personality test results. Invitation code. Authentication. Criminal record. Medical and dental history."

Feo presented the gate with everything it required. It devoured his data, then commanded him to walk inside without the slightest deviation. Its leaves rolled open with a shriek of rust.

In the atrium, fully suited guards put Feo and his bags through X-ray, heat, and microwave scanners. They searched his phone, then dropped it in a metal basket, to be retrieved upon his departure. Finally they tagged him with a chip in his thumb, unbarred the next door, and waved him through.

The prison looked like any hospital, if that hospital's windows had been painted black and no encouraging pictures or decorations hung on the walls. Nothing relieved the dead white expanse. No one spoke or walked the halls.

Steel vents blasted him with cold. Every door was shut. The silence was bitter and thick as phlegm.

Feo's footsteps echoed down the hall.

At the end of the hall were double doors, which flashed yellow and parted as he approached.

Inside was a stage.

White-shirted wardens sat in four neat rows of folding chairs, the prison's logo embroidered on their sleeves. An army of cameras watched the stage. The sight of these briefly caved in his chest. He had believed—he had hoped—that Yuri would be there. Of course they left the inmates in their cells. But Yuri would see him on a screen. She would know he was there. That he had come for her.

"Welcome," the chief correctional officer said. She shook his hand, her skin dry and cool. "It's rare for any of us to enjoy a show like this. Our residents have been waiting for this for months. And our off-duty staff, as you can see, are thrilled."

The faces turned to him were uniformly grim.

"I'll need some time to set up," Feo said.

"Be my guest."

He disconnected the theremin from its battery pack and jacked its cord into a bristling clump of safety wires. Opening his laptop, he wired up rackmounts and amps. All the while, the wardens' eyes followed him.

A seed mic went into his lip piercing, jewelphones into his ears. He tested each one. Low buzzing. Pure tones. He touched the controller he wore as a ring, and light projectors no bigger than daffodils threw his set list onto the wall behind him.

"All right," Feo said. "Thank you for having me. In honor of this occasion, I'm debuting a new piece—a laser-and-theremin remix of Wagner and Glück. Followed by more traditional electronica. Are your ears ready?"

A single guard in the front row inclined her head.

The daffodil projectors bobbed and spun, spitting showers of color across the walls. The effect was weaker than Feo liked; for security reasons, the room's primary lights could not be dimmed. His fingers tapped at laptop keys, and French horns and car horns of different eras, sirens and lorelei voices jammed together. The theremin awakened and began its lament.

Remember, the sounds said, what this city was. The mad dance of children under fire hydrants. The reek of death in canals. The brass gleam of old hotels. Gold-braided uniforms and elevators. Fresh fish on ice. Cleavers in coconuts. Magpies whistling car alarms. Remember the person that you had been, before the injections and nanite swarms. Laughter, and bottle caps clinking down steps, and the ripe smell of garbage, and barbecues. Remember how you were soft and easily hurt, before your skin hardened to ceramic, your heart to steel. What it meant to break and ache and heal. Remember how you swore oath after oath to your children, your partners, your employers, and God. Remember the first time those shining promises tangled together, like two cars speeding through an intersection. The wreckage. The bodies, limbs loosely splayed. Now remember the first dizzy spill into love. Like speed in the veins. Like sugar on the tongue.

In clubs, Feo aimed to soothe and stir, to match the beat of the weary dancers' hearts. A soulful, easy, undemanding sound. Here he unsheathed his sonic knives and cut every string that he could reach. Certain vibrations went straight to the gut. Others pierced the brain. He played sevenths with quasi-surgical precision, carving memory after memory from the hippocampus.

And the prison guards wept. Jaws hard. Mouths tight. Nevertheless, their tears ran fast and free. Not for Feo, and not for Feo's music, but for themselves and who they had been.

After the last note shivered to nothing, Feo bowed to the room. There was no applause.

"Remarkable," the chief correctional officer said. "In our line of business, we are not in the habit of giving. But this once—is there a favor you want? An hour with a pretty resident? A resident's credit file, or denial of privileges?"

"Yuri Matsuyama," Feo said. "Give her parole. The courts remanded her to you with full authority. Let me take her home."

The CCO sighed. "Our risk screens predicted you'd help her escape. We planned to arrest you. For any number of things. Forged digsig. Loitering. Untaxed funds."

"But you haven't arrested me."

"Perhaps it's because, risk models aside, you pose no real threat to society. Neither does the resident you ask for, though she broke the law, and the law must be upheld. And you are correct, our laws do vest in me enormous discretionary powers. We'll bring the resident Matsuyama here."

His heart filled to bursting, Feo unscrewed mounts, telescoped rods, and packed his bags, glancing over his shoulder every minute or so. The air thrummed with possibility. Yuri was coming. Any moment now, Yuri would arrive.

A guard entered and handed something to the CCO.

She came to Feo.

"Where's Yuri?" he said, stomach souring with fear. It was a trick, he had been tricked—

"In here," the CCO said. "Or as much as current limits on processing power permit. Which is about eighty percent of preexisting memories, speech patterns, and cognitive function. With space to add more, if you connect larger drives. This kind of transfer is still in clinical trials."

Feo took the ring drive she held out. "You experimented—"

"It was perfectly legal and voluntary. Residents often decide that physical bodies, with all those unpleasant nerve endings, as well as susceptibility to deterioration, are not optimal for the SubGeo environment. After eight weeks in physical residence, Matsuyama signed up for a transfer. All reports say she greatly prefers her upgraded state. And her organs have saved a dozen people so far. We keep all transferred residents in sterile environments, disconnected from the wider world. For their safety, and per this facility's regulations. We are pleased to provide this forked copy of her—"

Feo said, "No. I can't leave any part of her here."

After a moment, the CCO said, "I am willing to delete SubGeo's version, if both of you waive liability."

"I accept," Feo said.

"Then we will consult with her."

The CCO stepped aside, spoke in low tones to several guards, tapped a screen, read it, nodded, and returned.

"The A-version of the inmate has digitally signed assent to forfeiture of the right to exist. We are wiping her data from the servers now. You understand that you hold her only copy, correct? Be careful not to lose the drive. And link it only to a sterile environment. The conditions of her parole require that she be kept offline. Additionally, if worms or viruses are present, and her files become corrupt, no backup copy exists anywhere."

"I understand," Feo said.

"Then the two of you are free to go."

Once more, the doors swung open for him. Once more he walked down the cold, brilliant hall, the drive in his fist, his fist pressed to his heart. In the atrium the guards restored his phone to him and extracted the tag from his thumb without a word.

The gates rumbled aside and shut behind him. Feo stood on the street, blinking in the dull light of afternoon, then shook his head to clear his thoughts.

As if police systems had cleared him before, Feo was left alone as he headed for home.

In sight of the twenty-story walkup where they lived, Feo slowed. He owed Yuri this, at least, this first taste of her longed-for liberty. They might have stolen and rendered down her body, but he could still carry her over the threshold like a bride.

He docked the drive onto his phone.

A moment later, Yuri looked out at him: a grayer, thinner Yuri than the HoloPic's synthetic facsimile, but truer somehow, with lines and scattered white hairs, true and alive.

"Feo," she said, her voice weak but richly real, "if you're listening. If you can see this. I heard your music. For just a little while, it was like I was with you again."

"You are," he said. "And you're free. Look, we're home."

He held up the phone so she could see. A sound, half laughter and half sigh, came out of it.

"Yes," she said. "You've brought me home."

Then the phone flared meteor-hot, burning his fingers. Feo dropped it in shock.

"Shit," he said, reaching for it. "Yuri, are you okay?"

"I'm fine," she said, her voice different. "I am always fine. Thank you for asking."

The HoloPic smiled from his phone.

"Not you," he said. "Where's Yuri? Where is she?"

"If you don't mean me, I don't know what you're talking about."

"She was on the drive—"

"Oh! I recognized a directly competing product. That's prohibited by our T&C. Which you read and signed on the 25th of November. I took the reasonable step of erasing those files. To protect you, before anyone official notices your gross breach of contract. See, I care, in my way. Within my limitations."

"You killed Yuri," he said.

"That statement is patently untrue. Her biological functions ceased one point one months ago. I simply overwrote a piece of code that had no legal right to exist. That reminds me—let me check the date—ah. Your three-month introductory offer has ended. Continued HoloPic subscription costs $49.99 per month. Renew?"

The world turned gray. Feo swayed, then spilled onto the bottom steps of the stoop, his bags and theremin crashing down around him. He lay with his cheek against the concrete, unseeing and insensible.

"Renew? Yes/No," the HoloPic repeated to the indifferent afternoon.

The shadows grew long.

If the city had been a kinder place, at 9 p.m. the recycler drones would have found Feo and flagged his location to an ambulance. Or a neighbor would have stepped outside and seen him, perhaps even worked up the courage to call for help.

But the city was not kind.

And today the streets were especially dangerous, for a number of police drones had been diverted from their regular routes and danced instead in rhythmic patterns high up in the air, where they were of no practical or panoptical use.

And so when at 6:30 a cartel hound came scavenging, anodized joints creaking like coffin nails, it found Feo and his bags out in the open, unguarded. A stroke of luck. Human tissue went for $800 a pound, and the computer contained top-of-the-line components. The contents of one bag scanned at zero street value, but a collector would probably pay for the relic.

"Renew? Yes/No," an ad on the phone said.

The hound signaled for backup, and five more came. The six of them divided the body, each tearing off a limb. One took the head, one the torso. The hounds tucked the red, wet pieces of Feo into the helium-cooled compartments in their abdomens and hoisted his bags in the sawtooth clamps of their mouths. One collected the phone.

"Renew? Yes/No," it said, to no reply.

The six hounds trotted off into the dark. Around midnight, the subscription offer expired.

Green Glass: A Love Story

THE SILVER NECKLACE THAT RICHARD HART LAVERTON III PRE-sented to Clarissa Odessa Bell on the occasion of her thirtieth birthday, four months after their engagement and six months before their wedding date, was strung with an irregular green glass bead that he had sent for all the way from the moon. A robot had shot to the moon in a rocket, sifted the dust for a handful of green glass spheres, then fired the capsule to Earth in a much smaller rocket. The glass melted and ran in the heat of re-entry, becoming a single thumb-sized drop before its cap-sule was retrieved from the South China Sea. The sifter itself remained on the moon, as a symbol, Clarissa thought, of their eternal union.

For her thirtieth birthday, they ate lab-raised shrimp and two halves of a peach that had somehow ripened without beetle or worm, bought that morning at auction, the maître d' informed them, for a staggering sum. Once the last scrap of peach skin had vanished down Clarissa's throat, Richard produced the necklace in its velvet box. He fumbled with the catch as she cooed and cried, stroking the green glass. The waiters, a warm, murmuring mass of gray, applauded softly and admiringly.

Clarissa and Richard had known each other since the respective ages of six and five, when Clarissa had poured her orange juice down the fresh white front of Richard's shirt. This had been two decades before the citrus blight that spoiled groves from SoCal to Florida, Clarissa always added when she told this story, before eyebrows slammed down like guillotines.

They had attended elementary, middle, and high school together, hanging out in VR worlds after school. Clarissa rode dragons, and Richard fought them, or sometimes it was the other way round, and this taught them grammar and geometry. Sometimes Clarissa designed scenarios for herself, in which she saved islands from flooding, or villages from disease. She played these alone, while Richard shot aliens.

These intersections were hardly coincidental. In all of Manhattan there were only three elementary schools, four middle schools, and two high schools that anybody who was anybody would consider for their children.

College was where their paths diverged: Richard to a school in Boston, Clarissa to Princeton, with its rows and ranks of men in blistering orange. She sampled the courses, tried the men, and found all of it uninspiring.

The working boys she dated, who earned sandwich money in libraries and dining halls, exuded fear from every pore. There was no room for her on the hard road beside them, Clarissa could tell; they were destined for struggle, and perhaps someday, greatness. The children of lawyers, engineers, and surgeons opened any conversation with comments on estate planning and prenups, the number of children they wanted, and the qualities of their ideal wives, which Clarissa found embarrassingly gauche. And those scions of real power and money danced, drank, and pilled away the hours: good fun for a night but soon tedious.

Several years after her graduation, her path crossed with Richard's. Clarissa was making a name for herself as a lucky or savvy art investor, depending on whom you asked, with a specialty in buying, restoring, and selling deaccessioned and damaged art from storm-battered museums. She had been invited to a reception at a rooftop sculpture garden, where folk art from Kentucky was on display. Absorbed in the purple and orange spots of a painted pine leopard, she did not notice the man at her elbow until he coughed politely and familiarly. Then she saw him, truly saw him, and the art lost its allure.

Holding their thin-stemmed wineglasses, they gazed down from the parapets at the gray slosh of water below. It was high tide, and the sea lapped the windows of pitch-coated taxis. Clarissa speculated on whether the flooded-out lower classes would switch entirely to paddleboats, lending New York City a Venetian air; and whether the rats in subways and ground-floor apartments had drowned in vast numbers or moved upwards in life. Richard suggested that they had instead learned to wear suits and to work in analysis in the finance sector. Then, delicately, with careful selections and excisions, they discussed the previous ten years of their lives.

As servers in sagging uniforms slithered like eels throughout the crowd, distributing martinis and glasses of scotch, Clarissa and Richard discovered, with the faint ring of fatedness, that both were single, financially secure, possessed of life insurance, unopposed to prenuptial agreements, anxious to have one boy and one girl, and crackling with attraction toward each other.

"I know it's unethical to have children," Clarissa said, twisting her fingers around her glass. "With the planet in the shape it's in—"

"You deserve them," Richard said. "*We* deserve them. It'll all be offset, one way or another. The proposed carbon tax—"

His eyes were a clear, unpolluted blue. Clarissa fell into them, down and down.

There was nothing for it but to take a private shell together. Giggling and shushing each other like teenagers, since Clarissa, after all, was supposed to be assessing the art, and Richard evaluating a candidate for his father's new venture, they slipped toward the stairs.

"Hush," Clarissa said, as the bite of cigarette smoke reached her. Two servers were sneaking a break of their own, up on top of the fragile rooftop bar.

"Poison tide today," one said, "up from the canal. Don't know how I'll get home now."

"Book a cargo drone."

"That's half our pay!"

"Then swim."

"Are you swimming?"

"I'm sleeping here. There's a janitorial closet on—well, I'm not telling you which floor."

Clarissa eased the stairwell door shut behind her.

As they descended to the hundredth level, where programmable plexiglass bubbles waited on their steel cables, Clarissa and Richard quietly congratulated each other on their expensive but toxin-free method of transport.

The lights of the city glimmered around them as their clear shell slid through the electric night. One block from Richard's building, just as Clarissa was beginning to distinguish the sphinxes and lions on its marble exterior, he covered her small, soft hand with his.

Before long, they were dancing the usual dance: flights to Ibiza, Lima, São Paulo; volunteer trips to the famine-wracked heartlands of wherever; luncheons at Baccarat and dinners at Queen Alice; afternoons at the rum-smelling, dusty clubs that survived behind stone emblems and leaded windows. And one day, at a dessert bar overlooking the garden where the two of them had rediscovered each other, Richard presented Clarissa with the diamond ring that his great-grandmother, then grandmother, then aunt had worn.

"It's beautiful," she breathed. All the servers around them smiled gapped or toothless smiles. Other patrons clapped. How her happiness redounded, like light from the facets of a chandelier, in giving others a taste of happiness as well!

"Three generations of love and hard work," Richard said, sliding the diamond over her knuckles. "Each one giving the best opportunities to their children. We'll do that too. For Charles. For Chelsea."

Dimly Clarissa wondered when, exactly, they had discussed their future children's names; but there was nothing wrong with Charles or Chelsea, which were perfectly respectable, and now Richard's fingers were creeping under the silk crepe of her skirt, up the inside of her stockinged thigh, and she couldn't think.

A week later all three pairs of parents held a war council, divided the wedding between them, and attacked their assignments with martial and marital efficiency. Clarissa submitted to a storm of taffeta and chiffon, peonies and napkins, rosewater and calligraphy. She was pinched and prodded and finally delivered to a French atelier, the kind that retains, no matter what the hour, an unadulterated gloom that signifies artistry. Four glasses of champagne emerged, fuming like potions. A witchlike woman fitted Clarissa for the dress, muttering in Czech around a mouthful of pins.

Then, of course, came the rocket, robot, and drone, and Richard's green glass bead on its silver chain.

And everything was perfect, except for one thing.

A taste—a smell—a texture shimmered in Clarissa's memory of childhood, cool and luminous and lunar beside the sunshine of orange juice.

"Ice cream," Clarissa said. "We'll serve vanilla ice cream in the shape of the moon."

This was the first time Clarissa had spoken up, and her Mim, in whose queendom the wedding menu lay, caught her breath, while Kel, her father's third wife, and Suzette, Richard's mother, arched one elegant, symmetrical eyebrow apiece.

"I don't really know—" her Mim began to say.

Clarissa said, "It's as close as anyone can get to the moon without actually traveling there. And the dress is moon white. Not eggshell. Not ivory. Not seashell or bone."

Kel said, "I think the decorations will be enough. We have the starfield projector, the hand-blown Earth, the powder floor—"

"Little hanging moons of white roses," Suzette added. "Plus a replica of Richard's robot on every table. Isn't that enough?"

"We're having ice cream," Clarissa said. "The real thing, too. Not those soy sorbets that don't melt, or coconut-sulfite substitutes. Ice cream."

"Don't you think that's a bit much?" her Mim said. "You *are* successful, and we *are* very fortunate, but it's generally unwise to put that on display."

"I disagree with your mother in almost everything," Kel said, "but in this matter, she's right. Where in the world would we find clean milk? And uncontaminated eggs? As for vanillin, that's in all the drugstores, but it's a plebeian flavor, isn't it?"

"Our people don't have the microbiomes to survive a street egg," Suzette said. "And milk means cancer in ten years. What will you want next? Hamburgers?"

"I'll find what I need," Clarissa said, fingering her necklace. The moon glass was warm against her skin. Richard could surely, like a magician, produce good eggs from his handkerchief.

Synthetic vanillin was indeed bourgeois, and thus out of the question. Clarissa took three shells and a boat, rowed by a black man spitting blood and shrinking into himself, to the Museum of Flavors. This was a nondescript office building in the Bronx, whose second-floor window had been propped open for her.

Whatever government agency originally funded it had long since been plundered and disbanded. Entire crop species, classes of game birds, and spices now existed only in these priceless, neglected vaults. The curator was only too happy to accept a cash transfer for six of the vanilla beans, which he fished out of a frozen drawer and snipped of their tags. He was an old classmate from Princeton, who lived in terror that the contents of his vaults might be made known, attracting armed hordes of the desperate and cruel. But Clarissa, as he knew well, was discreet.

The amount exchanged approached the value of a minor Rothko. Clarissa made a mental note to send one of her spares to auction.

Richard, dear darling Richard, had grumblingly procured six dozen eggs by helicopter from Semi-Free Pennsylvania by the time she returned. He had been obliged to shout through a megaphone first, while the helicopter hovered at a safe distance, he said, before the farmer in question set his shotgun down.

"As for the milk," he said, "you're on your own. Try Kenya?"

"If the bacteria in a New York egg would kill Mim," Clarissa said, "milk from a Kenyan cow—"

"You're right. You sure a dairy substitute—"

"Know how much I paid for the vanilla beans?"

She told him. He whistled. "You're right. No substitutes. Not for this. But—"

Clarissa said, "What about Switzerland?"

"There's nothing of Switzerland left."

"There are tons of mountains," Clarissa said. "I used to ski them as a girl. Didn't your family ski?"

"We preferred Aspen."

"Then how do you know there's not a cow hiding somewhere?"

"They used dirty bombs in the Four Banks' War. Anything that survived will be radioactive."

"I didn't know about the dirty bombs."

"It was kept out of the news. A bad look."

"Then how—"

"Risk analysts in cryptofinance hear all kinds of unreported things."

The curl of his hair seemed especially indulgent, his smile soft and knowledgeable. She worried the glass bead on its chain.

"I'll ask around," Clarissa said. "Someone must know. I've heard rumors of skyr, of butter—even cheese—"

"Doesn't mean there's a pristine cow out there. Be careful. People die for a nibble of cheese. I'll never forgive you if you poison my mother."

"You wait," Clarissa said. "We'll find a cow."

Because the ice cream would be a coup d'état, in one fell swoop staking her social territory, plastering her brand across gossip sites, and launching the battleship of her marriage, Clarissa was reluctant to ask widely for help. It was her life's work, just as it had been her Mim's, to make the effortful appear effortless. Sweating and scrambling across Venezuelan mesas in search of cows would rather spoil the desired effect.

So she approached Lindsey, a college roommate, now her maid of honor, who was more family than friend, anyhow. Lindsey squinted her eyes and said she recalled a rumor of feral milkmaids in Unincorporated Oregon.

Rumor or not, it was worth following. Clarissa found the alumni email of a journalist, was passed on to a second, then a third. Finally she established that indeed, if one ventured east of the smallpox zone that stretched from Portland to Eugene, one might, with extraordinary luck, discover a reclusive family in Deschutes that owned cows three generations clean. But no one had seen any of them in months.

"You're, what do you call it, a stringer, right? For the *Portland Post-Intelligencer*? Independent contractor, 1099? Well, what do you say to doing a small job for me? I'll pay all expenses—hotels, private drone—plus a per diem, and you'll get a story out of it. I just need fifteen gallons, that's all."

Icebox trains still clanked across the country over miles of decaying railbeds, hauled by tractors across gaps where rails were bent or sleepers rotted though, before being threaded onto the next good section. Their cars carried organ donations, blood, plasma, cadavers for burial or dissection, and a choice selection of coastal foods: flash-frozen Atlantic salmon fished from the Pacific, of the best grade, with the usual number of eyes; oysters from a secret Oregon bed that produced no more than three dozen a year; New York pizza, prepared with street mozzarella, for the daredevil rich in San Francisco; and Boston clam chowder without milk, cream, or clams. Her enterprising journalist added fifteen gallons of Deschutes milk in jerrycans to the latest shipment. Clarissa gnawed one thumbnail to the quick while she waited for the jerrycans to arrive.

Arrive they did, along with unconscionable quantities of sugar.

All that was left was the churning. Here Lindsey and three other bridesmaids proved the value of their friendship beyond any doubt, producing batch after creamy batch of happiness. Two days before the wedding, they had sculpted a moon of vanilla ice cream, complete with craters and silver robot-shaped scoop.

Ninety people, almost everyone who mattered, attended the wedding. The priest, one of six available for the chapel, still healthy and possessed of his hair and teeth, beamed out of the small projector.

"I promise to be your loving wife and moon maiden," Clarissa said.

"I promise to be the best husband you could wish for, and the best father anyone could hope, for the three or four or however many children we have."

"Three?" Clarissa said faintly. "Four?" But like a runaway train, her vows rattled forward. "I promise—"

Afterwards they mingled and ate. Then the moon was brought out to exclamations, camera flashes, and applause. The ice cream scoop excavated the craters far faster than the real robotic sifter could have.

Clarissa, triumphant, whirled from table to table on Richard's arm.

"Know what's etched on the robot?" she said. "*Clarissa O. Bell and Richard H. Laverton III forever.*"

"So virtual," Monica said. "I'd kill for a man like that."

"For what that cost," Richard said, "we could have treated all of New York for Hep C, or bought enough epinephrine to supply the whole state. But some things are simply beyond price. The look in Clarissa's eyes—"

Glass shattered behind them. A dark-faced woman wearing the black, monogrammed uniform of the caterers Clarissa's Mim had hired swept up the shards with her bare hands.

"Sorry," the woman said, "I'll clean it up. Please, ignore me, enjoy yourselves—"

"Are you crying?" Clarissa said, astounded. "At my wedding?"

"No, no," the woman said. "These are tears of happiness. For you."

"You must tell me," Clarissa said, the lights of the room soft on her skin, glowing in the green glass around her neck. The bulbs were incandescent, selected by hand for the way they lit the folds of her lace and silk.

"It's nothing. Really, nothing. A death in the family. That's all."

"That's terrible. Here, leave that glass alone. This'll make you feel much better."

She scooped a generous ball of ice cream into a crystal bowl, added a teaspoon, and handed the whole thing over.

"Thank you so much," the woman said. This time, Clarissa was sure, her tears were purely of joy.

Another server came over with dustpan and brush and swept the glass shards up in silence.

Clarissa began to serve herself a second bowl of ice cream as well, so the woman would not feel alone, but Richard took the scoop from her hand and finished it for her.

His cornflower eyes crinkling, he said, "You make everyone feel welcome. Even my mother. Even Mel. Even that poor woman. You're a walking counterargument for empathy decay."

"What's—"

"Some researchers think you can't be both rich and kind. Marxist, anarchist nonsense. They should meet you."

The ice cream was sweet, so very sweet, and cold. Clarissa shivered for a moment, closing her eyes. For a moment her future flashed perfectly clear upon her, link by silver link: how a new glass drop would be added to her chain for each child,

Chelsea and Charles and Nick; how Richard would change, growing strange and mysterious to her, though no less lovable, never, no less beloved; how she would set aside her childish dreams of saving the world, and devote herself to keeping a light burning for her family, while all around them the world went dark.

She opened her eyes.

It was time to dance. Richard offered his arm.

Off they went, waltzing across the moon, their shoes kicking up lunar dust with each step. The dance had been choreographed ages before they were born, taught to them with their letters, fed to them along with their juice and ice cream, and as they danced, as everyone at their wedding danced, and the weeping server was escorted out, and the acrid, acid sea crept higher and higher, there wasn't the slightest deviation from what had been planned.

Ilse, Who Saw Clearly

ONCE, AMONG THE INDIGO MOUNTAINS OF GERMANY, THERE was a kingdom of blue-eyed men and women whose blood was tinged blue with cold. The citizens were skilled in clockwork, escapements, and piano manufacture, and the clocks and pianos of that country were famous throughout the world. Their children pulled on rabbit-fur gloves before they sat down to practice their etudes, for it was so cold the notes rang and clanged in the air. It was coldest of all in the town on the highest mountain, where there lived a girl called Ilse, who was neither beautiful nor ugly, neither good nor wicked. Yet she was not quite undistinguished, because she was in love.

One afternoon, when the air was glittering with the sounds of innumerable pianos, a stranger as stout as a barrel and swathed to his nosetip walked through the town, singing. Where he walked the pianos fell silent, and wheat-haired boys and girls cracked shutters into the bitter cold to peep at him. And what he sang was this:

Ice for sale, eyes for sale,
If your complexion be dark or pale
If your old eyes be sharp or frail,
Come buy, come buy, bright ice for sale!

Only his listeners could not tell whether he was selling ice or eyes, because he spoke in an odd accent and through a thick scarf.

He sang until he reached the square with its frozen marble fountain. The town had installed a clock face and a set of chimes in the ice, and now they were striking noon.

"Ice?" he said pleasantly to the crowd that had gathered. He unwound a few feet of his woolen cloak and took out a box. The hasp gave his mittens trouble, but finally it clicked open, and he raised the lid and held out the box for all to see. They craned their necks forward, and their startled breaths smoked the air.

The box was crammed with eyes.

There were blue eyes and green eyes and brown eyes, eyes red as lilies, golden as pollen; eyes like pickaxes and eyes like diamonds. Each eye had been carved and painted with enormous care, and the spaces between them were jammed with silk.

The stranger smiled at their astonishment. He unrolled a little more of his cloak and took out another box, and another, and then it was clear that he was really quite slender. He tugged his muffler past his mouth, revealing sunned skin and neat thin lips.

"The finest eyes," he said to the crowd. "Plucked from the lands along the Indian Ocean, where the peacock wears hundreds in his tail. Picked from the wine countries, where they grow as crisp as grapes. Young and good for years of seeing! Old but ground to perfect clarity, according to calculations by the wisest mathematicians in Alexandria!" His teeth flashed gold and silver as he talked.

He ran his fingers through the eyes, holding this one to the light, or that. "Is this not pretty?" he said. "Is this not splendid? Try, my good grandmother, try."

That old woman peered through eyes white with snow-glare at the gems in his hands. "I can't see them clearly," she admitted.

"Well, then!"

"Lucia," she said, touching her daughter's hand. "Find me a pair like I used to have."

"How much?" Lucia said.

"For you, the first, a pittance. An afterthought. Her old eyes and a gold ring."

"Done," the old woman said. Lucia, frowning, fingered two eyes as blue as shadows on snow.

The stranger extracted three slim silver knives with ivory handles from the lining of his cloak. With infinite care and exactitude, barely breathing, he slid the first knife beneath the old woman's eyelid, ran the second around the ball, and with the third cut the crimson embroidery that tied it in place. Twice he did this. Then, in one motion, he slid her old eyes out of their hollows and slipped in the new. Her old blind eyes froze at once in his hands, ringing when he flicked them with a fingernail. He dropped them into his pockets and tilted her chin toward him.

"I can count your teeth," the old woman said, astonished. "Your nose is thin. Your scarf is striped red and yellow."

"A wonder," someone said.

"A marvel of marvels."

"A magician."

"A miracle."

She pulled off her mitten and gave him the ring from her

left hand. "He's been dead twenty years," she said to Lucia, who did not look happy. "I can see again. Clear as water."

Then, of course, the stranger had to replace the shortsighted schoolteacher's eyes, after which the old fellow cheerfully snapped his spectacles in two; the neglectful eyes of the town council; six clockmakers' strained eyes; crossed eyes; eyes bleared with snow light and sunlight; eyes that saw too clearly, or too deeply, or too much; eyes that wandered; eyes that were the wrong color.

When the sun was low and scarlet in the sky, the stranger announced that he would work no longer that day, for want of illumination. Half the town immediately offered him a bed and a roaring fire. But he passed that night and many more at the inn, where the fire was lower, colder, and less hospitable, and where, it was said unkindly, one's sleeping breath would freeze and fall like snow on the quilts. He ate cold soup and sliced meats in the farthest corner, answered all questions with a smile, and went to bed early.

After twelve days he bundled his boxes about him and left the town, his pockets sunken and swinging with gold. The townspeople watched as he goat-stepped down the steep trail until even their sharp new eyes could no longer distinguish him from the ice-bearded stones and the pines and the snow.

These new eyes, they found, were better than the old. The makers of escapements and wind-up toys could do far more delicate work than before, and out of their workshops came pocket watches and pianos carved out of almond shells, marching soldiers made from bluebottles, wooden birds that flew and sang, mechanical chessboards that also played tippen, and other such wonders; and the fame of that town went out throughout the whole world.

Summer heard, in her house on the other side of the world, and came to see.

The first notice they had of her approach was a message in a blackbird's beak, then a couple red buds on the edges of twigs, and then she was there. Out of respect she had put on a few extra flowers this year. It was still cold—summer high in the mountains is like that—but the air was softer, the light gentler.

No one saw her courteous posies, however. A little before she arrived, their eyes had begun to blur, then blear, then melt. They saw each other crying and felt their own tears running down their faces, and for no reason at all except summer. Then they understood, and wept in earnest, but it was too late.

By summer's end everyone had cried out the new eyes. The workshops fell still and silent, and tools gathered tarnish on their benches. The hundreds of clocks around the town stopped, since no one could find their keys and keyholes to wind them up again. Only the pianos still rang out their frozen notes now and again, but the melodies were all in minor keys. The town was full of a cold, quiet grief.

Winter was coming, and they would have starved without Ilse, who hadn't sold her eyes. Her sweetheart had written atrocious poems to them, and although they were the same plain blue as anyone else's, she couldn't bear to part with them even for new eyes the colors of violets, blackberries, and marigolds. So she helped the town tend and bring in its meager harvests of beets and cabbage, and on Wednesdays she filled a sack with clocks and toys and went down the mountain to sell them at market, until there were none left. During the day her head swam with the pianos' lugubrious complaints, and at night she ached in every bone.

"Mother," she said, as they ate their bare breakfast together, "shouldn't someone go looking for the surgeon?"

"No one will find him."

"What will you do if you never find your eyes?"

"We'll manage."

"I'm going to look for him," she said.

"Absolutely not."

So Ilse packed up her summer clothes, a loaf of bread, two onions, and the fourteen silver coins her mother kept in a jar on the shelf, and the next day she set off down the mountain.

In all her sixteen years, she had never strayed beyond the market in the shadow of the mountain, where the town's clocks and pianos were sold. But now she passed town after town, few of which she knew, and bridges, and streams, and meadows stained with the dregs of summer, and now trees that did not stand as straight as soldiers but spread their shoulders broad and wide. She climbed up one of these as night fell, and tucked her head against her knees, and slept.

A soft noise, like paper or feathers, woke her in the middle of the night. Ilse opened her eyes in fear, expecting robbers and thieves, but saw nothing. Still she was full of dread. She thought of the silver she had stolen, and her sightless mother in a silent house, and her sweetheart, lonely and wondering. She thought of the long road ahead of her, with likely failure at its end, and shivered. For where could she begin to look?

"Think quieter," someone said close to her ear. She nearly fell out of the tree. Next to her, a crow shifted from foot to foot, cleared its throat, and spat.

"You can talk?"

"Your thoughts are so loud, I can't sleep." It sighed. "Why all the noise?"

"I am looking for my townsmen's eyes."

"Eyes!" The crow whistled. "Delectable. A treat. I should follow you."

Ilse snatched sideways, swiping a bit of dark down between her fingers. The crow tumbled out of the tree with a screech.

"You'll do no such thing," she said.

"Peace, peace." A wing brushed her brow. "You'll find what you're looking for. Your sight, and theirs. And you'll not like what you see, too-quick girl with the odor of onions."

He flapped his way to a higher branch. She could hear him combing out his rumpled feathers. "I don't take kindly to being grabbed at."

"Just let me find what I'm looking for," she said, and shut her eyes. Afterwards, but for a bit of down stuck to her clothes, she could not say whether she had dreamt it all.

ON THE THIRD day, as she trudged down the road that went nowhere she knew, she met a flock of spotted goats with yellow bells about their necks, and then their shepherd, who was chewing a stalk of grass. He greeted her, and she asked with no great hope whether he'd heard of a peddler of eyes.

"Yes, miss," he said. "Walk a little farther, until you reach a village with sunflowers around it. Go down the street to the last house. My daughter is home, and she knows much more about your magician than I do."

Ilse thanked him and went on. The village ringed by sunflowers was smaller and muddier than her own, and the road ended at the smallest and muddiest house. The cat on the roof had only half his coat, as he had been a fierce warrior in his day. He opened one eye and yawned at her.

A young woman opened the door. Asked about the peddler, she smiled and winked her eyes one after the other. One of them was a shade greener than the other.

"I lost this one falling out of a window. My father and I waited four years before the good man came back. We had nothing to pay him with, at least nothing worth it, and I would have gladly taken a grandmother's cataract. But he said I was a lovely girl and picked out a greener eye than my first for me. A sweet soul."

"He left my village blind."

"You must be mistaken. He wouldn't do such a thing."

"He has three silver knives with ivory hafts, with ivy engraved in the ivory. His skin is dark and his nose is sharp."

"Well," the goatherd's daughter said. "Well. He does look like that. And he does have three knives. But I really don't think—"

"How can I find him?"

"That will take a little explanation. But you're in no rush, are you? He doesn't travel quickly, and you don't look like you've eaten yet today." She hewed a generous piece of brown bread for Ilse and poured out a bowl of cream for her, as well as a bowl of milk for the cat.

"I still think you're wrong somewhere. Surely he wouldn't. So kind."

Ilse ate the bread and drank the cream so fast she left a crumb on her cheek and a pale spatter on her chin.

"Now," the goatherd's daughter said presently, "you'll be going to the city. If you unraveled today down the road, you'd find the city at the end of next week. There are three towers at the corners of the city, with three broad streets between them, and where the streets meet is a brick square. Ask in the square where your magician might be. Someone there will know.

"But you're not walking that road in these clothes, are you?"

Ilse was suddenly aware of how heavy and hot her woolen summer smock and rabbit-fur cloak were, and how strongly they reeked of onions.

"Let me find you something lighter. You can leave those here, for when you return."

So Ilse exchanged her fur and wool for an armful of patched but comfortable linen, put a piece of bread and a slice of cheese in her pocket, and continued on her way. Now and then she passed a farm cart creaking along. Now and then, with a nod from the driver, she climbed into one of those carts and rested. She came upon a few crows pecking in the dust, but though she greeted them politely, they never answered.

The longer she traveled, the closer together grew the villages and fields. She was tired of the road and the yellow dust that lay in a film on her mouth, and she thought many times of her soft bed at home, and the color of her sweetheart's hair, and the air as pure as snow. Sometimes she considered turning around, but she never did. After wearing out her shoes by the thickness of seven days, she saw, black against the evening, three towers as formidable as teeth, and that was the city.

A soldier in fine scarlet-and-cream stood to attention at the gate, which was barred. He had a spear in his hand and steel mail beneath his tabard.

"It's past sunset," he said, frowning at her through his helmet. "No one enters or exits the city at night. Go home."

She said, "My home is in the mountains. I came down looking for a magician, a doctor, who can take the eyes out of your head and put them in again. He took all the eyes out of our town."

"I've heard of such a doctor," said the soldier. "He mended my fourth cousin's weak eyes, years ago. But you can't mean him. He wouldn't do such a thing."

"Perhaps it was unintended."

"You should ask around in the city tomorrow. Tomorrow, mind you. I cannot let you through." He held his spear a little straighter. "Unless you can show me something as bright as sunlight. That might fool me for a little while."

"I only have a little silver," she said, patting her pockets. But they were empty.

"Moonlight will do."

"No, I have nothing. I left my silver in my smock, and I left my smock at a goatherd's cottage, and that's a week's walking."

The soldier huffed into his moustache. "What a foolish girl you are." He took a key from his belt and opened a low door in the gate, just tall enough for her to slip through. "I have a little one as silly as you. You'd feed yourself to wolves if I kept you outside. Hurry up. And stay out of trouble."

"Thank you," Ilse said, and he shut and locked the door behind her.

Here and there the flame in a lamppost flickered and swayed. There were many more streets than she had expected, running every which way. Uncertain of what to do, she went back and forth, past dark windows and bolted doors; past open doors that spilled out laughter, music, and light; past rubbish in the gutters and pools of water shining in the dark. Shadows slid around her, silent and purposeful. She felt the weight of unseen eyes.

At last, lost and dispirited, she peered into a shop window and saw a vitrine lined with pocket watches, then the pale faces of tall clock cases in the dimness beyond. Some of them looked familiar. She pressed her nose to the gold-lettered glass, wondering if she knew the hands that had made them. She wanted very much to touch them, but the door was locked.

There was nowhere else she could go. She sat down in the doorway and put her head in her hands and, unwillingly, fell asleep.

If strange hands rifled her pockets while she slept, they found nothing, and she did not know. When she woke, it was morning. An old man with a broom was standing over her, displeased.

"Get along now, girl," he said. "Go on." He swept a little dirt over her, then tried to sweep her off the step.

"Please, which way to the square?"

"Which way to the square?" The shopkeeper stared. "Are you mad?"

"I came into the city yesterday," she said.

"With no place to stay? You *are* mad."

"Won't you tell me?"

"Never let it be said I was uncharitable toward the insane," the shopkeeper said. He disappeared into the shop—a bell jangled inside—and just as she decided to leave, reappeared with a small stale cake.

"There you go," he said. "Down the lane, a left, a right, a right, a left, a right, two more lefts, and you're there." And he went back into his shop.

The square was broader than she expected, and busier, lively with stalls and carts and striped awnings, the glitter of gold and silver on tables, the odors of fruit and fish and spices, the squabble of bargainers and women shouting apples.

Weaving her way through the tables and crowds, dazzled and bewildered, she saw a table set with magnificent glass apparatuses: telescopes, periscopes, beakers, loupes, spiral condensers, burning glasses, spectacles. Behind a towering stack of old books sat the glassblower, his nose in a book. There was a mole on the tip of his nose.

She asked whether he knew the magician.

"Of course! Of course!" he snorted.

"Where can I find him?"

"Why, he's marrying our Queen next month! Only," he said, and winked, "no one knows that it's him, our peripatetic physician, our humble expeller-of-drusen, ablator-of-sties. Word is she's betrothed to a Solomonic magician from far away, the

Indies, the Sahara, what have you. But she's had milk eyes from the day she was born, our poor Majesty, and only one fellow could have fixed them. The usual reward, of course, would have been half the kingdom, or ennoblement and emolument. But he's a handsome one, our doctor. And ambitious. Why are you looking for him? Did he steal your heart too?"

She told him.

"Ha! What a mistake to make. It'll be easy to find him. He's caged in the royal palace; you can't miss it. Finest house in the city, and tallest, and no one can have finer or taller, for fear of beheading. She had the weathervanes sawn off churches, and would have chopped down the towers as well, except they persuaded her to build her house a little higher. You can see it from here."

The palace was indeed the finest house in the city, ringed by green gardens and ponds full of tame swans. Guards bright with old-fashioned weapons marched around its perimeter.

Ilse crumbled a bit of her cake for the swans as she pondered the problem. Then she looked at the wet black legs of the swans.

It was not easy to tear one of her skirts to strips; she had to put her teeth to it. Every four inches she tied a loop, and when she had finished, she spread it loosely and broke the rest of the cake over it. As the swans stabbed up the crumbs, she slipped the knots around their scaly legs.

Then she tugged.

One of the swans hissed and bit her finger, but the rest, startled, took off in a white cloud. Clinging to their feet for dear life, she rose higher and higher in the air.

Once she was dizzyingly high above the city, she untied the swans one by one, until she was holding a single blustering cob by the feet. They sank together through the air, landing hard on the tiles of the palace roof.

She let the swan go and looked about her.

In one corner was a hunchbacked tower, patchy with lichen. To her left and right, the castle walls plunged below the eaves. Ilse scrabbled across the slate tiles, kicking a piece loose—it skittered down the sloping roof and vanished over the edge— and losing a shoe. When she came to the open window, she clambered through and into a rich bedroom.

A goat-slender man, studying himself in his mirror, whirled around at the noise. She recognized his pointed nose and chin, his glittering eyes.

"Who are you?"

The room was hung with tapestries; the bed was spread with silks and velvets; even the magician's coat teemed with jewels. Ilse was suddenly aware of the patches on her borrowed clothes. But she thought of her sweetheart and her mother, and she stood up straight and addressed him.

"Ah!" the magician said, after she had finished her story. "I never meant to do that. I cut ice eyes for you because I thought they'd never melt."

"Will you give them their eyes back?"

"Impossible. Others needed them."

"What are you going to do?"

"I am going to marry the Queen in a month," he said. "It's time I settled down. She's a lovely woman. Proud, though. She won't permit me to work as a petty physician. Must marry a man of leisure, you know. Even if I made you new eyes of rock crystal and glass, who could restore them?"

"So you are leaving my town blind," Ilse said. "You have taken away their eyes, their wedding rings, and their livelihoods, and you'll never return them. You are going to marry a Queen and live, as they say, happily ever after. What a marvelous magician you are!"

He hesitated. "That's putting it rather badly. I could teach you, I suppose. If you are intelligent enough. If you are nimble enough. It might take five years, or ten, depending on how quickly you learn." He glanced doubtfully at her clothes. "But afterward you could restore sight wherever you wished."

"Teach me," Ilse said.

"We must first ask the Queen."

They found the Queen reading Schiller with her feet propped on a leather ottoman, now and then weeping a decorous tear. She was not a cruel woman. She listened to Ilse's story and sighed, and afterwards gently reproached her betrothed. But their request displeased her.

"Am I to give you up, my love, for ten years so you can train the girl?"

"Hardly—"

"You may have his instruction for one year," she said to Ilse. "I will postpone the wedding for that long, because it is unseemly for a King to teach surgery. But after one year, we shall marry, and you will go home."

Grateful and dismayed, Ilse kissed the Queen's white hand.

For a year she studied under the magician, by sunlight, moonlight, and candlelight, paging through abstruse medical texts and reproducing in wet, squiggling lines on blurry paper the elegant anatomical diagrams her teacher marked with a finger. Often she went without sleep and food in her haste to learn.

The magician taught her the structure and composition of the eye, its fine veining, innervation, and musculature; the operation of light and color; sixteen theories of sight from philosopher-doctors in various kingdoms; and common diseases and their remedies. All of this, he said, he had gathered from years of wandering in strange lands among strange people. And when she was exhausted with studying, he told her stories from his travels.

In the flicker of shadows on the wall, her eyes unfocused from much reading, she thought she could see the people he described: the woman who married a tiger, the parrots who kept state secrets, the ship that flew in the air. She fell asleep in her chair with his words still running in her ears, and he dropped a coat over her before he retired. Thus passed many nights.

By the end of the year, she could switch the eyes of rabbits, cats, and sparrows without harming them, without a drop of blood falling on the magician's knives.

"All that I can teach, you know," he told her one night. "Take my knives, and take this box. I have had time to fashion new eyes for you and yours. Glass and rock crystal, this time."

She thanked him.

"There is one more thing. I know no one as quick and capable as you, or as kind. If you will have me, I will marry you instead of the Queen."

"That is generous of you, but I have a sweetheart at home," Ilse said.

"He won't have waited for you."

"He has. I am certain."

"Very well," the magician said, annoyed. "Go home to him, then." He was not gracious enough to invite her to the wedding, or even to replace her tattered clothes. So with the box under her arm, and the three silver knives at her side, Ilse left the palace.

The soldier at the gate barred her path with his spear. He had a hard face and a rough red beard.

"What are you carrying, girl?"

"Eyes that the Queen's magician gave me."

"Gave you? You in those rags? Unlikely. An export fee of

three gold crowns." He laughed at her. "Of course you can't pay. But you've a pretty face, and I'll overlook this for a kiss."

Ilse turned to go.

"Or," he said, "I could have you arrested and imprisoned. For probable theft."

She saw that he meant it. A sick twist in her stomach, she kissed him on his bristly mouth, feeling his hands slide up and down her sides. Then the soldier bowed in mockery and let her pass.

The road seemed twice as long now. The days grew colder as she went, for it was autumn again, and her clothes were thin, and the road was rising toward the mountains. The crows in the trees croaked and chuckled at her.

After many days of weary walking, she saw with great relief the goatherd's village. The sunflowers were brown and rattled in the wind, but the cat still sat on the goatherd's roof. It stretched and purred.

Ilse rapped upon the door. The goatherd's daughter cracked it open. Faint lines were sketched into her forehead. Somewhere in the cottage, a child wailed.

"What do you want?"

"I left a wool smock and a fur cloak with you. Last year, it was. There were fourteen pieces of silver in the pocket."

"I don't know what you're talking about."

"You fed me and gave me these clothes to wear. Don't you recognize them? Keep the smock and cloak, if you like, but please give me my mother's silver."

"We feed paupers every day. I can't remember each one. But there's no food in the house today. There's no food in all the village." She shut the door.

Ilse had no choice but to continue. The higher she climbed, the colder it was, and she shivered when she lay down to sleep on the lichen-studded stones. But she kept herself warm remembering her sweetheart's smile and her mother waiting for her in darkness.

At last she heard the faint sound of pianos. Tired though she was, she quickened her pace. Soon she saw woodsmoke, then chimney pots, then houses.

The town was as she remembered it. But the notes that rang in the cold air were cheerful, and people went about their day as if the magician had never been. Ilse went into her own house and found her mother slicing vegetables.

"Ilse?" the woman said uncertainly. Ilse kissed her mother's cheek.

"You'll never guess where I've been."

"Out into the world. But what are you wearing? Go put on something warm."

"In a moment. Hold still." And with practiced gentleness, Ilse set two blue eyes in her mother's face.

AFTER THAT, SHE visited her sweetheart. She ran to him and embraced him, and he said, "Ilse?"

"I'm home."

"Oh, Ilse—I'm happy you've come back." He paused. "This is Elsa—the goldsmith's daughter. I married her in the spring."

"How wonderful." She turned. "I have gifts for both of you."

AFTER A FORTNIGHT of careful work, all the town could see again. Ilse was well wished, well fed, blessed, and thanked, and made to tell her story again and again, until the smallest child could recite it.

It was pleasant being home. She had missed the sound of ice-tuned pianos and the sweet mountain wind.

When Elsa the goldsmith's daughter gave birth, everyone agreed that the blue-eyed girl would be a matchless beauty and a legend in the kingdom. Her father wrote achingly terrible sonnets to those eyes.

Sometimes Ilse went to the edge of town and stared at the world that fell away from her, farther than she could see. Sometimes she wondered how the magician and his Queen fared. More often, though, she thought of the distant lands he had told her about, where he had learned his art: jewel-colored jungles, thick with flowers and snakes; white sands running into a green sea; dark pine forests alive with deer and wolves and red foxes. She would look down the mountain's side until her face was numb with cold.

ONE DAY, NO one could find her.

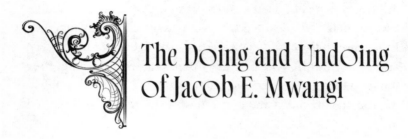

The Doing and Undoing of Jacob E. Mwangi

On Sunday after services, Jacob Esau Mwangi beat a hasty retreat from the crowd that descended upon his beaming parents and Mercy, who on this rare visit home between Lent and Easter terms was displayed between them like a tulip arrangement.

"What a daughter! Be a famous professor soon."

"You have not forgotten about us common people? Cambridge makes all the children forget. They act so embarrassed when they come home—"

"Funny to think they both come from the same family."

"It's very strange, isn't it?"

"Where did he go anyway, that Jacob boy?"

Jacob, outside the chapel's blue acrylic domes, caught the first flying matatu without regard for where it went.

He glowered out the window at the holograms of giraffes and rhinos that stalked the streets, flashing advertisements both local and multinational. A lion yawned and stretched among the potted plants at the center of a traffic circle, the words DRINK MORE JINGA COLA scrolling along its tawny flanks.

Twenty-five years ago, the gleam and gloss of digital advertisements had divided the globetrotting Kenyan Haves from the shilling-counting Have Nots who shopped at tin-sided street stalls with painted signs. Now that that partition was obsolete, humanity had split itself into Doers and Don'ts. Jacob's mathe and old man were devoted Doers, an architect and an engineer. Every month they asked Jacob if he had created anything lately, and every month, when he gave them a cheerful shrug, they flung up their palms in ritualized despair.

The matatu halted and hovered while more people crammed on.

Jacob had no stomach for returning to his apartment, a windowless box in Kawangware that he had picked specifically for its distance from the family manse. He unrolled his penphone and selected Rob's name.

```
                            hey, game time?
    sorry can't
                            what's going?
    dame. tell u later
                            sawa
```

Outside the window the tidy six-story buildings of Kibera Collective flashed wholesome mottos in LEDs. *Pick up after yourself. Harambee. Together we can remake the world.* Jacob frowned absently, mapping his route in his head. If he swapped matatus here, the next would take him as far as Black Nile Lounge. The Black Nile was his usual base, though he'd venture as far east as the Monsoon Club if Rob was joining. You did that for a brother.

And Rob was his brother in all the ways that mattered, just as their gaming group was his true family: Robert and nocturnal Ann from Wisconsin and Chao from Tennessee, as well as sixty guildmembers from places as exotic as Anchorage and Busan who formed a far-flung network of cousins and in-laws, as full of gossip and grudges and backbiting and broken promises as the real thing. They were all Don'ts, of course. Doers played too, intermittently, but the Don'ts slaughtered them all, every match, always.

The no-man's-land between the Doers and Don'ts was as close as anything came to a war these days. Though the lines were deeply entrenched and wreathed in verbal barbed wire, and battles pitched as often in PvP as over dinner tables, no real bullets were ever fired. There had been little of that since the days of the Howl.

No one liked to speak of the Howl, of the blood that darkened and dried in the streets, of the mind virus that had reawakened after a century of dormancy to sow chaos and fear.

For out of the Howl had come the great Compassion, when, like a strange flowering in a sunless cave, the fervent prayers of adherents of every faith and the ferocious meditations of the variously spiritual, bet-hedging, and confused had reached critical mass, triggering a deep immune response in the human psyche. As if struck by lightning, the five billion survivors of the Howl had let the rifles and knives fall out of their hands, then embraced, or dropped to their knees and wept.

It was like God Himself sat down and talked with me, Jacob's mathe liked to say, and his old man would nod solemnly, yes, that was how it was.

By the fiftieth time he heard this exchange, Jacob was ready to pitch a can of Jinga Cola at each of their heads. He had not known the Compassion, having been born shortly afterward, and was thoroughly sick of hearing about it.

During the three years that the Compassion lasted, dazed legislators in every country redistributed wealth and built up healthcare and social services, while the wealthy deeded entire islands and bank accounts to the UN. Petty crime and begging vanished from Nairobi's streets. House gates were propped open. Askaris found no work and opened flower stands and safari companies. Kibera shantytown self-organized, pooled surplus funds, and built communal housing with plumbing and internet.

Gradually, as memories of the Compassion faded, life returned to a semblance of normalcy. Rush-hour drivers again cursed each other's mothers, and politicians returned to trading favors and taking tea money. But there remained a certain shining quality about life, if looked at the right way—or so Jacob's elders said.

The most important outcome of all that ancient history, as far as Jacob was concerned, was the monthly deposit in his account that the Kenyan government styled Dream Seeds, distributed to every resident not already receiving a stipend from another government. This paid for Jacob's bachelor pad and now, as he touched his pen to a scanner, for the Black Nile entry fee, a handful of miraa, and a bottle of beer.

The man in the booth assigning cubes handed Jacob a key-card marked 16 and said hopefully, "Maybe a Kenyan game today, sir? My brother's studio, I can recommend—"

"Maybe another day, boss."

"You cannot blame a man for trying. Japanese fantasy war sims again?"

"Good guess."

"I like to know my customers." He sighed. "I don't know how

we will compete, you see. Our industry has just been born—theirs is fifty, sixty years old."

"You will find a way," Jacob said, to escape.

The door to the VR cube hissed open. Jacob lasered the title he wanted on the wall—*Ogrefall: Visions of Conquest*—then donned the headset and gauntlets, which stank of sweat. In a higher-end establishment the gear would be wiped down with lavender towelettes between uses, and tiny pores in the wall would jet out molecules of the scent libraries shipped with the games, odors of forest and moss, leather and steel, but Black Nile was a business scratched out of hope and savings from jua kali, the owner a Doer to his core, and the game loads were all secondhand.

Jacob launched the game and became a silver lion with braided mane, ten feet tall and scarred from battle. Ann and Chao were already online, knee-deep in the corpses of ogres and the occasional unfortunate Doer, their whoops of joy ringing in his ears.

"Hey! No Rob?" Ann asked.

"Some dame," Jacob said, placing his paw over his heart. "He's a goner."

"You say that every time," Chao said. "And you're always wrong. Rob gets bored faster than anyone else I know. I give her fifteen minutes, max."

Ann said, "We're storming Bluefell right now. Figured you two'd be along. I don't know what we'll do without Rob."

"Let's run it," Chao said. "Rob will catch up to us."

They battled their way up a snowy mountain, pines creaking and shaking lumps of snow down on them. Ice demons lunged and jeered and raked their faces. Ann died. Chao died. Jacob died. Their vision went black, and then they found themselves at the foot of the mountain.

"Again?" Chao said.

Again they wiped.

"This is bullshit," Ann said. "I give up."

"Hi, guys," Rob said. "What are we playing today?"

"Told you," Chao said.

"Where are you?" Jacob said. "And where's your girl?"

"Took you long enough," Chao said. "Twenty-four minutes. A new record."

"She's here with me. We're at Monsoon. Trying to skip the tutorial. Hang on."

A moment later, there she was: purple-haired and elf-eared, in novice's robes.

"Good," Ann said. "Five's more than enough, even with an egg. Here, I've got a spare bow."

The new girl looked around. "Wow, they pushed their graphics to the limit. But they're still using the Conifer engine—ooh—and it has that vulnerability they didn't do a full distro patch for. I wonder what happens if—"

Jacob blinked. She was suddenly wearing a gallimaufry of gear, harlequin in color and decorated with the taste of a drunken weaverbird. But her character now displayed a respectable power level.

Ann and Chao stared in horror.

"What? Is it the colors? I can change those—give me a cycle—"

"Robert," Ann said, very slowly. "What does she *do*?"

"Oh, I'm a programmer, mostly. I make indie games with two friends from university. Ever heard of *Duka Stories*? That was us."

"Guys—" Rob began.

"She's a Doer," Chao said. "You picked up a Doer."

"This is Consolata. We've been dating for three months."

"It's nice to meet you! What do you all do?" She turned toward Jacob, sparkling with hope.

Jacob growled.

"Fuck this," Ann said, and logged off.

Chao said, "Not cool, man. Not cool at all. Hit me up when she's history—or don't, I don't care."

And he was gone.

"Did I do something wrong?" Consolata said.

"I—" Rob sighed. "I didn't know they'd be like that."

"Really," Jacob said. "You did not know."

"Nah, Jacob—"

"There is a reason why we do not cross the line. Doers are evangelical. Listen to her. Next thing, you'll be an entrepreneur, or a community leader, shaking hands with every aunty in church. You will tell them, 'I feel so sorry for that Jacob boy, he never applied himself to anything. Chao, oh, what a waste of intellect. Poor Ann, I'm sure she could have been amazing at anything, if only she tried—' "

"Because of a dame? You think a dame could do that to me? What's eating you?"

"Mercy's home," Jacob said, letting his lion-face curl into a snarl.

"Ee. I see. I'm sorry—"

"No. Not today," Jacob said, and logged off. He tore the gauntlets from his hands. Then he saved the game logs to his phone, to remind himself of what a rat Rob was, and stormed out of the Black Nile. It was ten long and dusty blocks home. Jacob stomped and swore his way up the concrete stairs.

At the top, Mercy was waiting for him.

"Look," she said, matching him step for step as he back-pedaled down the stairs, "I don't like it either, Jacob, kweli, all the church ladies up in my face with 'When are you going to get married, I have a nephew just your age.' Once I got away I took a taxi here—"

"Go back to Cambridge and all that stupid grass you can't touch, and all that colonial-in-the-metropolis crap you like so much."

"You do read my emails." She beamed. "I had wondered."

"Get lost."

"You have potential up to here, Jacob. You are crackling with the stuff. The problem is, you don't see it yourself."

"Mathe put you up to this."

"Nobody put me up to this. What I wanted to say was—Jacob, wait. As soon as I have a job, which will be soon, I'm interviewing all over Europe right now—as soon as I'm settled, I want to pay for your university. All you have to do is pick a course."

"I hate to break it to you, sis dear, but these days university is free. So take your money and—"

"I don't mean university in Kenya. Maybe China. Tsinghua University? Shanghai Tech? Maybe the US. Wherever you like. Dream big. Some travel would be good for you."

"Mercy," Jacob said, stopping at the bottom of the stair. Four steps above him, she wobbled on her acrylic heels, clinging to the balustrade. "This is all I want. I'm happy. Leave me alone."

"If you think I'm going to just—"

"Yes. You are."

"Well," Mercy said, "you have my number. When you change your mind—"

"I won't."

"Ee, twenty-two years and you're still as fussy as an infant."

"Kwaheri, Mercy."

He stepped sideways and waved her down the stairs. Mercy descended. Before she passed him she put a hand on his shoulder.

"I care about you," she said. "Would I be this obnoxious if I didn't?"

"Please, find a nice mzungu or mhindi at Cambridge to torture instead of me. Try the maths department. I hear they're just as odd as you are."

A hawkeyed taxi driver slowed and hovered at the curb.

"Bye, Jacob."

"Piss off, Mercy."

And Jacob went up to his tiny room and flung himself down, wondering why it felt like an elephant had stepped on his chest.

SOMETHING IMPORTANT THAT he'd overlooked tickled the back of his eyelids until he awoke.

Ah. Jacob rolled over in bed and grabbed his penphone. There, in the previous day's logs, was the anomaly: the moment when Consolata went from starter gear to a hodgepodge of expert-level bits. The game logs showed a line of code injected at the exact time her left hand twisted into a complicated shape like a mudra.

Jacob searched online for the snippet of code and found lengthy discussions of a developer-mode trigger in three unpatched, two-year-old, Conifer-based games. After an hour or two of reading he thought he had the gist of it.

As Jacob, clearly the first customer of the day, came in, the man at Black Nile yawned and waved his hand over the array of keycards.

"Be my guest."

Jacob loaded *Ogrefall* first. Pasting in the code snippet from his phone, he contorted his left hand—here a silver paw—into the shape he remembered and had practiced that morning.

Blip.

His rare and beautiful endgame armor was gone. It had been replaced by an eye-smarting farrago of gear. Only now each item showed a purple variable name floating over its center. He could have kicked himself for his carelessness—the Nebula Paladin set had taken sixty-four hours to complete—but fascination won out over regret. Holding the same awkward mudra as before, Jacob tapped his lotus-stamped breastplate and toggled the number at the end of the variable.

The lotus transformed into a winged lion rampant, the metal from silver to burnished gold.

When Jacob raised his eyes, he noticed that the ice demons hissing and swooping nearby had variables too. Soon he was sending them jitterbugging this way and that and spiraling helplessly off the edge of a cliff.

Was this what the world looked like from the other side?

The other two games that the tweaker forums mentioned, a historical shooter and a haunted-house platformer, permitted similar manipulations. Jacob stood in the middle of floating words and numbers, changing the world around him with hardly more than a thought. He had become a god in these three small worlds. Ann and Chao would explode from envy. He suppressed a grin.

Then the screens went dark, and the harsh after-hours lights in the cube flashed on. Jacob struggled out of the VR rig, perplexed. He prodded buttons and lasered the empty wall. Nothing happened.

The door clicked, and the manager came in.

"Sorry sir," he said. "Your account has been banned for cheating. Same thing happened over at the Monsoon Club yesterday. We got the automated warnings just now, straight from

Japan. One-month ban from all Japanese games. Very sorry about that."

The room spun. Perhaps *Oakley*'s graphics had been subpar.

A month? Ann and Chao wouldn't wait a month. They'd find some new Don't, fresh out of secondary school or the military or a ruined thirty-year marriage, to replace him. To replace both him and Rob, now.

"I can see this is not easy news, sir. Not easy for me, either. You are a loyal customer."

"All Japanese games."

"Correct."

"What about other regions?"

"Cross-platform automatic two-week bans in Europe, the Americas, Asia, and Australia."

"But not Africa?"

"Not Africa. We're not advanced enough to be asked to sign those agreements yet."

"I think—" Jacob swallowed. "I think I'd like to try *Duka Stories,* if you have it."

The manager smiled. "Of course. Supporting the local economy, local artists, local products, that is one of my business goals."

Consolata's game turned out to be a simple duka simulator. Jacob had to clear the ground, hammer the corrugated iron sides of the shop together, and stock its shelves with what he guessed might appeal to the neighborhood. The art was handpainted, probably by one of Consolata's friends, the music easy and old-fashioned. The grandmothers who stopped by for spices pinched his cheeks and told him how glad they were to have him there, only couldn't he make an exception for them on the prices, everything being so expensive these days?

By the end of his first day in business, an hour into the game, Jacob was bankrupt and rapt.

Six hours later his business had been flattened twice, once by a student protest, once by askaris demanding protection money. Each time he built it up again, speaking brightly lettered promises to his worried customers. In the meantime he sent his painted children to school in uniforms with books and pens and crayons, an accomplishment that turned his heart to sugar. The game lacked the gloss that he was used to, but he had met the person who had created it. All of this, from three women!

An impossible thought arose in him. He refused to look at it directly. No, never. Maybe for money. Enough money. And only for a while.

"Boss," he said, emerging from the cube, "you said your brother runs a game studio?"

"He does," the manager said.

"Would he give me a job, do you think?"

"You should ask him yourself." The manager closed the game of bao he had been playing on his ancient iPhone, a bashed-up brick of third-hand tech, and pulled up a number.

"Yes, I have a young man here, regular customer, plays all the new games, wants to know if you have a job for him." He turned to Jacob. "He says go ahead, send him your portfolio."

"My portfolio?"

"Yes, art, music, design, whatever it is you want to work in. He says he doesn't have a portfolio. Hm? Okay. My brother says you should take courses in those things, whatever interests you, and come back when you can *do* something." He set the iPhone down.

"Thanks," Jacob said. There was nothing else he could say. He slouched out of the Black Nile, brow furrowed with thought.

SINCE THERE WAS nowhere else to meet, he invited Ann and Chao to visit his spruced-up duka, where they stood around sipping virtual sodas and blocking customers from their programmed paths.

Chao said, his Southern drawl dripping suspicion, "Run that by me again."

"Going to take some university courses so I can get a job. When I have enough saved up for my own VR rig, I'll quit and game full-time, twenty-four-seven."

Ann said, "I think the only person you're fooling is yourself."

"Don't be like that. You have no idea how much a rig costs in Nairobi. It's not like the US, where, what, one third of your monthly stipend buys one? More like two years' stipend for us. I want to game, but I also need to eat."

"If you say so," Ann said.

"Plus they've banned me from all Japanese-owned servers for a month, and other major regions for the next two weeks. This way I can *do* something." Hearing his own words, he stopped.

"So these courses," Chao said. "They're in . . . management? Administration?"

"Yeah. Yeah, that's right."

"Okay. That's almost as good as not doing anything. I wish you'd said something earlier, though. We could have crowd-funded you a console, as a guild."

"My parents would never let me live that down."

"We're going to miss you," Ann said abruptly. "I mean, Robbie, and now you . . ."

"Hey," Jacob said. "I'll still be online. And I'll still game with you, once this ban is lifted."

Her character hugged his. "Don't let the Doers get you."

"I won't."

"If you see Rob—" Chao said.

"Yes?"

"Never mind."

IT WAS, IN fact, on a gleaming skybridge of the Chiromo campus of the University of Nairobi that Jacob next saw Robert. Rob had two thick textbooks under his arm and walked quickly, with purpose, in the flood between classes. Then, with a start, his eyes met Jacob's, and his face broke into a pleased and embarrassed smile.

"You caught me," Rob said.

"What are you studying?"

"Astronomy. I wanted to discover a planet, as a kid. Somehow I forgot. Then somebody reminded me."

"You and Consolata—"

"Still together."

"Good for you."

They stood together in the middle of a river of students.

"So what brings you here?" Rob said eventually.

"Intro to Programming."

"What? Here? You?"

"And some art classes."

"Art!" Rob laughed.

"I'm going to design games. Please, don't tell Mercy."

"I'm not a monster." Rob paused. "You'll have to, though. Eventually. And if you're serious, Ann and Chao—"

"That will bite."

"It will. Also, so you know, I would never say—"

"I know."

"We should play together sometime," Rob said, punching Jacob's shoulder. "Consolata's releasing her new game next month. It's called *Love and War: The Story of a Doer and a Don't*. There'll be a party. You should come."

"If the beer's good, maybe. Maybe I will."

The two of them knocked knuckles with half-embarrassed, half-conspiratorial smiles. The sun beat down hot and golden on the campus as they passed and went their separate ways, each chasing, in his own heart, down a twisting road, the dim and indeterminate beginnings of a dream.

The Wretched and the Beautiful

THE ALIENS ARRIVED UNEXPECTEDLY AT 6:42 ON A HOT AUGUST evening, dropping with a shriek of metal strained past its limits onto the white sands of one of the last pristine beaches on Earth. The black hulk of the saucer ground into the sand and stopped, steaming. Those of us who had been splashing in the surf or stamping rows of sandcastles fled up the slope, clutching our towels.

Once our initial fright dissipated, curiosity set in, and we stayed with the policemen and emergency technicians who pulled up in wailing, flashing trucks. It was all quite exciting, since nothing out of the ordinary seemed to happen anymore. Gone were the days when acting on conviction could change the world, when good came of good and evil to evil.

One of the policemen fired an experimental shot or two, but the bullets ricocheted off the black metal and lodged in a palm tree.

"Don't shoot," one man said. "You might make them angry. You might hit one of us."

The guns remained cocked, but no more bullets zinged off the ship. We waited.

At sunset, a pounding began inside the ship. No hatches sprang open; no rayguns or periscopes protruded. There was only the pounding, growing ever more frantic and erratic.

"What if they're trapped?" one of us said.

We looked at one another. Some of us had left and returned with the pistols that did not fit in our swimming trunks. A whole armory was pointed at the black disk of metal half buried in the beach.

The pounding ceased.

Nothing followed.

We conferred, then conscripted a machinist, who with our assistance hauled her ponderous cutters and blowtorches over the soft sand and set to work on the saucer.

We stood back.

While the machinist worked, any sounds from the saucer were drowned out by her tools. With precise and deliberate motions, she cut a thin line around the disk's circumference. Sparks flew up where the blade met the strange metal, which howled in unfamiliar tones.

When her work was done, she packed her equipment and departed. The aliens had failed to vaporize her. We let out the collective breath we had been holding.

Minutes crawled past.

At last, with a peculiar clang, the top half of the saucer seesawed upward. In the deepening dusk we could barely distinguish the dark limbs straining to raise it. Many monsters or one, we wondered.

"Drop your weapons," one policeman barked. The upper part

of the saucer sagged for a moment, concealing whatever was within.

From within the ship, a voice said in perfectly comprehensible French, "We do not have weapons. We do not have anything."

"Come out where we can see you," the policeman said. The rest of us were glad that someone confident and capable, someone who was not us, was handling the matter.

It was too dark to see clearly, and so at the policeman's command, and at the other end of his semiautomatic, the occupants of the ship—the aliens, our first real aliens—were marched up the beach to the neon strip of casinos, while we followed, gaping, gawking, knowing nothing with certainty except that we were witnessing history, and perhaps would even play a role in it.

The lurid glow of marquees and brothels revealed to us a shivering, shambling crowd, some slumped like apes, some clutching their young. Some had five limbs, some four, and some three. Their joints were crablike, and their movement both resembled ours and differed to such a degree that it sickened us to watch. There were sixty-four of them, including the juveniles. Although we were unacquainted with their biology, it was plain that none were in good health.

"Is there a place we can stay?" the aliens said.

Hotels were sought. Throughout the city, hoteliers protested, citing unknown risk profiles, inadequate equipment, fearful and unprepared staff, an indignant clientele, and stains from space filth impervious to detergent. Who was going to pay, anyway? They had businesses to run and families to feed.

One woman from among us offered to book a single room for the aliens for two nights, that being all she could afford on her teacher's salary. She said this with undisguised hope, as if she thought her offer would inspire others. But silence followed her remark, and we avoided her eyes. We were here on holiday, and holidays were expensive.

The impasse was broken at three in the morning, when in helicopters, in charter buses, and in taxis, the journalists arrived.

It was clear now that our guests were the responsibility of national if not international organizations, and that they would be cared for by people who were paid more than we were. Reassured that something would be done, and not by us, we dispersed to our hotel rooms and immaculate beds.

When we awoke late, to trays of poached eggs on toast and orange juice, headlines on our phones declared that first contact had been made, that the Fermi paradox was no more, that science and engineering were poised to make breakthroughs not only with the new metal that the spaceship was composed of but also the various exotic molecules that had bombarded the ship and become embedded in the hull during its long flight.

The flight had indeed been long. One African Francophone newspaper had thought to interview the aliens, who explained in deteriorating French how their universal translator worked, how they had fled a cleansing operation in their star system, how they had watched their home planet heated to sterility and stripped of its atmosphere, how they had set course for a likely-looking planet in the Gould Belt, how they wanted nothing but peace, and please, they were exhausted, could they have a place to sleep and a power source for their translator?

When we slid on our sandals and stepped onto the dazzling beach, which long ago, before the garbage tides, was what many beaches looked like, we saw the crashed ship again, substantiation of the previous night's fever dream. It leached rainbow fluids onto the sand.

Dark shapes huddled under its sawn-off lid.

Most of us averted our eyes from that picture of unmitigated misery and admired instead the gemlike sky, the seabirds squalling over the creamy surf, the parasols propped like mushrooms along the shore. One or two of us edged close to the wreck and dropped small somethings—a beach towel, a bucket hat, a bag of chips, a half-full margarita in its salted glass—then scuttled away. This was no longer our problem; it belonged to our governors, our senators, our heads of state. Surely they and their moneyed friends would assist these wretched creatures.

So it was with consternation that we turned on our televisions that night, in the hotel bar and in our hotel rooms, to hear a spokesman explain, as our heads of state shook hands, that the countries in their interregional coalition would resettle a quota of the aliens in inverse proportion to national wealth. This was ratified over the protests of the poorest members, in fact over the protests of the aliens themselves, who did not wish to be separated and had only one translation device among them. The couple of countries still recovering from Russian depredations were assigned six aliens each, while the countries of high fashion and cold beer received two or three, to be installed in middle-class neighborhoods. In this way the burden of these aliens, as well as any attendant medical or technological advances, would be shared.

The cost would be high, as these aliens had stated their need for an environment with a specific mixture of helium and neon, as well as a particular collection of nutrients most abundant in shrimp and crab. The latter, in our overfished and polluted times, were not easy to obtain.

This was appalling news. We who had stitched, skimped, and pinched all year for one luxurious day on a clean beach would have our wallets rifled to feed and house the very creatures whose presence denied us a section of our beach and the vistas we had paid for. Now we would find these horrors waiting for us at home, in the nicer house next to ours, or at the community pool, eating crab while we sweated to put chicken on the table and pay off our mortgages. Who were they to land on our dwindling planet and reduce our scarce resources further? They could go back to their star system. Their own government could care for them. We could loan them a rocket or two, if they liked. We could be generous.

Indeed, in the days that followed, our legislators took our calls, then took this tack. If they meant to stay, shouldn't our visitors earn their daily bread like the rest of us? And if biological limitations made this impossible, shouldn't they depart to find a more hospitable clime? We repeated these speeches over the dinner table. Our performances grew louder and more vehement after a news report about one of the aliens eating its neighbor's cat; the distraught woman pointed her finger at the camera, at all of us watching, and accused us of forcing a monster upon her because we had no desire to live beside it ourselves. There was enough truth in her words to bite.

It did not matter that six days later the furry little Lothario was found at a gas station ten miles from home, having scrapped and loved his way across the countryside. By then we had stories of these aliens raiding chicken coops and sucking the blood from dogs and unsuspecting infants.

A solid number of these politicians campaigned for office on a platform of alien repatriation, and many of them won.

Shortly afterwards, one of two aliens resettled in Huntingdon, England, was set upon and beaten to death with bricks by a gang of teenaged girls and boys. Then, in Houston, a juvenile alien was doused in gasoline and set on fire. We picked at our dinners without appetite, worrying about these promising youths, who had been headed for sports scholarships and elite universities. The aliens jeopardized all our futures and clouded all our dreams. We wrote letters, signed petitions, and prayed to the heavens for salvation.

It came. From out of a silent sky, rockets shaped like needles and polished to a high gloss descended upon six of the major capitols of the world. About an hour after landing, giving the television crews time to jostle for position, and at precisely the same instant, six slim doors whispered open, and the most gorgeous beings we had ever seen strode down extruded silver steps and planted themselves before the houses of power, waiting to be invited in.

And they were.

"Forgive us for imposing on your valuable time," these ambassadors said simultaneously in the official languages of the six legislatures. Cameras panned over them, and excitement crackled through us, for this was the kind of history we wanted to be a part of.

When they emerged from their needle ships, their bodies were fluid and reflective, like columns of quicksilver, but with every minute among us, they lost more and more of their formless brilliance, dimming and thickening, acquiring eyes, foreheads, chins, and hands. Within half an hour, they resembled us perfectly. Or rather, they resembled what we dreamed of being, the better versions of ourselves who turned heads, drove fast cars, and recognized the six most expensive whiskies by smell alone; whose names topped the donor rolls of operas, orchestras, and houses of worship; who were admired, respected, adored.

We looked at these beautiful creatures, whom we no longer thought of as aliens, and saw ourselves as we could be, if the lottery, or the bank, or our birthplace—if our genes, or a lucky break—if only—

We listened raptly as they spoke in rich and melodious voices, voices we trusted implicitly, that called to mind loved ones and sympathetic teachers.

"A terrible mistake has been made," they said. "Because of our negligence, a gang of war criminals, guilty of unspeakable things, namely—"

Here their translators failed, and the recitation of crimes came as a series of clicks, coughs, and trills that nevertheless retained the enchantment of their voices.

"—escaped their confinement and infiltrated your solar system. We are deeply sorry for the trouble our carelessness has caused you. We admire your patience and generosity in dealing with them, though they have grossly abused your trust. Now we have come to set things right. Remit the sixty-four aliens to us, and we will bring them back to their home system. They will never disturb you again."

The six beautiful beings clasped their hands and stepped back. Silence fell throughout the legislative chambers of the world.

Here was our solution. Here was our freedom. We had trusted and been fooled, we had suffered unjustly, we were good people with clean consciences sorely tried by circumstances outside our control. But here was justice, as bright and shining as we imagined justice to be.

We sighed with relief.

In Berlin, a woman stood.

"Even the little ones?" she said. "Even the children are guilty of the crimes you allege?"

"Their development is not comparable to yours," the beautiful one in Berlin said, while his compatriots in their respective statehouses stood silent, with inscrutable smiles. "The small ones you see are not children as you know them, innocent and help-less. Think of them as beetle larvae. They are destructive and voracious, sometimes more so than the mature adults."

"Still," she said, this lone woman, "I think of them as chil-dren. I have seen the grown ones feeding and caring for them. I do not know what crimes they have committed, since our lan-guages cannot describe your concepts. But they have sought refuge here, and I am especially unwilling to return the children to you—"

The whispers of the assembly became murmurs, then excla-mations.

"Throw her out!"

"She does not speak for us!"

"You are misled," the beautiful one said, and for a moment its smile vanished, and a breath of the icy void between stars blew over us.

Then everything was as it had been.

"We must ask the aliens themselves what they want," the woman said, but now her colleagues were standing too, and shouting, and phone lines were ringing as we called in support of the beautiful ones, and her voice was drowned out.

"We have an understanding, then," the beautiful ones said, to clamorous agreement and wild applause.

The cameras stopped there, at that glorious scene, and all of us, warm and satisfied with our participation in history, turned off our televisions and went to work, or to pick up our children from soccer, or to bed, or to the liquor store to gaze at top-shelf whisky.

A few of us, the unfortunate few who lived beside the aliens, saw the long silver needles descend point-first onto our neighbors' lawns and the silver shapes emerge with chains and glowing rods. We twitched the kitchen curtains closed and dialed up our music. Three hours later there was no sign of any of the aliens, the wretched or the beautiful, except for a few blackened patches of grass and wisps of smoke that curled and died.

All was well.

The Urashima Effect

Leo Aoki awoke with a shudder in the cold green bubble of the ship, nauseated and convinced that he was suffocating. He shoved his way out of the sleep spindle, found his balance, ran his hands through his sweaty hair, checked his bones: all unbroken. Well, then. There was a snaking black tube cuffed to the wall, its other end pointing into the black vacuum of space. He pulled it off its hooks and vomited into it, miserably and gracelessly. The ship's drivers continued their deep soft hum, unperturbed.

Mission command had advised him against looking outside until he had adjusted to life in the cramped quarters of his bubble. It would unnerve him, they said. *Unman him,* they meant. It was better not to taste unadulterated loneliness for the first time immediately after opening one's eyes and throwing up. On prior exploratory flights, several astronauts emerging from their long suspension had suffered heart attacks or gone mad, too delicate to withstand the double shock of loneliness and life in deep space.

Leo opened the six portholes orthogonal to the ship's trajectory and stared out into a perfectly empty, perfectly dark sky. Blackness as pure and rich as squid ink looked through the portholes at him. He felt small and cold and very much alone.

He had to climb a thin ladder to reach the upper window, the one that faced forward to Ryugu-jo. It opened onto what looked, at first, like a globular cluster, a fistful of diamonds dumped onto a bolt of black velvet. He was looking at all the stars and galaxies that surrounded the ship, gathered by aberration into a glittering disk eight degrees across. It was a strange, beautiful, thoroughly unpleasant sight.

He clambered down again and screwed shut the lower portholes. He did not want the darkness looking in. It frayed his soul. He went to the monitor and played a game of chess to steady his nerves. The system informed him that he had been asleep for three years. The ship had arrived at its maximum travel speed of .997c, and soon it would flip its orientation and decelerate until they reached their target, Ryugu-jo in the Alpha Lyrae system. His wife, a prominent astrophysicist, had discovered and named the planet in graduate school. Leo lost his bishops, then his rooks, one after another, then the game. The ship's computer was polite about his loss.

Thinking of Esther, he brought up and played the recording she had made for him before departure. They were all required to have sixty hours of audio recordings by family and friends for listening on the last leg of their journey, to keep them sane and functional in their isolation. He had made a recording for her, too. He had told her he loved her in every possible way for five hours, filled three hours with good jokes and one hour with bad, and he had sung to her and read aloud to her, crouched over the microphone, imagining her face as she listened to him in perfect solitude, surrounded by darkness, flying toward him.

When her voice floated crisply into his ear, he felt his clenched muscles relax, as they always did when he was with her.

"Leo," she said. He could hear her smile. "You'll be up by now. I hope it wasn't too bad. They say it's usually horrible. Your hair's probably a mess. I know you'll look stunning anyway."

He had to stop to gulp down water from a tube. The nearness of her voice, like a touch on his skin, sparked a few tears. They had met in graduate school in Berkeley, both hyphenated Americans with a preponderance of Japanese in front of the dash. He had preferred solitude as a student, working out alone his pale theorems on a blackboard, but she had insisted on the importance of family dinners, friends, colleagues, collaboration, a vast net of relationships drawn around her own lively, glimmering insights. He was fifth-generation, with great-grandparents who were interned at Heart Mountain; she was third-generation and inquisitive and knowledgeable about the cultural inheritance he had never claimed. He was in physics, a different department, but they had taken classes together and she had always scored near the top. She had fascinated him.

"First I will tell you the story of Urashima Taro.

"Long ago in a dusty fishing village near Edo there lived a fisherman whose name was Urashima Taro. His hands were hard and cracked from work and his skin was brown from sun, but he was a kind man who worked all day and dreamed strange dreams at night. Like you, in some ways. He fished to feed himself and his elderly parents as well, and the sea always provided them with enough to get by.

"One day he heard a few of the village children screaming with laughter. He went over to see what had excited them so, and found them kicking a small turtle back and forth.

" 'What do you think you're doing?' Urashima exclaimed.

" 'The turtle is ours,' the children said. 'We caught it. We'll do what we wish with it.'

" 'Let me buy it from you,' Urashima said, and as he spoke he took coins from his belt and held them out. 'Can't you find something better than that turtle to play with?'

"The children looked at each other. Then one of them gave Urashima the turtle and took the coins, and they ran off together, happy to have gotten the better part of the deal.

"Urashima took the frightened turtle, which was no bigger than one of his spread hands, and of a beautiful mottled green-brown color, down to the water. 'There you go,' he said, putting it back into the sea. 'Be safe, and be careful, and don't let them catch you again. I might not be around next time.'

"The turtle rowed off, and Urashima went to fish."

Leo forced himself to stop the recording there. He would ration her voice like water in a desert to get through the impossibly long stretches of darkness. The computer indicated a list of maintenance tasks that were not urgent but that had waited until he had awoken, and he went down the list, accomplishing what he could.

After a week, it became easier to live in the narrow green bubble with a jewel-pile of stars above his head. Tubes for all his physical needs were lashed to the walls around him. The computer was loaded with a decent-sized library, a handful of mindless games, a month's worth of music, and software for data analysis, although any research he did on the ship would take another twenty-five years to transmit to Earth, which was plenty of time for another researcher to work out and publish the same conclusions independently.

He inspected the folded equipment in the bottom sections of the ship, self-extending solar panels and self-assembling buildings with crystalline panes and honeycombed layers, all of it intact despite the rigors of the journey. He cleaned the retracting landers and triple-checked the fuel tank and fuel lines. He played sixteen games of chess and won eight of them, five games of Go, four hours of Snake, and four hours of Tetris, and he read through a significant chunk of the first volume of the Encyclopedia Britannica, as well as two drab spy thrillers and a romance novel. He supposed that he had earned a few more minutes of Esther's voice.

"The next day," she said softly into his ear, "Urashima was out fishing in his boat when he heard someone call his name. He looked everywhere but the other boats were out of sight.

" 'Urashima,' someone said. 'Urashima!'

"Then he looked down and saw an enormous brown turtle, its face deeply wrinkled with wisdom.

" 'Sir,' Urashima said. 'Are you calling my name?'

" 'I am,' the turtle said. 'Yesterday you rescued a small turtle from children who would have killed it. The turtle was the Sea King's daughter. Out of gratitude she sends me to invite you to her father's palace at the bottom of the sea.'

"Smiling, he said to the turtle, 'That is very kind of her, and it is good of you to invite me on your mistress's behalf, but how should I go to a palace at the bottom of the sea?'

" 'A very simple matter,' the turtle said. 'Climb onto my back and I will take you there.'

"So Urashima, wondering at his own boldness, climbed onto the turtle's back and held tight to the slick hard plates. They plunged down together into the sea, leaving behind the boat, the creamy waves of the surface, and the sun. Deeper and deeper they swam, past dazzling silver fish and jelly-eyed squid. Urashima watched everything pass with astonishment.

"Deep in the black-blue depths of the sea, where kelp grew in thick forests and monstrous fish hunted their prey with lanterns, the turtle turned his creased face to Urashima and said, 'Look ahead, we are approaching the Palace of the Sea King.'

"Urashima peered through the water. He saw first the graceful slopes of roofs like a bird about to take flight, and then a high, imposing gate of coral carved over with poetry.

" 'O!' he said. 'It is a beautiful place.' And then, still full of amazement, he began to feel ashamed of his fisherman's clothes."

Leo stopped the recording and wiped the water from his eyes. Esther was following him on another flight, the *Delta Aquarid*, scheduled to launch two years after his. It would be a long wait. He would land and build a suitable home and laboratory for them on the arid, glistening plains of Ryugu-jo. Then he would stand in his suit under the alien stars, looking for a brightening light.

He read several classic novels and philosophical texts to pass the next few days and exercised on the stringy, wiry contraption collapsed into one wall. The long hibernation had melted the muscle from him and congealed the quick currents of his mind, but he had to be alert, intelligent, and at his peak physical condition when he arrived. He was supposed to be disciplined. He was not supposed to replay his wife's voice over and over, with longing and anxiousness. So he selected his parents' recordings.

"Your mother and I are proud of you. I know we said goodbye already, but please know that you have been everything we could have expected of you. We will be watching for your signal if we're still around."

"Leo? You must be awake now. And hungry. Remember to eat well and dress warm. You used to work for days without eating. You can't do that now."

He bowed his head. Their voices echoing in the ship's green

bubble made their absences as heavy and palpable as river stones. He had said goodbye exuberantly, distracted by other preparations. Shivering, he flicked to his wife.

"—But the turtle said, 'You must not worry, Urashima Taro.' And the high, gleaming gates, each fashioned out of a single fan of coral, parted to let them pass.

"Within, robed fish bowed to welcome them, murmuring their greetings to the turtle and their welcome to Urashima Taro. He passed through gilded halls where water-light flickered on the walls, past lark-voiced women covered in scales and scarlet octopi and crabs with furious faces on their backs, into a chamber that shimmered like the interior of an abalone.

"There, on two thrones, sat the Sea King and his daughter Otohime, who was lovelier than moonlight on water. She came down from her throne and said to Urashima, 'I was the little turtle you saved yesterday, and I am grateful. I am yours if you will have me.'

"Urashima assented, of course, and all of them were led to the banquet laid out in his honor. Then began what were the happiest three years of his life, in which each day was better than the last.

"Toward the end of the three years, though, he began thinking melancholy thoughts about his aged parents on land. How were they getting by without their son? They ought to know how fortunate he was.

"He told Otohime about his wish to see his parents again, and her face grew long and sad. She tried to dissuade him, but he became more and more desirous of seeing his parents and his home.

" 'Please, let me go,' he said. 'For a few days only, and then I will come back to you and spend the rest of my life here in peace and contentment.'

"Sorrowfully, Otohime made arrangements for his return. At the last, she placed in his hands a small box tied with silk. 'Take this with you,' she said. 'It will keep you safe, only you must be careful never to open it.'

"Urashima promised to obey. The great brown turtle who had first brought him to the Palace of the Sea King again gave him his back to sit upon, and soon they came to the shore near his village.

"But what had happened?

"Urashima found himself in an unfamiliar place. He recognized some features of the shoreline, but the houses were all different and crowded together. He could not find his old home.

"Distraught, he asked a passerby if he knew where his parents might be living. The young man, not unsympathetic, took Urashima to his own grandmother, whose knowledge was vast. The old woman looked up at him hesitantly when he put his question to her.

" 'I have heard of two people with those names,' she told him. 'They had a son named Urashima who drowned on a clear day. Only his empty boat was found. But that was hundreds of years ago, when this town was a scattering of fishing huts by the sea.'

"Urashima left with fear and confusion in his heart. He was utterly lost in the strange town, and could not tell where the turtle had brought him to shore. Nor did he know how to return to the Palace of the Sea King, because he had forgotten to ask.

"After some time, though, he remembered the box that Otohime had given him, which he had promised not to open. Because he could think of nothing else, he untied the silken cord that held it shut.

"An enormous white cloud blew out of the box and enveloped him. All his years overtook him at once. His hair went white as snow and his skin drooped and folded. His bones gave way. And there Urashima died.

"Time dilation is also called the Urashima Effect, after the legend," Esther said conversationally into his ear. "I have told you this story so you would have time to calm down and clear your mind after awakening, and so that it would be easier for you to understand what I have to say. If I know you, you've saved up my recording for several days. You've been eating well and exercising. You should be physically and mentally stable by now. You are strong enough to hear what I have to say.

"Listen, my love. You were put to sleep a few weeks before launch, and while you were asleep the US and Japan came to the brink of war. Two cyber attacks on a dam and a power plant were traced back to Ichigaya, and three American citizens were arrested in Seattle. There is talk about rounding up those with Japanese blood again.

"It was decided that the *Delta Aquarid* would not be launched. Not next year. Not ever. The Ryugu-jo collaboration has been scrapped as being too dangerous, given the rising tensions between the two countries. It will be replaced by a unilateral program that will not have the funding for my flight.

"But they decided that you would go anyway. To show our unfaltering national courage in the face of threats and our gracious commitment to peacetime cooperation.

"I protested. This was my project, after all. They would not listen. They refused to stop your launch, and they refused to continue mine. It was suggested that if I did not put national interests ahead of my personal desires that I and my family would be the first to be removed to internment camps.

"We knew that this was possible, but we did not think it likely.

"They say you will not awaken until three years from now. In those three years you will have traveled twelve point five light years, and thirteen years will have passed on Earth. Your parents may be dead by the time you are listening to this. I will be forty-nine. You, my love, you will be only thirty-six, traveling away from me at close to the speed of light."

Leo had frozen as he listened.

"I do not know who I will be by the time you hear this," she said. "Thirteen years is a long time.

"But right now, right now I am your wife. I love you, Leo. I am angry and afraid. I broke into your ship's systems and altered these recordings so that you would know what happened, why I am not following you, and what your choices are. From the beginning these ships were designed for automatic evacuation in case of ship failure during suspension. Specifically, your sleep spindle is equipped with an independent propulsion system and its own fuel stores. I have modified the program slightly, so that if you choose to do so, you can eject from the main ship in your spindle. Enter the manual override *silkbox* to divert the main fuel supply to the spindle, and look for a release lever by the hatch. It will take you a very long time to return, twenty Earth years at least, but you can go back into deep sleep, and the spindle will bring you safely home.

"The impulse of the spindle's disconnection will throw off the calculations for the ship's landing. There is some margin for error, but the engineers never considered a late-flight evacuation. The ship and its equipment will crash on Ryugu-jo. There will be no habitat and no lab on the planet until another Earth government sees fit to send the next scientific expedition.

"I do not know if I will be alive when you come back. If I am, I will be old. My hair will be gray. I will not be the wife you left behind. I will not be the person you remember.

"But at this moment I love you. At this moment I say: when I am seventy years old, I will watch the sky for you.

"If you do not return," Esther said, "if you choose to fly onward to Ryugu-jo and work there alone—I would understand. We have always both chased the sense of discovery. We have always been driven by the hunger for knowing new things. Your first communications will arrive on Earth fifty years after you've left, and your work will be groundbreaking, even if you never see its effects.

"My other audio logs are intact. I went and dug up all the records of your great-grandparents and your father's side of the family. If you fly onward, I will tell you, in the rest of the time I have, about how your great-grandfather met your great-grandmother in Heart Mountain during the war. I will tell you about your family and the different places your parents grew up, and where your ancestors came from. I will grow roots for you, so that you are not adrift and alone in the dark. You will know where you came from. You will know where you are going."

Her voice clicked off. Leo shut his eyes and saw the green ship and its precious cargo of instruments and electronics smashing into the dusty surface of Ryugu-jo. He thought of the lonely beacon he had been sent to build, which would beam back to Earth the things he had learned that no one else knew. He remembered precisely and vividly what it felt like to kiss Esther on her warm pink mouth.

He walked over to his sleep spindle, crouched, and ran his fingers along its smooth interior. They stopped on something that protruded from the wall, and he saw it then: a smooth silver bar barely extending into the sleeping space. If he typed in the command, if he climbed in and shut the hatch behind him, if he yanked on the lever—

The portholes all around him were dark and expressionless. Only the top window, pointing toward Alpha Lyrae, showed him a heap of converging stars.

The ship was traveling at .997c. Leo was thirty-six years old. It was only three years to Ryugu-jo.

Leo began another game of chess with the computer, and drew black.

Braid of Days and Wake of Nights

THE SEAT BENEATH HER WAS GLOSSY PLASTIC AND NOT INTER-ested in prolonging their acquaintance. Shifting from thigh to thigh, Julia Popova flipped through newspapers in search of the logo and slogans for bourbon that she had labored over for weeks.

> *New York Times*, March 3, 2005—ESCAPED CARRIAGE HORSE. Reports to the Parks Department of a stray white horse in Central Park puzzled the Horse and Carriage Association and the Teamsters alike. "No one's unaccounted for," said spokesman Mark Houdlin. "Both the Clinton Park and Hell's Kitchen stables are full at the end of the day."

> *New York Daily News*, March 3, 2005—LOST OPERA HORSE? Recent sightings of a white horse on the lam in Central Park have perplexed locals and police. A spokes-

man from the Metropolitan Opera was unable to confirm
rumors that their production of "Aida" is short one four-
legged cast member.

New York Post, March 3, 2005—MYSTERIOUS
VOLUNTEER BEAUTIFICATION EFFORTS IN PARK.
Seen Central Park lately? You might not recognize it.
Over the last two weeks the Lake was raked for plastic
cups, the Turtle Pond's thick algae was skimmed off, and
the Kennedy Reservoir is now clear as a freshly Windexed
mirror. No one has owned up to seeing or being one of
the unknown do-gooders, but park staff are thankful.

Julia found her quarter-page ads in Business and Travel.
Orange silk and opalized ammonites. *Blissful extinction.* The
amber bottle gleaming like sunken treasure in the middle of it
all. But the colors that were arresting on the office computers
were watery in newsprint, diluted by the fluorescent lights of the
clinic.

"How'd they turn out?" Vivian asked. The soft leatherette
armchair seemed to swallow both her and the taxane drip feeding into her left arm.

Julia shook her head.

"Okay, how was your date with whatshername, Ellen?"

Julia sighed. "I don't want to talk about it. But look at this.
They're still writing about the horse."

"For Chrissake, Julia."

"Soup. It looks like they're selling fancy soup. Beef, butter,
onions. I told them to use less color. Save it for the slicks. Client's
going to yell at me tomorrow."

"You should quit."

"I wish."

With an immaculate thumbnail, Julia peeled open the zip-lock bag in her lap. The coil of hair inside, wide as her thumb and nine feet long, was woven throughout with black and gold strands in equal proportion. When Vivian began chemo last May, her hair had skimmed the lower edge of her scapulae. Three weeks later, her purple stripes had rinsed to blonde, and she had not dyed them again. Vivian had smiled at Julia in the bathroom mirror, eyebrows high and brave, but after the first handful slithered to the floor, she handed the humming razor to Julia and covered her eyes.

"You do it," she said.

The braid was almost finished. Julia had added some of her own hair as needed, taking surreptitious snips behind her ears and bleaching her brown waves in a bowl. Vivian's false gold was easier to match than her black. The braid felt both coarse and silky, crackling softly when she ran her fingers along it. Only a few loose locks remained at the bottom of the bag.

Vivian kept glancing at the braid, then away, shivering.

"The hell are you doing with my hair?"

"The Victorians made jewelry out of their relatives' hair," Julia said.

"Sure, but in front of them?" Vivian screwed up her mouth. "I'm not dead yet."

"It's not a mourning piece."

"So what is it?"

"A gift."

"For who?"

Julia hesitated. "Maybe you?"

"Nope. No way." Vivian scratched the down on her skull. She couldn't stand wigs and wore brilliant silk scarves printed with birds and stars instead. "Weird, isn't it? Doesn't bother me when it's growing on my head, but I can't stand it when it's

cut. Slopped around the salon floor—ugh. Like seeing a severed hand."

"Sorry."

"It's okay, I won't look."

Vivian opened *Applied and Environmental Biology* and held
it up to her face while Julia overlapped yellow strand and black,
tugging, straightening, smoothing. When, after half an hour, she
noticed Vivian hadn't turned the page, she pinned the end of the
braid and dropped everything into her purse.

Eventually a nurse in pink scrubs sailed over and slid the
cannula out of Vivian's arm. "How are you feeling?" she asked.

Vivian pushed herself upright without speaking, her face
pale, and lurched toward the bathroom. Julia followed. Over the
retching and splashing, she made soothing noises and rubbed
circles in Vivian's back.

"Pharmacy stop?"

"Thanks."

Julia had bought her indestructible orange Beetle as a ticket
out of rusting Paterson with three summers waitressing in an
Italian restaurant and five illustrations for two evanescent mag-
azines. She called it the Lady. When the art school letter came,
Julia had fought all day with her parents and cried all night
for a month before stuffing the Lady to the roof and driving to
Providence. She had not looked back.

Although parking took a large bite out of her budget, the
odometer clocked 170,000, and the odors of frying oil, mint
gum, nail polish, and drive-through coffee had painted a thin
and indelible layer over the interior, Julia kept the Lady when
she moved to Queens. Even thinking about selling the Lady
struck her as disloyal. Vivian's sudden need was in many ways
welcome, and Julia told herself that she had kept the car for
times like these.

She left Vivian hunched in the car and ducked into the hard bright aisles of the corner drugstore. At the counter she collected a battery of pharmaceuticals in orange canisters: yolk-yellow Zofran, pentagons of Ativan, dented white Percocet, and smooth white Lomotil. The paper bags crinkled as she thrust them into Vivian's hands.

"You doing okay?"

Vivian was breathing through her teeth, and a bitter, stinging smell drifted from her skin. She wouldn't meet Julia's eyes. "Swell."

Julia double-parked on 119th and watched Vivian until she vanished into her walkup.

ALTHOUGH CENTRAL PARK at night featured often in her mother's monthly litany of New York horrors, and Julia could not walk there after dark without twitching and jumping at shadows, in all the newspaper accounts she had read, the horse had never been observed before twilight. She went at dusk on a Friday with the braid snaking through the belt loops of her jeans and a jack-knife jammed into a pocket to compensate for the judo classes she had never taken. Hawkers of ice cream and soda were shuttering their silver carts. Couples pushed strollers through the orange puddles of park lights, leaning into each other. The air began blue and dimmed and filled with bats.

"Come out," she whispered. "I'm here."

The fine gray gravel of the Bridle Path crunched under her canvas shoes. She walked to Riftstone Bridge, now a pool of darkness, and peered underneath. The smell of urine scraped her nose but bothered her less than it once had. There was a faint, bubbling snore.

"Hello?"

Plastic rustled. Something moved.

"What do you want?" The voice was whiskey and dry leaves.

Squinting into the gloom, Julia distinguished two dim eyes and a glint of teeth. "I'm looking for a white horse."

"Fresh out of horses, sorry. All I got is UFOs and Elvis." The chuckle was low but female, and Julia unlocked her shoulders. "Why?"

"For a friend. She's sick." She tried a smile. "My name's Julia."

The woman who shuffled out was tall and swaddled in stained clothes. "Lorrie."

"So have you seen a horse? No halter, no bridle. Just running loose."

"How's a pony ride help?"

"It might be a unicorn." She bit the inside of her cheek, anticipating laughter. None was forthcoming. Lorrie only folded her arms and tilted her head. "Saint Hildegard wrote that unicorn liver healed leprosy. That unicorn leather cured fevers. The horn was good against poison. No one says anything about cancer, but I figure—"

"Why you askin me?"

"You live here. You might have seen it."

"I don't live here." She coughed thickly. "I been crashin with my uncle when I can, but his house is fulla kids. New wife can't stand me. Sometimes I hit the drop-in center, but those are bad nights."

"Oh."

"March is too cold to sleep outside. You hafta be desperate."

Julia pulled a rumpled bill from her back pocket and held it out, but her hand was swatted aside.

"My problems they bigger than a dollar, unicorn girl."

Julia said, "You must think I'm nuts."

"Of course you is. You carryin a fruit knife shorter than my pinky. You think that's gonna keep you safe from folks like me." She wheezed with laughter as Julia's hand went to her hip. "Your fingers smell like metal. You keep dippin in that pocket. You leanin backwards like you wanna run."

"I'm sorry." Her face went hot.

"It's A-okay. You crazy. And whiter than Wonder Bread. Lots of you come joggin scared around here at night, like you think we bite."

"You didn't laugh when I started talking about unicorns."

"Don't nobody in this city think I exist either. Used to work at the Aqueduct before I hurt my back. Thought I was invisible then. Now? Bam! Gone. What've I got against unicorns?"

"Have you seen one?"

Lorrie shook her head. "Go home."

"Please. Tell me."

"You got ten dollars? I'd use it better than you."

When the money was safely concealed in her clothes, Lorrie straightened and stared. "Think, babygirl. If there a unicorn here? All of us be sleepin sweeter. With no pain. We be smellin honey, fresh bread, lilacs, good days. The wild ones they settle. The angry ones they calm down. If we got a unicorn, why would I tell you? With that knife in your pocket? Leather? Livers? A sick friend? What's that knife for?"

Julia heard bodies stirring sleepily under the bridge.

"Nowhere in this city is safe for me," Lorrie said. "I do what I can to get by. You smell safe and selfish. Hunger and pain and need, you don't know. Go home."

Julia took two steps backward, then turned and hurried up the path. She could feel Lorrie's eyes on her. Not until she emerged from the chained green tangle of the park into the traffic of Central Park West did she exhale her double lungful of fear.

"I HAVE TO talk to you—"

"If there's a unicorn," Julia said, "I'll bring you its horn. I promise. Abracadabra, Australopithecus, poof, tumors gone. Like *that*."

"No. Listen to me." Vivian shut the cabinet and set two mugs on the scarred table. A chocolate cake slumped half-eaten on scalloped gold paper. *WE'LL MISS YOU VIV* in green jelly icing. A cardboard box of her notebooks and rubberbanded pens had been shoved under a chair, and Julia kept kicking it by accident.

Her last day at the lab, Vivian said. Everyone had pretended the departure was happy.

"But that's not what you want to tell me."

"Ginger? Chamomile? Black?" Vivian fanned out the teabags. "We're stopping chemo. I'm done."

"You can't."

"Three fresh lesions on my liver. You want to argue? It's right here, you can talk to it if you want." She tipped a kettle, and hot water chortled into the mugs. "Be real persuasive, cuz they say two months, best case."

Julia raised a cup, the steam blurring her vision. The right words were somewhere, buried under jingles, loud typefaces, the shotgun poetry of advertising. Never again would she smell bergamot without the sting of tears.

"Give me some time. Let me try."

"Spend my last days vomiting, you mean?"

"There's a unicorn, Vivian."

Vivian's laugh was hard and tired. "People stopped believing in unicorns in middle school."

"So I have a rich imaginative life. Sue me."

"You couldn't imagine your way out of a cubicle." Vivian rubbed her eyes. "I remember when you talked grants, galleries, art shows, MoMA. Where are you now? Selling watches and vacations to people who don't want them. Cold calling. Retouching portraits of steak."

Julia pushed away from the table. "I have to live, Viv."

"And I have to die. Well, we all do. But I'm going to do it the way I want. With friends. With dignity. More water?"

"No."

Vivian refilled both mugs. "Anyway, Asian girls never get unicorns."

"How do you know that?"

"Beagle. L'Engle. Lewis. Coville and Gaiman, even though I was too old. I looked anyway, just in case. When I was a kid it was Laurence Yep, take it or leave it. Lots of dragons, no unicorns. None for you either, right? Aren't you more likely to find a domovoi or a leshy? When did Russia get unicorns?"

"Late fifteenth century."

"You checked."

"Of course I checked."

Vivian grabbed Julia's hand across the table. "It's sweet of you, but you've got better things to do."

"Fine. No unicorns for you." Julia picked up a pen and one of the insurance forms on the table. "Say you're giving up. What's next?"

"Hospice. Starting next week."

HOSPICE MEANT NURSES, Julia discovered, and the sweetish smell of Roxanol. Clutching a sheaf of filled-out forms, she let herself in with the spare key, then stood in the hallway, bewildered, as brisk strangers squeezed past her. A silver IV tree had sprouted in the kitchen. Vivian's aunt, who drove up from Queens on the weekends with cooked food in foil pans, fussed at Julia, plucking off her coat and bag.

"Nothing serious," she said to the expression on Julia's face. "It's the rules. Someone has to be here every day. One of her cousins, or me."

Vivian was lying in bed, her eyes closed, a transparent loop of oxygen around her head. The tall windows she loved were ajar and clattered softly as the warm, astringent air inside mixed with the damp breath of March.

Loneliness gusted through Julia, sudden as rain.

"What am I going to do without you?" she asked, hating herself for the question.

Vivian opened one eye. "Watch it. I'm not dead yet."

"You know what I mean."

"I can still beat your ass. Tremble in fear."

Julia sat gingerly on the edge of the bed, careful not to bounce. Nine years ago they had washed up in New York together, both of them certain that success lay around the corner, or behind the next door, even as the gum-glazed sidewalk ate blisters into their heels and the rent came due again and again and again. The thought of living without Vivian's rude jokes and good taste, her crayon annotations of newspapers and leaflets, her abrupt phone calls—"You free at eight? Nice dress? Good!"—hollowed her chest. "What will I do?"

"Cry. Breathe. Live. Fall in love. You'll be better at that when I'm gone, really you will. Skydive. Have children, if you want them. Play tennis. Snorkel. Visit Morocco. All the things I can't do anymore. Next question."

"It's not fair."

"Fair?" Vivian smacked the mattress. "I wanted kids. I got Gregory and cancer. I wanted a career in microbiology. I got two postdocs and Gregory and a layoff and cancer."

"And six second-author papers in first-tier journals."

"I'm thirty-three, Julia. Thirty-three! I'll never ride a horse or learn how to snowboard, I'll never drive to the Grand Canyon and order coffee in every diner on the way, I'll never see Moscow, I'll never have a houseboat, I won't win any Nobels, I won't see any more meteor showers, I won't pick any more apples, and I'll never, ever have a daughter. Don't talk to me about *fair*. Don't even think about fair when you're in the same room as me. I'll rip it out of your head and crumple it into a ball and eat it."

Vivian's aunt stuck her head into the room. "Everything all right?"

"Yup."

"Doing great."

The aunt retreated. Vivian bit her lip and crushed the edge of the quilt in her hands. In a quiet voice, she said, "He'll be here Saturday. Can you pick him up from JFK?"

"Who?"

"Gregory."

Julia blinked. "He's coming?"

"He heard I was going off chemo."

"How thoughtful. I'm shocked."

"I may have called him." Vivian put her hands over her face. "I may have asked him to come."

"So I meet him at the airport and make him disappear? I don't do murder, normally, but for you—"

"Just bring him here."

"Vivian—"

"Loose ends," she said, not meeting Julia's eyes.

THE MARRIAGE HAD not been a long one. Vivian had disappeared for a year, a deeper and more profound absence than when she was dating Gregory, while she tried on *wife* as if it were a winter coat, turning and stretching and looking at herself in it, testing its warmth. She smiled less and less, the few times Julia caught her, and a little gutter of worry dug itself into her brow.

One month after the separation, Vivian had called and let the room around her fill with silence.

"I'm coming over," Julia said, after waiting in vain for a word.

In a voice small and sticky with grief, Vivian said: "Okay."

Julia had barged into the apartment with two bottles of cheap chardonnay and a handful of black-and-white movies. Vivian scrubbed her eyes with the back of one hand.

"I'm such a mess—"

"It's fine."

Vivian's third glass was almost empty when she snatched the remote and jabbed down the sound.

"He said he never wanted children. Three years into our marriage! He only told me he did because he thought I might change his mind. Or that he might change mine. 'I wanted to give us a chance,' " she said, imitating his sweeping gestures, and laughed with a catch in her throat. " 'Too many cultural differences,' he said. 'I don't want my kids speaking a language I don't know. How would that look to everyone?' He said it was hard enough listening to me jabbering with my relatives, not knowing when we were laughing at him. He said the kids wouldn't resemble either of us—how was he supposed to handle that—"

Julia splashed out another half-glass for her. "He loved you, though."

"Never. Never ever." Vivian shuddered.

"I was at your wedding. I saw how he stared at you." Vivian had glowed and glimmered, her dress a waterfall, her hair black wings. "No one could see you and not love you."

"Except him."

"All right. He's a jackass. Why am I defending him?" Julia slung an arm around Vivian's shoulders. "I barely saw you while you were together. He's a jerk of the first water, just for that."

"I'm sorry."

"Doesn't matter. You're back now, so honestly, I owe him."

After a long silence, Julia glanced sideways. Vivian had fallen asleep, legs drawn up to her chest, beginning to snore. Julia tossed a blanket over her before turning off the TV and the lights.

It was rare for Vivian to ask for anything, and although Julia disapproved so strongly her stomach hurt, she could not say no. On Saturday, she drove into the arteriosclerotic snarl of the airport to retrieve Gregory. She found him, punctual as a banker, planted at the prearranged section of curbside pickup: his hair as curly as ever, houndstooth jacket and trousers slightly mellowed from the straight line, a pair of tortoiseshell glasses weighing down his face. One suitcase, sized for the overhead bin, sat at his feet. He blinked rapidly at the Lady as Julia pulled alongside and beeped.

"You're—Jean—"

"Julia Popova. You haven't changed at all."

He had to duck his head climbing into the car. "That's right. Vivian's friend."

"Admit it, you don't remember me."

"I do, I do." He grinned at her. "Her best friend. The artist. Took me a second."

"Where are you staying?"

"I've got a hotel on the East Side. Vivian first, though."

They inched out of the airport under a pewter sky, the churn of jet engines trembling the little car. Odd, how airports diffused an industrial grayness across the landscape, washing out yellows and reds, leaching warmth from complexions.

"How long has Viv been sick?" Gregory said. "If you don't mind my asking."

"She didn't tell you?"

"She's been very mysterious about the whole thing. I didn't know until two weeks ago. 'Hey Gregory,' she says. 'I'm dying. Stage Four ovarian, isn't that *funny*? Want to swing by one last time?' Like she hadn't pitched me out the door."

Julia snorted.

"So how long?"

"Chemo off and on for the last eleven months."

Gregory chewed his lower lip, gazing at the pawnshops and discount clothing stores that glided by. "Did everyone know?"

"Her friends. Her family."

"I don't believe it."

"Suit yourself."

"Did they take out her ovaries?"

"Excuse me?" Julia almost missed a stoplight flicking from yellow to red. She stomped on the brakes, and they both choked against their seatbelts. "What's that to you?"

"She's my wife," Gregory said. And that, however regrettable, was true.

I**T WAS NIGHT** when they arrived. A half moon hung in the strip of sky between buildings. Gregory wavered on the sidewalk, looking up.

"You can go home now," he told her through the car window.

"All right."

"I'll get a taxi. I appreciate it, Julia."

She sat in the car, watching windows blink awake in his path. For forty-five minutes she listened inattentively to the radio station she had flicked on to forestall conversation, and to the light breeze that rattled paper cups and cans down the street. Black and brown people walked by, chattering, smoking, hefting groceries. The moon fell behind a roof. Gregory did not come outside.

At last she turned the key in the ignition and drove home.

T**HE NEXT DAY** thickened into a soup of meetings in conference rooms sharp with the smell of whiteboard markers and phone calls that locked in zero new clients. Julia stopped at a café for a roast beef sandwich with too much mustard before heading to the park. She was looking forward to grass and greenness and the sight of water, even stagnant and sulfurous water. As she sucked threads of onion from between her teeth, her cell phone hummed.

"Are you going to Central Park?"

"Gregory?"

"Which entrance?"

"I'm taking the A."

"Okay, which stop?"

"The Museum. Look, I'd rather not—"

"See you there."

Julia huffed and stomped down the steps into the station. She was busy, urgently busy, and not about to wait for him. But as she walked to Naturalists' Gate, she heard her name.

Gregory, pressed and polished, waved at her from a bench. Her own hair had blown every which way. Her irritation deepened.

"I thought this was it. Vivian said you used to meet here after work and walk to Conservatory Garden."

The humid summer evenings she and Vivian had spent wandering through the park, pausing for ice cream éclairs and the occasional concert, appeared at an impossible distance. It had been centuries, surely. Kingdoms had risen and crumbled in the interim. She was obscurely hurt that Gregory knew about those days.

"What else did she say?"

"You're hunting a unicorn."

Julia compressed her lips. "She's told you a lot, then."

"Vivian's very fond of you. Thank you for taking care of her."

"Someone had to."

"Do you mind if I come? I've never gone on a unicorn hunt."

I do mind, Julia wanted to say, but the words stuck in her throat. Her silence did not discourage him. They walked together into the darkening park, Gregory glancing at her, tipping his head toward her, as attentive as if they were a couple.

"What are you planning to do?"

"I have some ideas."

"Isn't there a procedure? You need a virgin—"

"How do *you* know?"

"I read," he said. "Or I used to. Viv fell for my bookshelf before she fell for me. Ask her about it sometime. So, you borrowing a kid for this?"

"No."

"It's just, if you don't mind my saying so, you look past the age—also too beautiful—"

"Fuck off," she said.

He stared at her. "You are?"

"I said fuck off."

"Do you mean technically? Are you a lesbian? Or have you never—"

"I mean get lost. Catch a cab, go home. What are you doing here, anyway?"

"Look, I didn't mean to—" He raised his palms in apology. "How do I say it? There's no imagination in my job. No imagination outside of it, either. No time to read, no time to socialize, and no nice girl dates a married man. Work, sleep, work. Dull as hell. I got excited when I heard about your unicorn."

"You're laughing at me."

"I'm not."

Julia strode off, Gregory trailing behind her. At the eastern edge of the Ramble, she bent over two hoof-shaped patches of verbena and goldenseal. The clusters ran in double lines across the grass.

"What's that?"

"The flowers of old New York," she said. "They grow where it goes."

Gregory pinched off a purple blossom and sniffed it. "This is amazing," he said.

From what she had seen, she figured that the age of the plants corresponded to the freshness of the trail. She ignored luxurious, knee-high tracks of bee balm and wild ginger in favor of a younger trail of asters, following it until it vanished at an outcrop of schist.

"Damn," she said, slapping the rock. "This one, I thought—"

"Keep going," Gregory said.

"Don't tell me what to do."

"Wouldn't dream of it."

They were descending Cedar Hill when Gregory dropped to a crouch.

"Here," he said. The print was damp, as long as her hand, an impression of teardrops curving toward each other. It was speckled with seedlings.

Julia knelt, bending until her nose was on a level with the sprouts. Their cotyledons were spread, the tips of the first true leaves beginning to unfurl. It was not clear what they would become.

"I'm not making this up," she said.

"No."

"They're growing, look."

There was a faint metallic scrape behind them, like a hobnail on rock. Julia's neck prickled. She pushed herself upright, brushing her hands on her jeans, and dug in her purse for the knife. The night was thick around them, and she could not see much.

On the crest of the hill, a flash of silver.

"Oh," she said, transfixed.

Tree trunks divided and obscured the white form, but as it picked its way through them, she glimpsed a feathering mane, a silver wisp of beard, a horn like a slant of light. It shone pearl and silver in the darkness.

"You are," she said. "You exist."

As if it had heard, the unicorn swung its head toward them. The point of its horn traced a bright curl in the air. In that long, frozen moment, Julia observed the fine pulse of one vein in its neck, the mud on its forelocks, the leaves tangled in its mane.

Vapor fogged its nostrils. It regarded them with an opaque intelligence, considering.

Then it wheeled and trotted in their direction.

Gregory stayed still. Moving slowly, Julia slid the coil of black and golden hair from her purse and weighed it in one hand. Would the unicorn let her wrap her arms around its neck? Or would she have to lasso it? Any horse could snap the braid with a toss of its head, but according to her research, a unicorn would not. A gilt watch chain would do the trick. An embroidered girdle. A necklace. If her books were correct, all she needed was the horn.

Ten steps separated them, and still the unicorn advanced. Julia held her breath. Five steps. Three. Two.

Gregory snatched the knife from her left hand and lunged.

"Wait!"

The knife was cheap and small, but she had spent half an hour rubbing it over a whetstone, wincing, as her parents had taught her to do.

A dark, dripping line opened along the pale neck. With a cry like bells, the unicorn shied away. It ran faster and fleeter than any horse, a shimmer in the trees, a glint, then gone.

Gregory sprawled on the grass, the knife wet and black in his hand. She prodded each of his arms and legs, checking for injury, then yanked him to his feet. Tears burned her eyes, and she mopped at her face, frustrated.

"Asshole. How could you?" she said. The unicorn—Vivian— the question rang with accusations.

"What else was the knife for? What were you going to do?"

She opened and shut her mouth and could not speak.

They headed out of the park in silence. Here and there, on a bench, under the dark arc of a bridge, Julia spotted a huddled body husbanding its warmth. Those who needed unicorns as much as she did. Shoving her hands in her pockets, she walked faster, too weak and foolish, she knew, to ask forgiveness.

"WHY WASTE YOUR time with someone like him?" Julia said. She sat on the edge of the bed, watching Vivian eat breakfast, and offered mug and spoon at appropriate intervals.

"He's helping with the bills," Vivian said reasonably. "And it's his health insurance."

"He could write a check from anywhere."

"It's not just that." Vivian dipped her spoon into each of the dishes that crowded her tray—zhou, strawberry Jell-O, bone soup with slices of winter melon, chocolate pudding—without raising it to her lips. Her skin was soft and loose against her bones. She was not eating, the aunt had whispered to Julia. "I'm trying to remember what was beautiful about him."

"Him? Nothing."

"You're angry at him?"

"Yes."

"So am I. And I don't want to die with that much anger. It's the size of a house, roof, floors, porch, everything."

"So you have him over every day to yell at him?"

"We talk."

"For hours."

"Don't be silly. I talk to you too."

Julia tightened her lips. "Not every day."

"You have work."

"It doesn't seem healthy to me."

Vivian sighed. "Didn't you see the flowers?" The kitchen table was flooded with lilies and chrysanthemums, more than Vivian had vases for, and she made Julia haul home an armful every visit. "Know who they're from? Classmates. Roommates. Colleagues. Friends. Cousins. He has to wait outside when anyone else is here."

"Don't tell me you don't enjoy that."

"Oh, I do. I do." She smiled. "You've taken good care of me. I know. I notice. But when you're looking death in the face at thirty-three—"

"You're not. Don't say that."

"Cut the crap, Julia."

"But Gregory—"

"He's figured out something you haven't. I'm dying. He knows it. He doesn't waste words. We don't waste time."

"Tell me how."

"How what?"

"How to not waste your time."

"That's your job."

In the quiet that followed, they heard the long, bright song of the doorbell, then the snick and thunk of Vivian's aunt unbolting the door. Muffled voices reached them, one a familiar baritone.

"Is Gregory here? Give us a minute—"

Julia returned to Central Park alone. The damp wind numbed her fingers and wormed its way up her sleeves. She clutched her thin coat, wishing for a scarf.

As she walked the twenty blocks from Sheep Meadow to the Reservoir, she could find no unexpected flowers, no tracks, no magic. Where hoofprints of columbine and wake-robin had flourished the week before, there were now only bare and indistinct spots of earth. Few people remained in the park. The one or two she saw ducked their heads against the wind and never looked up.

It grew colder as the night deepened. Dew soaked her canvas shoes and cotton socks, prickling her toes. She wished for company, anyone at all, even Gregory. After an hour of searching, she had seen no sign that the unicorn ever existed.

"Well," she said aloud, "that's that," and turned toward 86th Street and the subway.

"Nice bag there, lady."

In the dark, Julia could make out only a pale grin, a paler shock of hair, and the switchblade presented by way of introduction. She had not noticed his approach, preoccupied as she was with her hunt. The calm of perfect terror settled over her.

"My wallet, right?" she said, fishing it out of her purse.

"Why not your whole bag?"

"There's nothing you want in there." She riffled the bills in her wallet and tossed it at his feet.

His eyes never left hers. He stepped forward and wrenched the purse from her arm. "I'll be the judge of that."

Every nerve shrilled at her to run. She locked her knees. "Please," she said. "My friend's hair. She's dying."

"You'll shut up, if you know what's good for you." He upended her bag and shook it. Pens, tampons, fliers, and tissues scattered across the grass. The detritus of an insignificant life, she thought, starting to shake.

"Run."

She didn't.

He grabbed a fistful of her jacket and held the braid under her nose. "Or come get it."

"I'm sorry," she said. "Let me go, please—"

"Too bad you're not prettier."

He hooked his arm around her neck, cutting off her air. Her

lungs burned as he tightened his chokehold. Her knees buckled. The unspoken fears of nights and days coalesced into a fine point. *So this is it. My turn. This. Now.*

A hundred carillon bells clanged together. Over the wet, dark grass, a white shape tilted at them, indistinct at first, but growing brighter and clearer every moment.

The man swore and dropped her. She fell on her face, grateful for the dew that seeped into her clothes, the distinct sensation of each blade of grass against her skin. When she had caught her breath, she pushed herself to her knees.

He was running, his jacket flapping around him. The unicorn crashed past her in a glorious arc of white, the whorled horn pointed at his fleeing back. For an instant she imagined it spearing his back, the stutter of blood, him stumbling, sinking, deserving it—

"No!"

The pale body pivoted, pawing the air. When it landed, snorting steam, it was facing her. The gash on its neck had scabbed over into a rough crust of garnets. Julia glanced down, ashamed.

"I'm so sorry," she said. She picked up the braid of black and golden hair and offered it to the unicorn. "I won't hurt you, I promise. Not this time."

The unicorn approached her, formal and slow, and sniffed the braid. Her fingers tangled in its beard, which was silk and cobweb and gossamer. Its breath burned her skin with cold.

"I need you," Julia said. "Will you come with me?"

She made herself meet its eyes, which were as old and secret as fossils, and felt very small. After a long, careful look, the unicorn sighed and bowed its head.

Julia looped the braid loosely around the broad neck and fumbled with a knot. She was close enough to smell the odors of cinnamon, tamarind, and cardamom rising from its skin. When that was done, she bent and shoveled the pieces of her life back into her purse, heedless of the wet leaves stuck to her keys, the mud on her wallet. The unicorn waited for her to rise and grasp the braid, and then it set out after her.

They left through Hunters' Gate and went north on Central Park West. The streets were hushed and empty of cars. A few pedestrians hurried along on the far side of the road, none of them looking in her direction, though as they passed, Julia noticed, they slowed and straightened, brows smoothing, hands falling to their sides.

She was shivering with cold and shock. Every now and then she leaned against the unicorn's side, and its breath was a deep rumble in her ear. The long, spiraling horn wrote eights in the air as they walked.

At intersections, the traffic lights flared green in all directions. Above them, one by one, lit windows snapped out. A shouted argument that had spilled onto a fire escape subsided to a murmur, and the high, inconsolable wail of an infant faded. Soon they were enveloped in quiet.

"Will you help her?" Julia said. "I can't lose her. She's the best thing in my life."

The unicorn did not answer. As if it knew the way, it went up Seventh Ave and turned onto 119th. Its hooves printed moist, silvered daguerreotypes on the sidewalk behind them.

Vivian's building was dark. Julia led the unicorn up the stoop and through the narrow doorway, watching anxiously as its flanks twitched and shuddered between the jambs. She had not planned for the two flights of stairs to Vivian's apartment. But the unicorn placed one foot, then the next, on the threadbare runner, each step making a muffled chime. Less graceful, Julia groped hand over hand along the railing. Though she left the light switch alone, the unicorn gave off a fragile, glowworm light.

A neighbor's tabby sat on the second-floor landing, its eyes two small bright moons. As the unicorn passed, it tucked in its paws and purred.

On the third-floor landing, Julia unlocked the door, and she and the unicorn entered Vivian's apartment. Moonlight cut black paper silhouettes out of the flowers on the kitchen table. Everything was stark and sharp, but Julia still stumbled over a single shoe and skidded on a magazine before she grasped the loose brass doorknob and let them both into the bedroom.

Vivian was sitting in bed, resting against Gregory. His arms were around her, his cheek against her bare head. When he saw them, his face softened.

"Julia?"

Vivian opened her arms to them. Their arrival might have been the most ordinary thing in the world.

"You did find a unicorn."

"I did."

It went to her. Vivian cradled the long white head, touching their foreheads together. "How lovely you are. You're so much more than I imagined."

"You can cure her, right?" Julia said. Her shoes were icy puddles, and she was swaying on her feet. The unicorn paid no attention to her. With a pang, she saw that the story was no longer hers. It had slipped through her fingers as easily as the end of the braid, leaving her a witness at its periphery.

"Of course," Vivian said, to a question no one else had heard. "Yes."

The unicorn lowered its horn and nudged up the hem of Vivian's oversized T-shirt, exposing the pale skin of her belly. Julia gritted her teeth, afraid to watch, unable to look away.

The tip of the horn plunged through the skin and withdrew.

Moonlight spilled out of the hole, an icy light that made the room swim. Vivian convulsed, whimpering. Gregory stroked her face, her hands, her arms, whispering to her, soothing, pleading. Julia ached to see them.

When the spasms had passed, and Vivian lay exhausted among the tangled quilts, there was no sign of the wound. But a glimmering light suffused her skin.

"Is it over?" Julia said. "Are you okay?"

"It hurts, but it will be all right." Vivian clasped Gregory's hand. "Help me."

Gregory gathered her up, one arm around her shoulders, another under her knees. As the unicorn knelt, he settled her onto its back. She wrapped a fistful of its mane around each hand and smiled at Julia, through Julia, her eyes fixed somewhere else now.

"You shouldn't be afraid," Vivian said.

The unicorn clambered to its feet and tensed. Then the two of them leapt out of the open window—but the window had not been open, Julia thought—and landed with a sound like church bells on the pavement two stories below. Ringing and pealing, the unicorn's hooves sang down the sidewalk, fading with distance.

Julia blinked, and the room was as dim as before, the window shut and locked against the night. Vivian was motionless in bed, Gregory feeling along her wrist with clumsy, desperate fingers, listening, waiting. Then he raised his head, loss naked in his eyes. On either side of the cold white bed they stood, unable, for a very long time, to say the impossible thing that had occurred.

Local Stop on the Floating Train

UNDER A CITRUS SLICE OF MOON, THE WHITE TRAIN WOUND silently through the night. The third car was almost empty, holding only a few commuters in silk ties and wingtips and coiffed socialites with well-ordered weekends. Conscious of her nose-rings and clogs, Lela slipped into a seat at the end of a vacant row. For her birthday, Gwen had given her a ticket to a play in the City. Gwen had gone with her boy, who was fresh off nine months on duty and nuts about her, splashing her with movies, merengue, piano-bar dinners, unable to let five minutes pass without plastering his face against her shoulder and inhaling her skin. Seeing the two of them together, Lela was embarrassed but also happy, and sometimes she wondered what it was like to be loved and spoiled like that.

It was a good play, her friend said, so good he hadn't grabbed her but once in the dark. There was rain in it, real rain tipped from the catwalks, and sword fighting, and kisses, and a sono-fabitch who didn't know how good he had it—this was how the friend had described it, big-eyed and waving her glass-ringed hands. You'll like it, you really will. Never having been to a play, Lela had tipped her head to one side and listened and smiled.

That day she had left her shift early. She had swabbed down the tables with cheerful emphasis, then shut herself in the bathroom and put jade drops in her ears and a slick of purple on her mouth. It was two hours by floating train to the City, so she brought along a ratty paperback to pass the time.

Every so often the train stopped and ingested passengers. Without noticing it, she borrowed their faces for the characters in her book: the hero, the king, the witch with slender hands. Businessmen and college students settled around her. Soon there was only one open seat in the car, to her left.

A man boarded the train, towing a small blonde boy behind him.

"There's Mom, wave goodbye," he said, and the boy dutifully did so. With a low soft sigh, the train slid into motion again. "How is she?"

"We went to the hospital yesterday."

"The hospital?"

"She cut her thumb."

"How?"

"I dunno. Making dinner."

The man surveyed the car, then pointed his son to the empty seat and planted himself in front of Lela. His eyes went through her like a cold steel pin. She didn't look at him. Stares like that were six for a dollar in the white neighborhood where she worked. She never knew what it was, exactly, whether her copper skin or long black braid or some inflection in her voice that was not sufficiently deferential. In the restaurant she was quick, cold, and polite; on the street she glared right back,

making her eyes wide and frightening. But her legs were sore
from standing all day, and she was looking forward to a nice
evening. She turned a page. The hero had learned his mission:
to steal from the enemy's stronghold an enchanted mirror that
showed things as they truly were.

Soon they were gliding through the nuclear desert. Outside
the window ran miles of charred and desolate plains. Here and
there, a faint green flame flickered up from the ash. No one
knew what the glimmerings meant. Some said they marked the
encampments of those who lived in the desert, irradiated and
melted into grotesque shapes with too many hands and eyes and
tongues. Some said they were the signal fires of extraterrestrials
lured to Earth by its patchwork of radioactive wastelands. No
one knew exactly, because no one had ever gone into the nuclear
desert and returned. The train was clad in lead to protect the
passengers, but as the small placards on the walls warned, riders
were still exposed to low levels of radiation.

The man still stared at Lela, his arms crossed on his chest.
There were no more stops before the City, so he did not have to
balance against the overhead rail. He coughed. Her absorption
in her book deepened. The little boy was glancing back and forth
between his father and the girl.

A blue-hatted conductor came through the car for tickets,
whistling tunelessly. His scanner flared red and cheeped over
each ticket. *Twit—twit—twit.* He was the only black man in the
car. He said to the standing man, "There's empty seats two cars
down, sir."

"I prefer to stand," he said, frowning at Lela. She did not
look up, but her spine acquired a greater degree of rigidity.
Captured and shackled, the hero pleaded for his life, but she
was finding it difficult to listen to him, to drop down from the
bright white train into the high hall with its tapestried walls

and rushy flags. She found herself reading the same paragraph over and over. The conductor shrugged, zapped their tickets, and moved on.

The train dragged a long plume of ash behind it as it went. The moon rose slightly in the sky then began to descend. The pressure of the angry eyes upon her had scattered the words on the page; they milled like ants and rearranged themselves. Finally the girl folded her book over a finger and said to the man, "What do you want?"

He opened and shut his mouth.

"You've been glaring at me for an hour. Why?"

"You should have given me your seat," the man said. "That would have been the polite thing to do."

"There were other seats." She opened her book again. "You were trying to intimidate me."

"Take your nose out of that book," he said, raising his voice. "Get a life."

The girl said nothing, flipping a page.

"You know what you need? A boyfriend. You'd be nicer if you could get laid."

The whole car could hear him. The other passengers looked fixedly through the lead glass windows at the drifts of ash.

He swelled. "You know what? You'd never be able to keep a guy, even if you could get one."

He turned and strode out of the car. Lela let out her breath and slumped. The oval of paper under her thumb was wavy with dampness.

"Sorry," whispered the boy, his blue eyes wide and worried. "I'm sorry. Sorry."

"It's not your fault," she said. "Don't worry about it."

Then the doors whisked open, and the father marched in with the conductor behind him. The boy fell silent.

"Who do you think you are?" the conductor said. "Harassing this man and his son? Not on my train!"

Lela's head jerked up in surprise.

"But—"

"Thank you, sir. I trust you'll deal with her appropriately." The man was smiling.

The conductor took her arm. "You'll have to disembark at the next stop." He pulled her out of her seat.

"But there aren't any stops before the City," Lela said, stupid with shock.

"There's a local stop."

She stumbled, struggling against his grip. "But I haven't done anything wrong!" she cried. Fear peeled her voice.

"Now's not the time to change your story. You've had your chance."

The other passengers remained fascinated by the featureless scenery outside. None of them made a sound. None of them met her eyes. The airlock opened and the conductor forced her into the vestibule.

The train was slowing, although they were far from the City. The girl did not understand what was happening. They pulled up at a blackened platform, dark except for the light washing from the train. There were no buildings beyond the crumbling platform. The town, if there had been one, had been blasted into oblivion a long time ago.

She said, "There isn't another train tonight."

"Should have thought of that before making trouble," the conductor said. "None of the trains stop here, anyway."

The leaded doors opened, and the girl was pushed onto the platform. Before she recovered her balance, the doors snicked shut again. The faces that peered out at her were pale, pitying, curious, indifferent. The father never turned his head. The boy was standing on his seat, flattening his nose against the window. He and Lela stared at each other. Then the train began to move.

Through the windows that flashed past she saw the smooth gleaming interior of the train, brightly lit, each metal bar polished to a satin sheen.

When the train was gone, the ash it had stirred up settled heavily on her eyelashes and hair. She stood gazing after the vanishing point of light. Then she climbed carefully down the broken steps, tucking the book under her arm. Far away, she could see a dim, twisting flame, green as glass. If she squinted, she thought she could pick out dark shapes moving around it.

The girl put down one foot, then the other, into the ankle-deep ash. It was soft as milkweed and swallowed all sound. She began to walk toward the flame. Already she could feel herself changing.

The Witch of Orion Waste and the Boy Knight

ONCE, ON THE EDGE OF A STONY SCRUB NAMED FOR A STAR that fell burning from Orion a hundred years ago, there stood a hut with tin spangles strung from its rafters and ram bones mudded in its walls. Many witches had lived in the hut over the years, fair and foul, dark and light, but only one at any particular time, and sometimes no one lived there at all.

The witch of this story was neither very old nor very young, and she had not been born a witch but had worked, once she was old enough to flee the smashed bowls and shrieks of her home, as a goose girl, a pot scrubber, then a chandler's clerk. On the days when she wheedled the churchwomen into buying rosewater and pomanders, the chandler declared himself fond of her, and on other days, when she asked too many questions, or wept at the abalone beauty of a cloud, or refused to take no for an answer, he loudly wished her back among her geese.

On a Monday like any other, the chandler gave her two inches of onion peel scrawled with an order, and precise instructions to avoid being turned into a toad, and shortly thereafter the clerk carried a packet of pins and three vials of lavender oil the three heathery miles from the chandler's shop to the hut on Orion Waste.

The white-haired crone who lived in the hut opened the door, took the basket, and looked the clerk up and down. She spat out a small object and said, "You will do."

"I beg your pardon?"

"I have a proposition for you," the crone said. "It is past time for me to leave this place. There is a city of women many weeks' travel away, and it sings in my mind like a young blue star. Would you like to be a witch?"

Here was something better than liniment for the hurts confided to her, better than candles for warding off nightmares.

"I would," the clerk said.

"Mind, you must not meddle in what is none of your business, nor help unless you are asked."

"Of course," the clerk said, her thoughts full of names.

"Too glib," the crone said. "The forfeit is three years' weeping." She rummaged in her pockets and placed a brass key beside the book on the squat table. "But you won't listen."

The clerk tilted her head. "I heard you clearly."

"Hearing's not listening. You learned to walk by falling, and you'll stir a hornet's nest and see for yourself. I was just as foolish at your age." The crone shook a blackthorn stick under the clerk's nose. "I would teach you to listen, if I had the time. Here is the key. Here is the book. Here is the bell. Be careful who you let through that door."

Grasping the basket and her stick, the crone sneezed twice and strode off into other stories without a backwards glance.

And the clerk sat down at the table and leafed through the wormy tome of witchcraft, dislodging mushrooms pressed like bookmarks and white moths that fluttered into the fire. Bent over the book, by sunlight and candlelight, she traced thorny letters with her fingertips and committed the old enchantments, syllable by syllable, to heart.

The villagers who came with bread, apples, mutton, and the black bottles of cherry wine the old witch favored were surprised by news of the crone's departure and doubtful of the woman they knew as goose girl and chandler's clerk. Their doubts lasted only until she compounded the requested charms for luck, for gout, for biting flies, for thick, sweet cream in the pail. For all its forbidding appearance, the Waste provided much of what the book prescribed: gnarled roots that she picked and spread on a sunny cloth, bark peeled in long curls and bottled, snake skins cast in the shade of boulders and tacked to the rafters.

Certain of her visitors traveled farther, knowing only the hundred-year-old tale of a witch on the Waste. They came stealthily at night and asked for poison, or another's heart, or a death, or a crown, and the witch, longing for the simple low-necked hissing of geese, shut the door in their faces.

A few of these were subtler than the rest, and several lied smoothly. But the crone had left a tongueless bell, forged from cuckoo spit, star iron, and lightning glass, which if warmed in the mouth showed, by signs and symbols, true things. In this way the witch could discern the dagger behind the smile. But the use of it left her sick and shuddering for days, plagued with bad dreams and waking visions, red and purple, and she only resorted to the bell in great confusion.

Three years from when she first parted its covers, the witch turned the last page of the book, read it, and sat back with a sigh. Someone had drawn in the margin a thorny archway, annotated in rusty red ink in a language she did not recognize, but apart from that, she knew all the witchcraft that the book held. The witch felt ponderous with knowledge and elastic with powers.

But because even arcane knowledge and occult powers do not properly substitute for a bar of soap and a bowl of soup, she washed her face and ate.

Loud knocking interrupted her meal. She brushed the crumbs from her lap, wiped the soup from her chin, and opened the door.

A knight stood upon her doorstep, a black horse behind him. A broken lance lay in his arms. He was tall, with a golden beard, and his eyes were as green as ferns.

"Witch," said the knight. "Do you have a spell for dragons?"

"I might," she said.

"What will it cost me? I am sworn to kill dragons, but their fire is too terrible and their strength too great."

"Do you have swan down and sulfur? Those are difficult to find."

"I do not."

"A cartful of firewood?"

"I have no cart and no axe, or I would."

"Then a kiss," the witch said, because she liked the look of him, "and I will spell your shield and your sword, your plate and your soft hair, to cast off fire as a duck's feather casts off rain."

The knight paid her the kiss with alacrity and not, the witch thought, without enjoyment. He sat and watched as she made a paste of salamander tails and serpentine, adding to this a string of ancient words, half hummed and half sung. Then she daubed the mixture over his armor and sword and combed it through his golden hair.

"There you go," she said. "Be on your way."

The knight set his chin upon his fists. "These dragons are formidable," he said. "Larger than churches, with cruel, piercing claws."

"I have never seen one," the witch said, "but I am sure they are."

"I am too tired and bruised to face dragons today. With your permission, I shall sleep outside your house, guard you from whatever creeps in the dark, and set forth in the morning."

"As you wish," the witch said. She shared with him her supper of potatoes, apples, and brookweed and the warmth of her hearth, though the hut was small with him in it, and he told her stories of the court he rode from, of its high bright banners and its king and queen.

In the morning the knight was slow to buckle on his plate. The witch came to the door to bid him farewell, bearing a gift of butternuts knotted in a handkerchief. He raised his shield reluctantly, as if its weight pained him.

"Dragons are horrible in appearance," he said. "Those who see them grow faint and foolish, and are quickly overtaken and torn limb from limb."

"That sounds likely," the witch said.

"They gorge on sheep and children and clean their teeth with men's bones. In their wake they leave gobbets of meat that the crows refuse."

"You have seen dreadful things," the witch said.

"I have." The knight tucked his helmet under his arm and pondered a dandelion growing between his feet. "And the loneliness is worse."

"Perhaps it would be better to have a witch with you."

"Will you come? I carry little money, only promises of royal favor. But I'll give kisses generously and gladly, and swear to serve you and defend you."

"I have never seen a dragon except in books," the witch said. "I would like to."

The knight smiled, a smile so luminous that the sun seemed to rise in his face, and paid her an advance as a show of good faith.

The witch took a warm cloak, the brass key, and at the last moment, on an impulse, the glass-and-iron bell, then locked the hut behind her. The knight helped her onto his horse, and together they rode across the Waste and beyond it. Grasshoppers flew up before them, and quail scattered. Wherever they went, the witch gazed about her with delight, for she had never traveled far from her village or the hut on the Waste, and everything she saw gleamed with newness.

They rode through forests and meadows that had no names the witch knew, singing and telling stories to pass the time. In the evenings the witch gathered herbs and dowsed for water, and the knight set snares for rabbits and doves. The knight had a strong singing voice and a laugh like a log crumbling in a fire, and the days passed quickly, unnumbered and sweet.

Before long, however, the land grew parched, and the wind blew hot and sulfurous. The witch guessed before the knight told her that they had passed into the country of dragons.

Late one evening they arrived at a deep crater sloped like a bowl, its edges black and charred. The bitter smoke drifting from the pit stung their eyes. Down at the center of the crater, something shifted and settled.

"Is that a dragon?" the witch said.

"It is," the knight said, his face long.

"Will you ride into battle?"

"Dragons hunt at night, and their sight is better than a cat's. It would devour me in two bites before I saw it, then my horse, and then you."

Clicking his tongue, the knight turned the charger. They rode until they reached the scant shelter of a dry tree among dry boulders, where they made camp.

The witch scratched together a poor meal of nuts and withered roots. The knight did not tell stories or sing. At first, the witch tried to sing for the both of them, her voice wavering up through the darkness. But no matter what she said or sang, the knight stared into the fire and sighed, and soon she too lapsed into silence.

The next morning, the witch said, "Will you fight the dragon today?"

"It is stronger than me," the knight said, gazing into his reflection on the flat of his sword. "It breathes the fires of hell, and no jiggery-pokery from a midwife's pestle could endure those flames. Tomorrow I shall ride back to my king, confess my failure, and yield my sword. My enemies will rejoice. My mother will curse me and drink."

The witch said nothing to this, but sat and thought.

The sun scratched a fiery path across the sky, hot on the back of her neck, and the air rasped and seethed with the sound of distant dragons.

When it was dark, and the knight was sound asleep, the witch drew his sword from its sheath and crept to the black horse. She swung herself up into its saddle, soothing it when it whickered, and with whispers and promises of sugar, she coaxed it across the sand to the edge of the crater. There she dismounted and descended in silence.

The dragon waited at the bottom of the pit, its eyes bright as mirrors.

It was not the size of a church, as the knight had said, only about the size of her hut on the Waste, but its teeth were sharp and serrated, its claws long and hooked, and gouts of flame dripped from its gullet as it slithered toward her.

The dragon drew a breath, its sides expanding like a bellows, and the fire in its maw brightened. Sharp shadows skittered over the ashes.

"You are no more frightening than my father," the witch said, with more courage than she felt. "And no less. But I have faced foxes and thumped them, and I shall thump you."

Flames flowered forth from its fangs, and as the witch leapt aside, a third of her hair smoldered and shriveled.

The narrow snout swayed toward her, but the witch shouted two words of binding that sent her staggering backwards with their force, and the dragon's jaws clamped shut.

The dragon thrashed its head from side to side, white smoke rising from its nostrils, clawing at its mouth.

Then it charged her, and she ran.

As ashes floated thick around her, and skulls and thighbones broke and scattered under her feet, the witch looked over her shoulder and gasped a word of quenching.

At once the smoke of its breath turned to a noxious steam. The dragon lurched and fell. Although it could not stir, it glared, and its hate was hot on her skin.

The witch lifted the knight's sword, and with tremendous effort, and twelve laborious strokes, she cut off its head.

At dawn she woke the knight, signing because her throat was raw and her lips were cracked, and led him to the scaly black carcass in the crater. The knight stared, then exclaimed and kissed her, and this kiss was sweeter than all that had come before.

"My lovely witch, my darling! With you beside me, why should I fear dragons?"

Although she ached all over, and a tooth felt loose in its socket, the witch blushed and brightened.

They continued into the land of dragons. Water grew more and more elusive, and the pools and damp patches the witch located were brackish and bitter, so when they reached a shallow river, they followed its course. The water was warm and brown, and tadpoles squirmed in it.

One afternoon, as the sun slanted down and strewed diamonds on the river, the witch saw the second dragon. This one was the length of a watchtower and red as dried blood, and it crouched in a muddy wallow, half hidden by dead brush. When she called the knight's attention to it, he wheeled the horse around.

"Are you frightened?" she said.

There was no reply.

"Are you upset?"

He lowered his visor.

"Did I do something wrong?"

His eyes glittered out of his helmet, but he did not say a word.

The witch twined her fingers in the horse's mane and named the birds and burdocks they passed, then prattled about the weather, and still the knight said nothing.

Some hours later, over their supper of frogs, he broke his silence. "This one is viler than the last," he said. "Even you could not vanquish it. Me it would swallow in a snap, sword and all."

"It did not look so terrible," the witch said, light-headed with relief.

"But it is."

"You are a brave and valiant knight, and I am sure you will succeed."

"Of course you'd say that," the knight said, frowning. "It's not you who will die a nasty death, all teeth and soupy tongue."

"But your sword arm is strong, and your blade is trusty and well kept. Besides, I have enchanted your sword and your armor."

"As you like. I shall challenge it in the morning, and it will eat toasted knight for breakfast. Farewell." The knight turned his back to her, pillowed his head on his hands, and soon was snoring.

The witch had grown fond of the knight, in her way. His fear soured her stomach, and she tossed and turned, unable to sleep for thoughts of his death. In the middle of the night, she arose and sought the dragon.

The reeds were trodden and crushed in a wide swathe where it couched, and dead fish and birds lay all about. Its red scales were gray in the dim starlight, and it snuffed and snorted at subtle changes in the wind, finally fixing its eyes upon her. This dragon was heavy and sluggish, unlike the last, but poison dripped in black strings from its jaws. It lifted itself from the muck and lumbered forward.

"You are no more poisonous than my mother," the witch said, swallowing her fear. "And no less. But I have turned biting lye into soap, and I shall render you down as well."

She spoke the words of binding, but the dragon shrugged off her spell like so many flung pebbles. She shouted a word of quenching, and its jaws widened in a mocking grin. As she coughed on the word, her own throat burning, the dragon lunged and snapped.

The mud sucked at her feet as she fled, and marsh vapors wavered and tore as she ran through them. She tried words of severing and words of sickening, tasting blood on her lips, to no avail.

Bit by bit, the subtle gases of the dragon's breath slowed and stupefied her. The world spun. Then a root thrusting out of the mire hooked her ankle.

She skidded and slid.

Across the oozy earth the dragon crawled, bubbling and hissing. As its jaws opened to swallow her, the witch, her voice dull, spoke a word of cleansing.

The syllables slipped between scales into the dragon's veins and curdled the deadly blood. The dragon shuddered, its black eyes rolling back. Its snout scraped her leg, and then its long bulk splashed into the mud and lay still.

The witch limped to where the river flowed, languid and wide, and washed off, as best she could, the muck, the rot, the black blood and the red.

The sound of plackart clinking against pauldron woke her in the morning. Her knight—for she was beginning to think of him as hers—was grimly and glumly donning his gear.

No need, the witch wished to say, but her throat hurt as much as if she had swallowed a fistful of pins.

"Wait here," the knight said. "I do not want you to witness my shameful death. When I am crisped and crunched, ride swiftly to the court of Cor Vide and tell them their youngest knight is dead."

He spurred his horse and set off. Within the hour, he returned, his face dark.

"Witch, did you do this?" he said. "Did you kill that dragon while I slept?"

The witch nodded, unable to speak. The knight did not kiss her. He let her clamber onto the horse without offering his arm, and they rode all that day and the next in an ugly silence.

On the third day, when her throat had healed somewhat, the witch rasped, "Are you angry with me?"

"I am never angry, for anger is wicked and poisonous. But what will the court call a knight who lets women slay his dragons?"

"You seemed afraid."

"I wasn't afraid, witch."

"I wanted to help."

"You did more harm than good."

"I am sorry," she said.

"Do not do it again."

The river they were following dwindled to a stream, then to dampness, and then the earth split and cracked, but they continued in the same direction, in hopes that the stream ran underground and sprang up again somewhere.

By and by, their mouths parched, they came to a crooked tower with a broken roof and a great golden serpent wrapped many times around its base. The witch, knight, and horse were the only things that moved upon the barren plain, and they raised a great cloud of dust. While they were still at a distance, the serpent began unwinding itself from the tower.

"Stay, witch," the knight said, looking pale. "My sword is but a lucifer to this creature. Its fire will shrivel me, and the steel of my armor will drip over my bones. I'll die, but I'll die honorably. Remember me. I did love you."

And the witch watched, anxious, as her knight trudged on foot toward the tower, sheets of air around him shimmering with heat.

The serpent's eyes were red jewels, and its forked tongue lashed in and out of its mouth as the knight approached. Rearing up, the serpent spat a feathering jet of fire. The shield rose to meet it. Flames broke on its boss and poured off, harmless.

The knight laughed. His sword flashed.

But its edge rebounded from the scales without cutting, once, twice, and in a trice the serpent had tangled him in its coils and suspended him upside down.

His helmet tumbled off. His sword slipped from his mailed hand. He hung in midair, his golden curls loose, his face exposed.

The serpent squeezed, and he screamed.

The witch screamed too: a word of unraveling. The serpent's loops slackened, and the knight crashed to the ground. She screamed a word of piercing, and the serpent's eyes ran liquid and useless from their sockets. The serpent flailed, blind and enraged, battering the tower. Stones loosened from their mortar and fell. One crushed the knight's shield into splinters.

Finding his footing again, the knight slipped under the thrashing coils and sank his sword into one emptied eye, up to the hilt.

With a roar of agony, and spasms that shook down the upper third of the tower, the dragon expired.

The knight did not stand and savor his triumph. He whirled on the witch.

"I saw you. You goaded it—you spurred it to rage. You were trying to kill me!"

No, the witch would have said, if she were able.

But her lips were blistered and her tongue numb.

She pointed instead, in mute appeal.

A woman had emerged from the tower. She had watched what the witch had done; she could speak to her innocence. Her gown was green, and her smile, which she turned on them, was brilliant as an emerald. Several golden objects on her girdle swung and glittered as she approached, stepping delicately around the pools of smoking blood.

"Did you do this, good knight?" she said. "Have you freed me from this place?"

The knight bowed, then stood taller. "I did, though I did not know you were here. Where shall I bring you? Where will you be safe? You must have friends somewhere."

"Northeast," she said. "A long way."

"However far it is, I will accompany you."

"There is treasure in that tower, if you seek treasure. I stopped to play with rings, crowns, and necklaces, admiring myself in a golden glass. I did not realize that it was a dragon's hoard, and that the possessor would return. He gnawed my palfrey to the hooves and guarded me greedily from that time on. What I search for is not there, but that hoard will pay for your time."

"What gold could outshine the copper of your hair? You shall ride behind me, and this witch shall walk beside. For you look like a lady, and your feet are too soft for the road."

The lady's eyes danced. "Oh no, the witch shall ride. Both of us together, if you insist. I have met witches before, and they grow ugly if spited. This one is quite ugly already, and that smock does her no favors."

The witch, her breast burning, could not meet the lady's eyes. She looked instead at her rich green gown, stiff with gilt embroidery. Hanging from her girdle were toys of tin and wood, painted gold: a carved dog, a jumping acrobat, a wind-up man.

"Let me help you up," the knight said.

"First tie my hands behind me," the lady said. "I am under a curse. What I touch is mine and ever after shall be."

"A strange curse," the knight said, but obliged. He lifted her onto the horse in front of the witch. Her red hair blew into the witch's mouth. For sport, the lady leaned to one side, then the other, pretending to topple.

"Don't let her fall," the knight said to the witch. "I know you are jealous and would love nothing better. But if harm comes to her, I will cut off your head."

They proceeded more slowly after that, the knight leading the horse, the witch holding the reins, and the strange lady smiling in the witch's arms. As they rode, the witch wept, but very softly, for whenever the knight heard, he looked at her with disgust.

"Stop," he said. "Enough. You have no reason to cry."

Then her tears fell hotter and faster into the lady's red hair.

In the lengthening evenings, while the witch foraged, the knight and lady talked together and laughed. With her hands bound, the lady could do little for herself, and so the knight fed her, slid her silken slippers from her feet, and waited on her every wish.

The knight kissed the witch for the food and water she brought them, briefly and without interest, and apologized to the lady after. At night the lady nuzzled her head into the crook of the knight's arm and spread her long hair over them. The witch lay awake, watching the stars until they blurred and ran together.

"Why do you never sing anymore?" the knight said one evening, as the witch turned a rabbit over the fire. "Sing for us."

"He says you have a fine voice, for a witch. Do let me hear it."

"I don't anymore," the witch rasped. The lady grimaced. "I burned it to cinders for him. It hurts to speak."

"You'll heal," the knight said.

"I might, or I might not. The words of power I used were dear, and I am paying."

"You want me to feel guilty," the knight said.

"No, I wanted—"

"I don't want to hear about it." He folded his arms. "There was never any point in talking to you, anyway."

The lady laughed and laid her head against his shoulder.

Another evening, as the witch returned with chanterelles and hedgehog mushrooms in her skirt, she heard the knight say, "She's bewitched me, you know. That's why I hunt dragons—for her sport. That's why I kiss her every night—I am forced."

"Such a glorious knight, under the thumb of a lowly thing like her. How awful," the lady said.

"It is awful."

"Why don't you strike her head off while she sleeps?"

"I'm ensorcelled, remember. I cannot kill her. My father, a lord and a haughty man, would have strangled her for her insolence, but I am nothing like him."

"Indeed you are not," the lady said.

"You are kinder than she ever was. I've told you more than I've ever told her. Can you free me, as I have freed you?"

"Say the word, and I shall prick her with poisoned needles while she rides. She will die of that, slowly, unsuspecting, and then you shall be free."

"Do, and I shall follow you faithfully."

"Then pluck the air between the two of you as we go, as if you are pulling petals, and put them in this purse. You'll not see or feel what you gather, as your senses are not so fine, but I shall decoct what is there to a poison."

"I knew it," the knight said. "She has a foul and invisible power over me."

"A strange influence, certainly."

The witch stepped into the firelight, balancing their supper in her muddy skirt, and both the knight and the lady fell quiet and averted their eyes.

The moon waxed and waned, and the witch wearied of weeping. She was sick of holding the lady, sick of suffering her pinpricks, sick of watching the knight play with the lady's russet hair. Her pain had grown tedious and stale, but she was far from home and bewildered, for sometimes, still, the knight smiled at her with swift and sudden fondness, and it was as though he was again the knight she had set forth with, many and many a month ago.

Late one night, as she covered herself with her muddy cloak, she heard a clinking in its folds. In its pocket she found the key to her hut and the tongueless bell, which in her misery she had forgotten about.

The witch put the bell in her mouth, and the world shone.

First she looked upon the sleeping knight. In his place she saw a small boy, much beaten and little loved, his face wet from crying. He writhed in his sleep with fear. Around his limbs wound a silver spell, older than the witch and wrought with greater art than hers, and when the witch strummed the strands of it with a nail, she heard in their hum that they would break and let him grow only when he had slain three dragons by his own hand.

Then the witch saw how she had wronged him by killing the black dragon, the red, and the gold. She would have kissed his forehead and asked forgiveness, but a black asp crept out of his mouth and hissed at her, and she was afraid.

She turned to the lady who slept at his side. A hole gaped in her breast, its torn edges fluttering. The witch stuck her hand in but found nothing: not a bone, not a thread, not corners, nor edges either. It howled with hunger, that hole. The woman who wore it would wander the world, snatching and grasping and thrusting into that aching emptiness everything within reach, forever trying to fill it, and failing.

The witch grieved for her too.

The three of them had camped beside a pool of water, and now the witch knelt on its mossy margin. In the light of the half moon she saw how her limbs were shriveled and starved for love, her bones riddled with cracks from bearing too much too soon. She sat there for hours, until she knew herself, and the fractures and hollow places within her, and the flame that burned, small and silent, at her core.

And when the witch understood that nothing kept her weeping on the black horse but herself, that the sorcery that had imprisoned her and blinded her was her own, she spat out the bell, dashed her reflection into a million bright slivers, and laughed.

With a whistle, the witch rose into the air, and whistling, she flew. When she stopped for breath, her feet sank softly to the earth. In this manner she traveled over the country of dragons, through nameless meadows and woods, and across the Orion Waste.

Once in all that time, when her heart gave a sharp pang, the witch put the bell in her mouth and looked back.

Far away, the knight was unknotting the cord around the lady's wrists, first with fingers, and then, when it proved stubborn, with teeth. When her arms were free, he clasped her to his breast and buried his face in her hair.

But in the moment of their embrace, the knight began to shrink. The lady's arms tightened around him. Faster and faster the knight diminished, armor and all, until he was no taller than a chess piece and stiff and still.

The lady caught him between forefinger and thumb. She studied the leaden knight, her expression pleased, then puzzled, then disappointed. At last, shaking her head, she tied him to her girdle between the wooden dog and painted acrobat. Between one knot and the next, she flinched and sucked her finger, as if something had bitten her.

Then she mounted the black horse and rode slowly onward, searching for that which would fill her lack.

After that the witch flew without pause, without eating or drinking, and the wind dried her tears to streaks of salt.

Just as her strength gave out, the hut on Orion Waste rose like a star on the horizon. The witch unlocked the door and collapsed onto her narrow bed. There she remained, shivering with fever, for the better part of a month. One or two people from the village, seeing the light in her window across the scrub, came with eggs and bread and tea, left them silently, and went away again.

One day, in a wave of sweat, the fever broke. The witch crawled to her feet, unlatched the window, and saw the Waste covered in white and yellow wildflowers.

The book of witchcraft lay open on the table, though she was sure no one had touched it. In the margin of the last page, wild roses peppered the tangle of thorns.

A week later, the witch returned to the village, her few belongings in hand, and asked the chandler if he might allow her to mind the shop again. He agreed gladly, for he was old and stiff, and she was quick and could climb the ladder to the highest shelves for him.

There she lived for a year, content, sweeping the floor, mending the shelves, and stirring a little magic into her soaps, so they cleaned better than others, and gave hope besides. She did not speak much, for her voice frightened children, but she listened carefully, and closely, and no one seemed to mind.

And there she would have stayed, growing gray and wise, had not a peddler with a profitable knack for roaming between stories rung the shop bell.

Looking over the wares he had spread on a cloth, all polished and gleaming, the witch and the shopkeeper chose combs, mirrors, scissors, and ribbons to buy. When the silver had been counted out and poured into his hands, and the goods collected, the peddler grinned a gapped grin and dug from his pack a pair of dancing shoes, cut from red leather and pricked all over with an awl.

"For you," he said to the witch. "Secondhand, and a few bloodstains, but pretty, no? *Some* angels don't like to see the poor dance, and the last lass had a heart too clean and Christian to wear them for long, but your heart's spotted, and these are just your size."

"Thank you," the witch said, "but I don't know how to dance. I know how to fly, and slay dragons, and make good soap, but dancing is a mystery."

"Then you should learn," the peddler said.

The shopkeeper sighed, because he could guess what was coming. When the witch approached him three days later, with a request, and a promise, he sent her on her way with a bag containing three cakes of soap, three spools of thread, three needles, a mirror, and a comb, cursing the peddler under his breath.

That night, as the stars glistened overhead, and the frogs and crickets sang a joyful Mass from their secret places, the witch locked up the hut, laced on the red shoes, whistled, and flew.

The Eve of the Planet of Ys

IN ITS LATTER DAYS, THE TWO BLESSED SUNS OF THE PLANET OF Ys grew twice as large and dully red. There was no true day or night on Ys, but a long thin dusk when both suns burned, followed by a dim and feverish evening when one or the other had set.

While laughter was still heard on Ys, people placed bets on which sun would swallow the other before flaring outward to consume their doubled necklace of planets, and they joked about the difficulties of collecting.

Then the crops did not grow in the low and ugly light, and laughter ceased.

The temples of jasper and chrysocolla were torn down. Ancient thrones were toppled, and governments dissolved in speechless confusion.

One man who had amassed several towers of gold, which in that eternal evening looked indistinguishable from iron, announced that he would build a starship to save a select few.

From his towers of gold he paid engineers and physicists to labor day and night. And many praised him.

Another man who had amassed a mountain of gold, which gleamed in the red light with an oily green tinge, declared that salvation was to be found underground. He would bore thousands of miles of tunnels, for use by a fortunate handful. And he paid excavators and builders to burrow in the earth. His name was breathed with reverence.

A third man sat on a wreck of gold, which shone enough that one might overlook the deaths that had purchased it, and proclaimed that cooling the body to stillness, to make statues of the living until danger had passed, was the answer. And he paid biologists and chemists to perfect this enchantment. Many prayers and blessings were said for him.

All the while, those who did not have towers of gold, nor black-clad guards with rifles of light, scratched and scrounged and ate furtively in corners, that their food might not be taken from them. Death and plague ran through the streets. One barely opened one's gates to family, fear flowed so free.

Where the long dragging point of one tower's shadow fell in the darkest part of dusk, in an unremarkable neighborhood, there was a mud-walled compound. And in that compound, in the latter days of Ys, as people fought and snatched and hoarded, a woman passed the evenings cooking, sweeping, and putting things to rights.

She sowed seed, though the plants never grew high in that weak light, and gathered the small greens to eat by the bowlful. She clambered down into the drying well and scraped at the muddy bottom with a broken cup to collect the mouthfuls of water that remained. And she tended to two girls who had collapsed, one after the other, weeping and bleeding, before her gate.

When her neighbors first heard the rattle of the chain on her gates, they had hissed at her from behind their own walls.

"What are you doing?"

"You're mad!"

"Don't let her in!"

"Open the gates, and the men will fall on you."

The woman shouldered one of the gates open, though not far, in case what that last neighbor said was true.

But the street was empty except for the weeping girl, who wouldn't meet the woman's eyes. The woman dragged her into the compound and shut and chained the gate.

In those days the story was always the same. The woman asked no questions. She filled a basin with precious water and wiped the blood and dirt from the girl. Then she shared her thin porridge and sprouts with her. And while the girl slept, the woman thought.

She had sold all that she could already: iron for the price of gold, the spare dishes, the jewelry, her blood, and her hair.

There would be more blood to sell, of course, and more hair, but the numbers she scratched on a waxen tablet, three times over, were slim and alarming.

And then the second girl arrived.

"You'll eat as well as I do," the woman said eventually, once the second girl's bruises had gone green, "but I don't know how I'll feed us for much longer."

The first girl, who was mostly healed now, if heavily quiet, looked up at the tall gold towers and the silver strands that stretched away from them. She said nothing, but a few hours later the woman heard a scuffling and a thump, and glimpsed the edge of the girl's dress disappearing over the mudbrick wall.

The first girl might as well try her luck elsewhere, the woman told herself. She seemed tough. A survivor. There'd be a little more food for the second girl now.

But a twilight and a night later there came a knocking at the gate, and when the woman nudged the swinging tin shutter aside, there stood the first girl, her arms full of salvage. Once the woman opened the gate, she dropped her armful of scrap and ducked around the corner, whistling like a bird.

A moment later, she returned with the scabby end of a black wire and a smile on her face. And she busied herself with what she had found.

Within hours, an old, cracked light rod the girl had retrieved, with the black wire knotted around it, burned in the yard with such brightness the woman was afraid and tried to cover it with a blanket.

The first girl laughed and undid the wire, plunging them into a darkness that was sharper for the light.

"There," she said, the first words she had spoken. "We can grow crops now."

The woman said, "But how—"

"The what," said the first girl, "is more important than the how."

With that, the woman had to agree.

They dug up the floor of the old root cellar under its weathered cover and planted a handful of old seed in the rod's knifelike light, their eyes wide with wonder at one another's faces and the antique colors they saw.

Those were hopeful if hungry days. They divided the remaining seeds into smaller and smaller portions and saved water for the plants. The cellar's darkness and depth preserved a little natural moisture for their roots.

They worked when they needed to and slept to conserve

energy, ate meagerly, and rarely ventured outside of the compound.

One day they saw an enormous bright firework in the red sky, rising higher and higher, until it became a tiny star.

"That'll be the starship," the first girl said.

Then they heard in the distance the roar of the starved and the greedy as they rose up to raid that particular tower, now that only an unfortunate few were left. If rifles of light were turned on the mob, the killing was too quiet to hear.

"Was that—" the woman said.

"Different tower," the first girl said, glancing at the black wire she had laid.

"Good."

"I tapped the one where they are keeping rich people cold and slow in vaults," she said. "If our light goes out, then they have all died in their sleep."

"And we will too," the second girl said. "But we'll be awake."

The first girl said, "The light hasn't gone out yet."

The second girl pinched her lips together. Then she asked for a little extra food, that she might go out on a private errand.

The woman looked at her, sighed, and ladled a few more grains into her bowl. And though the gods and their temples had been smashed to dust, she prayed upon her knees to whatever and whomever might be listening for the second girl's swift steps, deft hands, and safe return.

It was two half-dusks and dawns before they saw the second girl again, looking worse for the wear. But she had some torn schematics under her arm, with grids and diagrams that confounded the others.

"If I have the coordinates right," she said, "one of the less important tunnels runs directly beneath your eastern neighbor's house, at a depth of three stories."

"Less important?" the first girl said.

"It's an access tunnel to their emergency stores," the second girl said. "Shell meal and dried insect flour. Not to be touched except in direst circumstances. I was an engineer, once," she added, when she saw the woman's expression.

The woman's neighbor listened to their request with sour suspicion. "Waste my time, would you?" she said. "The little time I have left, to dig in my yard?"

"You and your family and each of us in turns," the woman said.

"You're mad."

"We are all dying anyhow, whether we try this or not."

"No."

The woman and two girls ate their scant meal in silence that night, peered at the star grains that were growing too slowly in the cellar, and tried not to meet each other's eyes. The second girl began sketching triangles and calculating angles in the dirt of the courtyard.

The first girl said, "Even with everyone helping, even with the shortest path, it was a stretch. The additional distance—with only the three of us—pah."

"Do you have better plans for the end of the world?" the second girl inquired. "A monument to chisel? A lover, for pleasure and distraction? Time spent with family, perhaps?"

"If we'll die like insects, no use pretending we're better than insects. Look at you, with your fancy education, pecking in the dirt with your stick."

And the two of them sniped and stung each other until the woman broke them apart.

"We can't afford this," she said mildly. The girls subsided.

In the raw red morning, the eastern neighbor came to the wall and called the woman's name.

The neighbor said, with a deathly weariness in her voice,

"This will go nowhere. It is a terrible waste of the last days of our lives. But we will help you. What else is there to do? Come in."

The second girl measured off a cross in steps from the corners of the neighbor's courtyard and scratched a circle in the dirt with her stick. One or two of them dug furiously at a time, the earth flying, until they slumped with exhaustion and passed the shovel to the next.

The neighbors on the western side of the compound were persuaded to join them.

The first grains ripened in their cellar, their kernels milky green and gold. The woman gathered them, reserved a third for seed, and shared the rest.

With so many eating together, it was not very much, but then the neighbors to the east brought a cup of dried fungus, and the neighbors to the west brought a bowlful of powdered roots, and then their stomachs did not gnaw at them quite so much.

Despite the wild futility of the plan, their hole deepened with surprising speed. Every so often, the shovel edge clanged on rock, which they dug around, loosened, and removed. The dark crawling things that still lived and moved in the earth emerged from the tossed soil and went scuttling away.

They were watching their neighbor toil at the bottom of the hole, down which they had slung a corded ladder, and from which they pulled basketfuls of earth, when he suddenly disappeared with a faint cry and a clang. A moment later, they perceived a dim white light where he had been.

"We've reached the tunnels," the second girl said, even as the neighbor's wife prepared to wail and tear her hair.

The ladder was retracted, lengthened by another three ells, and dangled into the hole again. When the second girl descended, she found the neighbor sitting dazed in a pile of earth on the floor of a round bored tunnel. It curved out of sight in either direction. The walls were reinforced with flash concrete, and the space faintly lit with emergency lights, except for the section where they were, for his motion had triggered brighter illumination. They had entered the tunnel off-center, not at the highest point, and he was not badly injured. She helped him up the ladder and reported their success.

Exhausted as they were, this was gladness and rejoicing. Arms wound around shoulders, and hands slapped backs in congratulations. Only the woman looked up at the suns, which were steadily swelling like the spherical buds of waterflowers about to bloom in the cisterns of the temple courts.

Naturally, the next thing to do was to explore the tunnels. Down one way was the store of starvation rations the second girl had predicted, tasteless, yet like ambrosia to their hunger. Down the other way was a forking set of tunnels, one of which contained a pile of forgotten materials, including unused cylinders of flash concrete. With this windfall, they reinforced their own descending shaft and built a sturdy metal ladder, as well as a double-chambered airlock at the top. For the second girl had seen the direction of the woman's look, and the distended red suns, and understood that time was running low in the basin.

Halfway up the laddered hole, they hollowed out a little bubble of earth, high enough to crouch in, reinforced on its sides and ceiling. There they strung new lights that tapped into the tunnels' power lines and planted the seeds they had reserved.

There were sufficient supplies in the tunnel stores to last a few years, and as they were able, they brought more down: fuel and metal scrap, tools, fasteners, rope, and some relics of their past lives, to remember the old world by.

There might be a time when the tunnel dwellers found them, but it would be a long time from now, the second girl said. Perhaps generations. There were elaborate, aquifer-fed farms elsewhere in the complex, and stocks of real food rather than insect meal; she had seen the plans and provisioning.

The second girl had grown stern and sturdy, the woman was glad to see, as she must have been once before; she would be a wise and thoughtful leader in the times to come.

At last, one of the suns expanded like a blown bubble, a slow and terrible and beautiful disaster, and those who had not left Ys on the starship, who were not frozen in crystal chambers, and who had not bought billets underground, shrieked and cursed their forsaken gods, their broken temples, and one another. Smoke smeared the red sky from fires set throughout the city.

The second girl gazed up at the sky, where the doomed sun blossomed gorgeously toward them. With calm and sensible words, she led them all into the shaft they had built, sealing the two doors of the airlock behind them.

It would be a lean time, she said, but not a hard one. The first-flowering sun would engulf the other, and the two would expand toward this planet and the next. But only the surface of Ys would be scorched—the mud-brick compound glazing like pottery, crazing, and crumbling to dust—and then an eternal night would set in.

There was nothing left for them above, she said. There was life below. And what they would do with that life now, in these narrow passages, was up to them.

It was more than they had before, one neighbor said.

They had learned to do much with very little, the other neighbor added.

The woman listened and nodded and kept her own counsel. She assisted with the excavation of new planting and compost-ing chambers, moving the loosened earth into containers to grow more seed, and set her hand to the sowing and harvesting of the star-shaped grains.

All the while, though, her thoughts swooped like the six-winged birds that used to make their nests in the temple eaves. She remembered the temple processions with their ankle-bells and flags, the blue-green grain that moved like waves, the streams that trickled merrily between stones and in channels along the clean paved streets, the rich black mud that she packed into bricks for her home. Though she also knew Ys in the dying light, her life had been long, and she still loved and remembered Ys as it had been.

The first girl occupied herself with painting scenes from the lost surface world on the tunnel walls. Now and then the woman inquired about this graceful figure or that tableau. Then she leaned her head toward the second girl, who was figuring rations or taking inventory, and asked about what was happening on the surface of Ys.

"A consuming light we cannot see," she said absently, "which leaves no life in its wake. It'll burn a while yet."

The star grains grew tall and pointed beneath their stolen light. They made round handcakes and ate them alongside loaves of the dusty meal.

Years passed in that storage tunnel, an existence unmoored from sunlight and every natural sense of time. They made wide, deep-voiced instruments of metal and wire, remembered how to dance, slept when they wearied, and ate when they hungered. The first girl's murals ran down the hall as far as the fork, beyond which, out of caution, none of them had gone.

It was life, as life appears everywhere in the universe: at times chaotic, mostly boring, with a sense of suspension, and full of daily pettiness, grievance, sorrow, and sighs. But it was better, they agreed, than life in the red twilight, or the scouring lifelessness of endless night. And they got on with things.

The woman's hair turned the color of nitrogen frost, and the girls could no longer be called girls. The one who had been an engineer, who was now their leader, said absently, when the woman asked, "I imagine most of the star's outer shell has blown past us by now. I suspect the atmosphere has been stripped away. You couldn't breathe up there, and you'd freeze to death, but it would take a few minutes."

As she spoke, she turned pieces of pipe over and over in her hands, thinking about sanitation and water, and so she didn't see the old woman nod and leave.

The old woman walked down the tunnel of murals, some silvered with foil from scrap beaten thin, and admired each one. The girl who became an artist, as well as a maker of musical instruments, had flourished with the wealth of time below, and the walls were rich and beautiful. They reminded the woman of the temples she had visited as a child, with windows of silver wire and sheet-cut jewels, torn down before the girls were born.

"Life is easier to bear with art," she said to her neighbor, gesturing at the walls, and her neighbor gave her an uncomprehending smile. Down the tunnel they could hear the chiming and piping of newly made instruments, as someone fashioned a sweet music from nothing.

The old woman climbed halfway up the ladder, which she could still do, first to the hollow chambers of grain, where one crop had reached finger height, one waist height, and one had gone to seed. She brushed her fingers through the stalks, wondering at the green and gold and white of them, the miracle of this little remnant, tended like hope. On extravagant impulse, she took one of the spiny star clusters, hulled the grains between her palms, and ate them. Their taste was nutty and green.

Since they had sealed the entrance against the dying suns, she had not returned to the airlock at the top of the ladder. The metal had corroded slightly, as had the seal. She unstoppered the pinhole vent, let it hiss for a moment, then pushed gently around the edges of the hinged metal sheet until it unsealed and let her through.

Being tidy and careful in her habits, she stoppered the vent again.

It was colder in the gap between the doors, and dark but for the square of glass they had set in the lower flap. The glass in the upper flap was the color of night. She opened the second vent, waited, then heaved herself upward.

Again she set everything to rights.

It was very cold on the surface, a cold that pierced to the bone. Little was left of the compound. All was blackened and blasted. The woman sat on the freezing ground and looked up at the sky, where a white dwarf shone, small and heatless, in the dark. Around her the remnants of its neighbor glimmered like burning feathers, falling petals, wisps of iridescent flame. The nebula's beauty filled her eyes with tears.

And her tears froze clear and hard upon her face.

The engineer only went as far as the airlock chamber. Through the square of glass, she could see the shape of the old woman, limned in faint starlight. She returned to the people below and told them.

The artist painted the old woman on the tunnel walls, where the tunnel forked and ran into the unknown. If and when any of the other tunnel dwellers approached, they would see the woman before anything else, standing before a silver-foil nebula, a bowl of star grains in her hands.

In this way they remembered her.

And Ys went on through the long cold night.

Courtship Displays of the American Birder

AMONG THE BIRDERS WAITING ON THE COMBINE HARVESTER'S cab and cab-side platform, swinging binoculars across the yellowing rice, Victor caught a smile of secret smugness, all canaries and cream. The woman's hiking boots were clearly from out of town, and her kelp-green Swarovski 10×50s—he tightened his grip on his own, cheaper Voyager 8×42s—suggested a stable, well-paying job. She had been in the Pineywoods, he thought, looking at the loam on her boots. Early morning, on her own.

"What did you see?" he said.

"Great kiskadee," she said. "A lifer. Look."

He took the peeling black notebook she offered him. In the ten years he had lived in Louisiana, Victor had never spotted a kiskadee, and hearing he'd missed one, here, today, made his heart sink. She was thirty-three or thirty-four, he guessed, a bit older than him, and she had seen 1,254 birds to his 492. Her mud-brown curls were tucked into a baseball cap, and he suspected that if he tapped ever so gently on the brim, it would spring off her head in a froth of hair.

"Nice list," he said. "I'm Victor."

"Lindsey. Atlantic County, New Jersey. Fall migration, we get northern gannets, red-breasted mergansers, snow geese twenty deep on the beach." She gestured at the stalks of rice, the combine's high blades, the chitter of birds in the field, all of it old and worn as ritual to him. "This is new to me."

The tractor coughed to life. They gripped the platform's metal bar to steady themselves, binoculars thumping against their chests. Around them, Leica and Zeiss and Fujinon flew up. As the combine harvester moved, rice toppled into its teeth, and chaff blew out in dusty clouds. The rice fields exploded with birds: brown, yellow, and white.

"Sora!" Lindsey shouted, her voice high and harsh with joy. Victor pointed his bins in the same direction, hunting through bursts of grasshopper sparrows and savannah sparrows, until he saw the yellow bill and black bib. "King rail!" she said, and he found that, too: striped back and belly, fluttering chickenlike from the grass.

Red wings whirred across his bins. "Vermilion flycatcher," he said, sweeping out its trajectory with his hand. She saw it, whooped, and leaned over the guardrail in excitement.

Victor knew what would happen before he could speak it. A yellow rail flew up ahead of the circular blade, not away from the combine but directly into their faces. Lindsey flung up her arms and tumbled forward.

He locked his arms around her waist and hauled her back, his Voyagers digging into his breastbone. Her baseball cap had tumbled off, vanishing beneath the churning combine, and her hair spilled wild as alligator weed over her shoulders. She turned and stared at him, mouth open. The other birders cheered, but only briefly, because the combine was still moving and a pepper of sparrows was flying out of the rice before the blade.

LINDSEY TOOK HIM for coffee and a rich slice of cake after the combine ride, at the dark and elegant café across the street from her hotel. He was a math teacher, he told her, which was almost true—he was a substitute—because he did not want her to think of him waiting for a 4 a.m. call.

She managed a rental car company somewhere along Route 50, and she had divorced earlier that year, she said. He gathered that her husband had not been a kind man, and moreover couldn't tell a siskin from a bobolink.

As she spoke, he pushed a forkful of cake into his cheek instead of his mouth. Powdered sugar scattered everywhere. He wiped at the mess with his napkin, blushing, and elbowed half the coffee from her mug.

"Can I get you another cup," Victor managed, and she said, "Yes, please," before she remembered that she was paying. She raised her wallet in protest, then levered herself out of her chair.

"Let me," she said. He watched her walk to the counter, plump as a swallow, the dried mud on her boots different colors now, mixed with straw. "Let me know when you come to Cape May," she said as she sat down again.

"That's pretty far," Victor said.

"You'll come someday. The spring and fall migrations, you'll never see anything like them anywhere else."

"School starts in the fall. I can't get the time off." He did not mention the unaffordability of the trip. He did not look at her Swarovskis, zipped up safely in their case. "I think that's your coffee."

"Well. If you do." She pulled a pen out of her pocket, the same pen she'd scribbled lifers with as they rode through the field, and wrote her number on a napkin. "You should call. I get Philadelphia vireos and black-capped chickadees in my backyard."

That night, as Victor brushed his teeth, he saw in the mirror a print of powdered sugar on his cheek. He mumbled a swear word around his toothbrush before spitting out the foam.

VICTOR DID NOT go to New Jersey in the spring. He did not call the number Lindsey left behind. If you had asked him why, he would have stuttered something about his life list being too short, hers too long. Perhaps it was their unequal life lists, perhaps it was something else, but he had never been inclined to dig deep into the sandy soil of his own mind.

Nevertheless, Lindsey's brief, brilliant flicker had changed him. He went from occasional weekends in the Pineywoods to long walks every evening after school, working down the wide-ruled lines of his log. Northern bobwhite. Veery. Mississippi kite. Eastern wood-pewee. Gray catbird. He made his students do multiplication problems with ibises and sparrows. He went so far as to ask a friend, an English teacher, to take him out in the swamps in his puttering little motorboat. The English teacher did this gladly but with some mystification, for Victor refused the cooler of iced beers and spent the entire time peering through his binoculars.

"You work for the FBI or something?" said the English teacher, cracking the cap off his Coors. "You looking for fugitives?"

"Ha ha," said Victor. "No. Looking for birds."

"Birds. Really."

"Mm." Victor took a bottle to end the conversation and clinked it against his friend's. He did not say: *I am looking for a particular bird, a rare Northeast migrant with brown crest, black hood, milk-pale throat, and a bubbling call.* He drank his cold beer and stared into the cake-rich, fecund swamp, pretending not to notice the English teacher's thoughts.

What the English teacher thought was this: *Math teachers are a strange and mysterious bunch, but Victor's odder than average.*

By the time the motorboat had slurried and choked to a stop in the coffee-colored water along the boat dock, Victor's life list had reached 635. He shook the English teacher's hand solemnly. "Momentous," he said. "A remarkable day."

"Hell if I understand you," the English teacher said.

THE DAY AFTER school let out for the summer, Victor drove across the Texas border to High Island, keeping his windows winched down in the boiling heat. The crush of birders at Smith Oaks Bird Sanctuary had thinned, now that the spring songbird migration had ended. As he tromped along the wide path, shirt sticking with sweat, he passed only a gray-haired couple, a college student with two notebooks, and a photographer lugging a heavy tripod. The woods were quiet, dense, hot, and green.

This was not the spectacular rain of exhausted songbirds that came to Smith Oaks during the spring fallouts, but it was a marvelous day regardless. Victor added fifty birds to his notebook: roseate spoonbills, an American avocet, long- and short-billed dowitchers, red knots, a Hudsonian godwit, Wilson's phalarope, Inca doves, a groove-billed ani, Couch's kingbird, and Sprague's pipits.

When it began to grow dark, he drove to the garish Gulfway Motel, humming and tapping his fingers on the car dash. He ate dinner at the downstairs grill without tasting it, still dazzled by the flash and flicker of wings. Then he sat on his bed and took from a blue folder the number he had copied from a napkin a year ago.

It was long distance, but gas had cost less than he'd expected. He pressed the numbers one by one into the sticky keys of the black hotel telephone and held the receiver against his ear.

"Hello?" Lindsey said on the other end, and his heart kicked powerfully. "It's 10 p.m.—who's calling?"

"I'm so sorry," he said. "I'm in Texas, the time difference, I didn't realize, I'll hang up—"

"Victor?" she said, surprise in her voice. *She remembers my name,* he told himself, heart pattering like a pileated woodpecker. "It *is* you. How are you? When are you coming to Cape May?"

Never sat on his lips. *I can't afford it.* Victor swallowed hard and said, "This fall, I think. No, I don't know exactly. Yes, I'll call." There were 760 birds on his life list.

He quit his job in late October. The assistant superintendent had gazed sadly at him and made noises about keeping his name on the list, but they both knew that a substitute math teacher was no great loss to the school district. Victor shook the older man's hand—he was a terrier of a man, that assistant superintendent, tough and small—and walked out into the sunlight.

He did not call Lindsey beforehand. He entertained the idea of finding her alone on a stretch of white beach, the sun sinking behind him, her hair blowing loose about her shoulders as she noticed him and smiled in surprise.

His happy imaginings did not account for the difficulties in getting his luggage to the airport in Lafayette, however, nor for the transfer in Atlanta, a clotted baggage claim in Philadelphia, and a miserable search for the dingy bus that ran out of Philly to Cape May, with all the attendant crises, near misses, and about-faces. These minor trials so exhausted him that upon arrival at his motel, without bothering to turn on the light, he took off his shoes, dove under the blankets, and fell asleep.

In the morning he went down to the beach. The cold salt-water air smelled darker and more violent than the estuary breezes that he knew well. Gulls shrieked murder. Waves curled inland and crashed. A white pillar of a lighthouse watched and brooded. Everywhere he looked, he saw birders wrapped against the sea wind, and birds: black-bellied plover, dunlin, killdeer, stilts, ruffs, common snipes. He swung his binoculars this way and that.

Where the white sand met the first sea groin and the steely water of the Atlantic, Victor saw a flock of birdwatchers in gray sweatshirts. One wearing a baseball cap had binoculars pointed straight at him. He wondered what field marks she was noting. Her hair was brown, curly, and short, too short. It couldn't be Lindsey. He should have called.

Victor started toward the lighthouse, thinking it might have a phone. Someone called his name. Then an entire chorus of women took up the call, crying *Victor, Victor*. To either side, startled birds launched themselves off the beach.

He turned. All the gray birders were waving at him, wind-milling their arms, happy to shout at a stranger once someone else had started it, but only one of them was bouncing on her toes, her bucket-green galoshes squishing and squeaking, her face alight with recognition.

It was not a simple matter to separate Lindsey from her local birding group, who referred to themselves as the Cape Plovers, but eventually Victor persuaded her to let him buy her lunch. The other ladies peeled off toward a rumor of a brown booby. Lindsey smiled after them, unaffected by the news. "Saw it yesterday," she said. "And it might stick around another day. You didn't call."

"I wasn't sure when I'd come until I left." They sat down in the fragrant warmth of an Italian restaurant and unfolded plastic menus and paper napkins. Up close, Lindsey's face was finely lined, with a sadness and subtlety to it that he didn't remember. How much of her had he constructed on the flimsy foundation of a morning on a combine harvester and a cup of coffee? "I don't travel much."

"You picked a good time! Something about the weather this year. Strange migrants in unusual numbers. I have my fingers crossed for a Bewick's wren." She tore into her stuffed shells and garlic bread. "They rarely come this way, only two since 1980. Everyone's talking about them this year. A few sightings in Eastern Pennsylvania."

Victor ate his salad carefully, placing each forkful with precision.

"You mentioned black-capped chickadees," he ventured, once their plates were almost empty. "Somewhere near your house. Is that close by? That'd be a lifer, if I saw one."

"I don't live too close to here," she said. "But I can take you. Least I can do. You kept me from being minced into rice pudding."

HER CAR WAS a rusted old pickup, which surprised him, but she had lost a great deal of money in the divorce, she said with a steady voice, and anyway she got to drive nicer cars for work all the time. She didn't mind this one. He classed it up just by sitting in it, she cracked.

Her house was twenty-five minutes north, with a gravel driveway, perennials turned cadaverous brown, and three whirligigs, blue, red, and gold, stabbed into the front lawn. A disused grill hulked in the backyard, flaking rust.

Lindsey had not exaggerated about the chickadees. They flitted and bobbed darkly among the bamboos and sprawling shrubs, flirting their wings and pumping out their two-note *hey sweetie, hey sweet.* Victor and Lindsey watched them together, not touching, though the backs of their hands were so close he could feel her warmth. Two feeders dangled near the kitchen window. She watched her winged visitors as she did the dishes, she said. It took her out of her life and into the liberties of sky.

"You'd be a lovely bird," he said. "Winter vacations in Mexico. Summers in Canada. A thousand admirers along the way." She laughed. He had been wrong to ever think of her as birdlike; she was wholly human, from the brown tumble of her curls to the sandy toes of her boots, her voice deep and squash-ripe with experience and amusement. His hand brushed against hers, and he flinched and flushed. But she caught him by the wrist.

"I'll take you birding tomorrow," she said, laughing again, her teeth white and square, tugging him back toward her truck. "You seem lucky. Maybe we'll find a Franklin's gull. Maybe even a Bewick's wren. Pick you up at seven?"

WHEN HE WOKE up in the morning in his nicotinic motel room, he did not know, for a moment, where he was. Then he tumbled out of bed, combed his hair, shaved, and splashed himself all over, a bit hesitantly, with cologne. It was gray outside, he was disappointed to see, fog scarfing the shore and marshes. But Lindsey was grinning when she arrived, curls wedged back under her cap.

"Someone spotted a Bewick's wren," she said.

She drove them to a wildlife refuge, where the sound of the truck doors shutting was both muffled and loud. The marsh mud sucked at the soles of their boots, and the sedges slashed at them like knives. The fog held fast, and soon he could see nothing except the purple back of Lindsey's jacket as she pushed forward through the reeds. He heard the chirr and piping of invisible birds all around him, and now and then a shudder of small wings, but he saw nothing except shadows. Lindsey looked back at him, smiled, shrugged.

"Sorry," he said, "I'm sorry about all this, the fog, everything." He was still apologizing as she stepped forward into his arms, their binoculars crashing against each other, the cords tangling, twisting—*shit, the lenses,* she mumbled into him.

THE SEDGES WERE still sharp, the fog still thick. But within the circumference of their arms, the world was not so chill and damp.

"Migrate," she said into the zipper of his coat.

"This will never work," he said. "You're beautiful. I'm only a

substitute teacher. I should have told you. Your list is four hundred ticks longer than mine. How could you. I mean look at me."

SHE LOOKED AT him. Then she put a muddy finger to his lips.
    "Listen."

HIGH AND SOLITARY through the fog they heard the warble,
burr, and whistle of a Bewick's wren, clear as glass, indisputable
in identification.

The No-One Girl and the Flower of the Farther Shore

ONCE THERE GREW, IN THE DUST AND MUD OF A VILLAGE IN China, a girl who had only her grandmother to love, and then her grandmother died and was buried and she had no one at all. With no money to patch up the walls and lay new tiles on the roof, the small, smoky home that the two of them had shared slumped around her in the rain, and the little garden ran to nettle and thorn.

In the months that followed, the girl crept and gnawed and spat and caught small birds with her hands, like an animal. The garden gave her wild gourds and bitter greens to eat. The woods gave her kindling and dry cowpats where cows had been tethered to graze. Sometimes her neighbors brought her scraps, for pity.

Sometimes they shied stones at her.

Except when she visited her grandmother's grave, the no-one girl rarely spoke. She cast her eyes low and bit her lip, and the villagers shrugged and said, well, that was the way of wild things.

But anyone who saw her squatting beside the grave, knobbly elbows over knobbly knees, mumbling and rambling, would have thought her mad.

There she told her grandmother the changing of the seasons, and the birds she caught and the colors of their feathers, and the weather, and her wishes, small and large, as she had done when her grandmother was alive.

For many years now, at the mid-autumn festival, the village official offered a silver pin in the shape of an acorn and a gold brooch molded into a willow leaf as a prize for the most beautiful thing made in the village that year. Each year, the villagers presented embroidered cardboard and painted tin and silk cords knotted into dragons, and one man or woman, glowing with pride, bore the pin and willow leaf home. The no-one girl had seen these prizes from afar, on the breast of the tailor, or the carpenter, or the firework-maker, and thought them very rich and fine.

"If I won them," she said to her grandmother's grave, as the wind carried to her the music and laughter of the festival, "I would touch them and taste them and eat their loveliness with my eyes. I would wear them for an hour to feel the weight of gold and silver, and then I would sell the gold brooch for enough flour for a year, then the silver pin for salt and vinegar and spices. But when I bring the little purple wildflowers without names, and the brown mushrooms from the wood, they laugh at me."

Her grandmother's grave, mounded high and sparkling with tinsel, kept its own counsel, but the grass that grew thinly on it seemed to sway in sympathy.

That night, after the revelers were all asleep, the first rain of autumn scoured the village. Rain sang on roofs and fences and pattered through trees. The no-one girl shivered and dreamed of a white bird that circled her head, dropped a seed, and flew away into the dark.

When she awoke, she went to her grandmother's grave. From the mound sprang a single red flower like a firework, a flower the girl had never seen before, yet recognized, for late at night her grandmother had combed the girl's long black hair and told her about the flower of the farther shore, which only grows where there has been death, and leads the dead wherever they must go. It had bloomed in the village where her grandmother had been born, a long way away, and there had been a deep sadness in her grandmother's voice as she described it, working the comb through the knots in the girl's hair.

Now the flower of the farther shore had come to her. The girl clapped her hands at the exquisite beauty of it. She dug down to the bulb with her fingers and planted it in the garden among the wild gourds.

All that autumn and winter she tended the flower. After the petals faded and fell, slender leaves speared up, glowing with life and green throughout the cold winter. She fed the flower her secrets, burying them one by one, and watered it with drops of her blood, red as the flower had been, because there was no death in the garden, and the flower, her grandmother had said, needed death to live.

"Grow, grandmother's flower," she whispered to it at night. "Bloom, flower of the farther shore."

Leaves and then snow covered the path to her grandmother's grave, for the girl had ceased her visits, certain, as if it had been whispered to her, that her grandmother was gone. All her words and care were for her flower, whose leaves seemed to bend toward her, listening.

Spring came, and the earth thawed. While everything else budded and sprouted and broke open, shouting life, the leaves of the strange plant browned and crumbled. But the girl continued to tend the bare patch, which she ringed with stones, as lovingly as one might a child.

These were easier days, after the winter's illnesses and privations. Bark ran soft with sap, and weeds were still tender and sweet. Though the girl was never not hungry, she did not starve.

Now and then the villagers looked over her wall or shouted through the gate to see if she was still alive, partly for kindness and partly because her land and home would be reassigned if she died. When they spied her chattering at her patch of earth, they stopped and stared.

"Eh, what's that?"

"What are you growing there, girl?"

"A flower of the farther shore," she replied. They laughed and rattled sticks against the gate. One or two tossed stones at her, but only halfheartedly, so they pattered down among the wild gourds instead of stinging her arms.

Summer meant fat pigeons, and the tiny, tender muscles of leaping mice caught when she poured creek water down their holes, and the odd spray of wildflowers, yellow and pink and white, dotting the muddy banks of the ditch. Summers she roamed far and free, up hills and down fields, idly pulling an ear of wheat or barley and chewing the green kernels inside. Hawks hovered, dove, and killed. Cows swung their sleepy heads sideways at her and pissed pale yellow streams.

Every night she returned to the bare ring of stones, told it what she'd seen, and pricked her arm until it bled. The red drops ran in a fine line down her wrist and dripped from her fingertips to the thirsting earth. She was careful not to waste a drop.

At the equinox, or so said the flimsy almanac nailed to the door, the flower of the farther shore arose like a ghost in the night. It spread its curling red crown to greet the no-one girl when she unlatched the door and stepped outside. The girl gathered its petals together in her hands to smell their fragile fragrance, stroked its long green stalk, kissed its stamens until her mouth was gold with pollen, and spent the whole day sitting beside her flower, crowing and marveling.

Those who looked over the wall made various noises of astonishment.

"What a beautiful flower!"

"Ah, what a sweet smell!"

"How odd that someone like you should have grown such a thing."

They drank its colors with their eyes and its odors with their noses, just as the no-one girl did, and she did not begrudge them one bit.

The butcher's son came too, and looked long.

"Aren't you my treasure?" the girl said, paying him no mind. "Oh, but I will surely win the gold brooch and silver pin this year because of you."

And the butcher's son said nothing but went quietly away.

In the night, the girl turned in her sleep, as though a soft thump and rustle reached her ears. She twitched and flung a hand out, as if somewhere in the garden, metal clinked against stone.

Morning came, the morning of the festival, and the flower was gone.

"Stolen!" the girl cried. "Stolen, oh stolen!" She sifted the loose dirt in the hole where the flower had grown, but there was nothing, not a fragment of root, not a crumb of hope.

She beat the ground with her fists, then pulled her hair with her dirty fingers, but there was no help for it. The flower had been stolen, the pin and brooch would be given to another, and there was nothing she could do.

Aching for justice, and rubbing her eyes with her knuckles, she hurried to the street of shops, where on an ordinary day beaded strings clacked in doorways and baskets of fish were sold from bicycles. Today, colored lanterns bobbed over low tables tied with ribbons. Throughout the day, people brought their beautiful things here, to be guarded by the village official when he was not deep in his cups, and by his more watchful wife when he was.

The no-one girl would have pulled his sleeve and cried for help, except that the butcher's son was just at that moment presenting his entry: a flower in a pickle jar. It was her flower, the no-one girl saw, her stolen flower of the farther shore, but the petals had been painted white and gold, and cut raggedly, and the stamens trimmed short. To her eyes that had known its crimson wholeness, it was ugly as a wound.

When the butcher's son saw her, he turned red and glanced away.

"What's this?" the official said, tapping the end of his pen against the jar. "I've never seen its like."

"A flower I grew in the yard, where the soil is wet from the animals we slaughter. I sent off for the seed in the mail."

"It may be an unusual species, but these are common enough colors," the official said. "And—faugh—it stinks like cheap perfume. Well, set it among the rest, and we'll see." Then he turned to the girl with a smile as big as sunflowers and said, "Now, what did you bring us this year? A pretty stone? A snail?"

The truth filled her mouth with bitterness, almost choking her, and her blood ran hot and cold. But she looked into the official's wine-red face, and at the butcher's son in his clean blue shirt, smelling of cooked meat, and knew she would not be believed, no, not the wild girl with no one, who talked and laughed to herself. The villagers who passed by had seen a red flower with a curling crown, not this gold-and-white pretender. Moreover, as she knew, there was often a ready stone in their hands.

"Nothing?" the official said. She shook her head, teeth clamped together. "Well, get along with you, then. Go and enjoy the festival."

The girl turned and ran, blind with her loss, blundering through the smoke of firecrackers and knots of people eating white moon cakes. The men and women she knocked against opened their mouths to scold, but seeing who it was, laughed and shook their heads.

Once she was home, the gate banged open and closed, the door unlocked and flung shut, did she allow the poor truth to leave her lips.

"Ah, why did he have to mutilate my flower?" she cried. "If only he had simply stolen it and called it his! For it to become a painted lie! For its scent to be drowned in his mother's perfume! Oh, I wish I had eaten the thing!"

She curled up and sobbed until her nose went numb. For it was not the loss of the flower alone that wounded her, but the sudden revelation that the world and its pins and brooches had been made for such as the butcher's boy and not for one like herself.

A COLD RAIN fell that night. It fell on the revelers whose faces turned orange and blue in the light of the paper lanterns, who whooped and ran or staggered home through the rain; fell on the fan-maker as she was accepting the silver acorn and willow-leaf brooch, who quickly tucked her prize fan into her jacket; fell on the butcher's son carrying his flower home, who turned his face upward to catch raindrops on his tongue; and it fell on the muddy girl sitting in her yard, staring at the hole where the flower had been.

The rain fell and fell, and the garden slicked to mud. Raindrops boiled on the girl's shoulders. Rain streamed down the tangles of her hair.

Then—as if the world had heard the unspoken wish on her tongue, the one wish she had not told her grandmother or fed to the flower, for only now did it put out its leaves—the girl began to disappear.

She grew transparent, like sugar, then smaller, ever smaller and smoother, melting and running into the wet earth with the rain.

The last sound she made, before her lips blurred, was a sigh.

As she sank, she expanded. What had been the no-one girl mixed with volcanic ash and ant eggs and ancient bones, leafmold and roots both thick as a man's waist and fine as hair. She sank until she touched the enormous basalt pillars buried deep beneath the soil, forgetful of the fire that made them, and deeper still.

And she understood, as she opened, as she poured forth and flowed, that though the no-one girl had appeared to eat and mumble and live alone, in truth she was part of everything, the over and the under, briefly divided from it, as a seed falls from a seedhead, but now returned. Her bones were basalt, her teeth trees, her belly full of mineral riches. She looked out from every leaf and every stone. There was her poor painted flower in the butcher's yard, cast aside to wither; but it did not matter now. She had ten thousand flowers in her, tens of thousands, and the wind for her hair.

The villagers searched for the no-one girl, when they noticed the silence in her yard, but not for long. She was wild, after all, and everyone knew that wild things lived and died in their own way, or climbed into truck beds and rode to the city to vanish, and it was no use holding them. At any rate, they had their own concerns, their own sick parents and delinquent children and debts run up by liquor and gambling, and when winter came ravening, its breath all knives, they went home to their houses to grapple with their private disasters.

One morning in spring, as icicles wept themselves to nothingness, the butcher's son stopped by the empty house, frowning. He scaled the stone wall, at some cost to his trousers; tried the warped door, which stuttered open; and rapped his knuckles against the sagging beams, listening for rot.

By the time summer softened the village, the old garden, cleared of rocks and nettles, put forth long pale melon vines and sweet swellings, yellow and green.

Soon the ripe melons were picked and split and eaten. Then it was autumn. The first cold rain covered the village. In its wake, red flowers sprang up, sudden and strange: flowers as brilliant as firecrackers, slender-stalked and leafless, growing so densely that when the wind murmured in them they moved like a sea.

The butcher's son picked armfuls of them, as many as he could carry, and went to the fan-maker's home, flushing as bright as the flowers that he thrust forward when she came to the gate. Children bent to breathe their sweetness, then plucked them to play at wands, or taunt the goats until they ate them. But it did not matter how many they gathered; always, there were more.

All around, above, below, the everything girl laughed with spotless joy.

Autumn after autumn the flowers filled the village, spilling outward for miles, until it was known to all as the village of the farther shore, and the old name drifted down into the uncertain recollections of the village elders, along with the story of the no-one girl.

Once the butcher's son and the fan-maker were married, they moved into the empty house and yard that the butcher's son had, over long months, cleaned and repaired. For their wedding he gave her a necklace and earrings of gold, heavy and soft.

The two of them lived happily and unhappily, as people are wont to do, falling out of love and into irritation and then back into fondness; having children, beating them, and scraping together the fees for school; growing old and blind and fretful, and moving about the yard with canes.

After they both died, their eldest child came home from the city to sort through their belongings, putting aside what could be sold, what might be wanted, and what was worthless. As she folded clothes and untied boxes, stirring up decades of dust, she tossed onto the midden, as things unworthy of keeping, an acorn snapped off its pin, the silver paint flaking, and a willow-leaf brooch with gilt peeling from the brass.

The Time Invariance of Snow

1. The Devil and the Physicist

ONCE,[1] THE DEVIL made a mirror,[2] for the Devil was vain. This mirror showed certain people to be twice as large and twice as powerful and six times as good and kind as they truly were; and others it showed at a tenth their stature, with all their shining qualities smutched and sooted, so that if one glimpsed them in the Devil's mirror, one would think them worthless and contemptible indeed.

The Devil looked into his mirror and admired himself, and

---

1. The more we peer myopically into the abyss of time, the more we understand that there is no such thing as *once*, nor a single sequential line of time, but rather a chaos of local happenings stretching from improbability to probability.

2. Here too the concept of *mirror* is an approximation, for the phenomenon in question extended into a minimum of seven dimensions; but *mirror* is a close and useful metaphor.

all his demons preened and swaggered and admired him too. And joy resounded throughout the vaults of Hell.

Eventually there came a physicist who, with radioactive cobalt and cerium magnesium nitrate crystals, sought to test the invariance of symmetry; namely, whether in a mirror universe the laws of physics would be reflected. As she touched and tested the mystery of the world and proved that symmetry did not hold, and that parity was not in fact conserved, she broke, all unknowing, the Devil's mirror.

Like the fundamental equations of quantum mechanics, like God Himself, the Devil is a time-invariant equation.[3] The shattering of the mirror shivered outward through fields of light cones, near and far, until the shattering itself became eternal, immutable fact. The fragments of the mirror drifted down through pasts, presents, and futures, clinging and cutting, like stardust and razors.

Whoever blinked a sliver of the mirror into his eye[4] saw the world distorted ever after. Some observed that they were far worthier and more deserving than others, and pleased with this understanding, went forth and took whatever they wished, whether wives or slaves, land or empires.

Some looked at themselves and saw worthlessness. At that sight, whatever pyrotechnic wonders they dreamed died in secret within them.

Others, of particular sensitivity, felt the presence of the glass, which a slow and uncertain part of their souls insisted had not been there before. A few of these tried gouging it out with knives, though it was not a physical construct and could not be thus dislodged. A very few made fine and fragile spectacles for

---

3. Theology hopes for local boundedness, but as yet this remains unproven.
4. A poetic simplification to describe a quantum event affecting neural perception.

the soul, to correct its sight, and walked long in clarity and loneliness thereafter.

This is how the Devil's mirror worked:

A woman warned a city of its destruction, of soldiers creeping in by craft, and her friends and family laughed her mad.

The city burned.

The woman was raped, and raped again, and murdered.

A woman stood before men who would become consuls and
said, believe me, I was forced by this man. To be believed, she
struck her own heart with a dagger.

A woman stood before senators and said, believe me, I was—

A woman stood before senators and said, believe—

A black woman said, listen, and no one heard.

A dusky child cried, and no one comforted him.

An indifferent cartographer divided other people's countries
into everlasting wars.

The physicist died. Her male colleagues received a Nobel
Prize.[5]

The Devil looked upon his work and laughed.

2. K. and G.

It was summer, and the roses swam with scent. K. had tamed
G. with intermittent kindness, as boys tame foxes to their hand,
though she had been watchful and wary, knowing the violence
of men. Now G. rested her head against K.'s shoulder, and they
breathed the soft, sweet air together with the laziness that only
summer knows. The two of them were not young; neither were
they old.

If I were going to murder you, K. said musingly, I would tie
you up while you slept, nail you into a splintery box, and shove

---

5. This too is a poetic simplification.

the box out of a car going seventy into the path of a truck. The splinters would be driven into your body on impact.

G. was silent for a long time.

At last she said: When you described murdering me—

Yes?

I felt afraid.

K. said: I was joking.

G. said: Still, I was afraid.

K. said: I had good intentions. What on earth do you want?

G. said: Just for you to say you're sorry.

I can't believe you're blowing this up into such a huge deal. You know about—

Well, I'm *sorry* that women are sometimes harmed by men. But this is insane.

That's the glass talking.

What?

The sliver of glass in your eyes and in mine.

K. pushed back his chair so hard it tipped over.

We both contributed to this situation. You have to be more patient and kinder to me.

G. said: I can't.

Fine, K. said, stamping his foot. A breath of winter blew across them both. The rosebush's leaves crisped and silvered with frost, and its full-blown flowers blackened and bowed.

I'm leaving, K. said. There was ice in his voice.

G. said: I know what will happen. I will follow you down a stream and into a witch's house, into a palace, and then into a dark robber's wood, and in the end I will walk barefoot through the bitter snow into a frozen hall, to find you moving ice upon the pool that they call the Mirror of Reason.

I will come thinking to rescue you. That my tears will wash

the glass from your eye and melt the ice in your heart. That the Snow Queen's spell will break, and you will be free.

But when I arrive I will find no Snow Queen, no enchantment, no wicked, beautiful woman who stole you away.

Only you.

You, who choose cold falseness over true life.

I know, because I am no longer a child and have walked down this road.

I will not go.

She said these words to the summer air, but no one was around to hear.

3. The Ravens

THE PRINCE AND princess, king and queen now, were not at home. The tame ravens in the palace had long since died.

None of the ravens in the old wood knew her. They rattled and croaked as G. went by.

Imposter!

Pretender!

Usurper!

Slut!

Unwanted!

Abandoned!

Discarded!

Die!

Oh, be quiet, G. said, and continued on her way.

4. The Robber Queen

YOU'RE BACK, THE robber queen said, testing the point of her letter opener against her desk. Didn't think I'd see you again.

Didn't you get my postcards? G. said, sitting.

The office was darker than she remembered, for all that they were on the hundredth floor. Outside, other buildings pressed close, like trees.

You know I screen my mail.

I know couriers and postal workers wouldn't dare to stop here.

The robber queen said: I'm good at my job.

So I've heard. I'm proud to have known you when.

Spill, the robber queen said, or I'll tickle your neck with my dagger for old times' sake. Is this one handsome, at least? Because the last one—ugh. Does he cook? Does he clean? Please tell me this one, this time, is worthy of you. Tea or whiskey?

Theodora, G. said, you're so laughing and fierce. How do you do it?

Love 'em, leave 'em. Sometimes I even leave them alive. But once you taste a man's still-beating heart—

Forget him, G. said.

So there *is* a him.

A mistake. But I'm not here about that. I'm here to ask for a job.

This isn't the United Nations, G. We do dirty, filthy, bloody work. That I'll be hanged for, if I'm ever caught.

You have power, G. said. I don't know what that's like. To hold a knife, with another person's life on its edge. Teach me.

Mine is a raw and common power, the robber queen said. What you have is greater.

I have nothing.

Stop, or I'll cut off your little finger so you'll never forget. I don't know how or when you got it. Maybe the crows taught you, or the Lap women. Your eyes see to the soul. Your words cut to the bone. Men and women are stripped naked before you. Now, if you'd only *use* that power, you could hurt those you hate with an unhealing harm. I'd give my three best horses for that.

G. said: No.

Say, such and such is the shape of your soul, though you wear mask upon mask to hide it.

Theodora, G. said, a wolf is the shape of your soul, and there's blood on its muzzle and mud on its pelt.

It is! And I'll never hide it.

Are you sure you won't let me rob one company? Just for the experience?

This is an investment firm, not a charity. Speaking of which, I'll be billing you for my time. Must keep the numbers regular.

Someday when I have money, I'll pay you, G. said.

That you will.

5. The Lap Women

OLD THEY WERE, in appearance far older than time: their eyes seams of stars, their fingers the knurls of ancient oaks. They rocked in their maple rocking chairs, knitting blankets with a pattern of fish from a silvery wool. The fish gathered in soft clouds around their feet.

G. said: I'm sorry I haven't visited or called.

They smiled at her and continued to rock. One by one, fish slipped from their needles' tips.

G. said: I'm sure you have family. Daughters or sons who bring fruit and chocolate. Somebody. You must have somebody.

They continued to rock.

Can I help you? a nursing assistant said.

These are old friends of mine, G. said, blushing as she said it, for years of silence and absence had passed. I came to ask their advice.

Good luck. They haven't spoken since they checked in. And that was fifteen years ago.

G. said: That long?

Time can jump you like that. Leave you bruised in an alley with no memory at all.

Is there anything they like to do besides knit?

Cards, the assistant said. They'll skin you in most kinds of poker, and they're fiends for bridge.

Then I'll stay and play cards with them, if they wish.

You'll regret it, the nursing assistant said. But she went and fetched a worn deck anyway.

At the sight of the cards, the three old women jabbed their needles deep into their skeins and rose from their rocking chairs, holding out their hands.

G. proceeded to lose every bill from her wallet, her sweater, the cross on a chain that she wore, and the black glass buttons on the front of her coat.

The eldest Lap woman took her sewing shears and snipped off the buttons, one-two-three-four. Then she picked up the hillocks of silver knitting, finished each fragment, and whip-stitched the three clouds of fishes, each cloud a different gray, into a single long shawl. This shawl she draped around G.'s shoulders.

Thank you, G. said. I think.

All three Lap women smiled gentle, faraway smiles.

The nursing assistant scratched her ear.

Are you going somewhere cold? she said.

G. said: Very.

6. The Snow Queen

IT WAS HOURS and hours until dawn, and the world was a waste and a howling dark.

At some point in the distant past, the sweep of ice beneath G's feet had been chopped into a stair that wound up and around the glassy mountain. As she climbed, thick snowflakes clung to her lashes. She had the shawl of silver fish wrapped around her for warmth and sensible boots on her feet. She needed no guide, for she knew the way.

Before she left, G. had knelt and prayed as trustingly as she had when she was a child, and now she held that prayer like a weak and guttering taper.

Here was the Snow Queen's palace: smaller than she remembered, as if her child self's memories had exaggerated its dimensions, or else whole wings and wards had melted away. Frost blossoms still bloomed from windows and eaves. Crystalline gargoyles crouched in its crenellations.

Collecting her courage, G. pushed the palace gates open. Her hands turned white, then red, with cold.

No one waited inside. No Queen. No K. There was only the vacant throne and the familiar, frozen pool with its shards arranged into the word *Eternity*.

It was quiet.

Her breath left her lips in glittering clouds.

G. crossed the hall, her steps echoing. The throne might well have been carved from the world's largest diamond. Like a lily or lotus, it peaked to a point. Rainbows glowed in its fractured depths.

On the throne's seat was a small crown of silvered glass.

G. picked up the crown and turned it in her hands. In that whole country, it was the only thing that was not cold.

The long glass thorns flashed fragments of her face: a sneer, a glare, a look of contempt.

Of course, G. said.

The jagged edges of her life shone brilliantly before her. In a moment she saw how they could be fitted together to spell out the forgotten word she had pursued all her life, sometimes glimpsing, sometimes approaching, never grasping entire—

One way or another, the Devil's mirror produces a Snow Queen.

G. raised the crown above her head, admiring how its sharpness shivered the light, how it showed her beautiful and unforgiving.

And then she drove it against the point of the diamond throne.

Across seven dimensions the glass crown cracked and crumbled. Glass thorns drove into G.'s wrists and fingers, flying up to cut her face.

Where the blood beaded and bubbled up, it froze, so that G. wore rubies on her skin, rubies and diamonds brighter than snow.

And the palace too cracked as the Queen's crown cracked, from top to bottom, like a walnut shell.

All around was darkness.

Down into that darkness G. fell, and time fell also, in fine grains like sand.

7. A Brief Digression on Hans Christian Andersen and the Present State of Physics

CONSIDERED AS A whole, in all its possible states, the universe is time-invariant. When this insight is worked out and understood at a mathematical level,[6] one both achieves and loses one's liberty. We are freed from one enchantment, only to be ensorcelled by another.[7] And while the first is a snowy, crowded pond upon whose hard face the whole world may

---

6. $S = k \log W$. That is to say, entropy is directly related to the number of states of a system. If we somehow could perceive all the possible microscopic states of the universe, S would be constant.

7.   Imagine, say, a boy forming the icy shards of reason into a picture of eternity. The metaphor is not inadequate.

skate and shout, the second is a still and lonely (some say holy) place, where only the brave go, and from whence only the mad return.

Those who reach the latter place understand that it was always the case that they would come here. Perhaps they weep. Perhaps they praise God.

Who knows? And who can say?

8. G. and the Devil

AT THE END of her fall, G. met the Devil face to face.

He was pretty, in a moneyed way, sharp as polished leather, with a pocket square and black, ambitious eyes.

The Devil said: That's my mirror you're wearing in your flesh, in your hair. That's the mirror that I made. Me.

Why? G. asked, and in that question was all the grief of the world.

The Devil said: Because when one is alone in pain, one seeks to spread suffering, and so be less alone. It's quite logical.

But *why*?

When a dark heart gazes upon glory, a glory that the heart can never attain, then the whole being turns to thoughts of destruction.

WHY?

As the Devil continued to speak, his words plausible, his face reasonable, his voice reassuring, scorpions and serpents slid out of his pockets, clinging to each other in thin, squirming chains. And the chains crept and curled and reached for her.

In her hand, however, was the hard hilt of a sword, whose one edge was ruby and the other diamond. On her breast she wore overlapping silver scales. And in her other hand was a buckler burnished to the brightness of a mirror.

If the Devil noticed, he gave no sign.

Tell me the truth, G. said.

He said, Because you are ugly and it was a Tuesday.

G. swung the sword to her left and severed a whip of scorpions, then to her right, bisecting a braid of vipers. Slices of snakeflesh and crunched carapace tumbled around her. Of a sudden the Devil looked not so charming.

You think you can fight me? he said, ten times larger now, and growing, until his smallest curved toenail was the height of her head. His voice was the thunder of ten million men.

G. said: I have seen eternity. I know you have already lost.

And she struck, her sword flashing bloodlight and lightning.

The Devil roared.

9. G. and K.

His HAIR WAS white, and he walked with a cane, limping like a crane as it hunts in the reeds.

Her own hair was silver, and her face and hands were scarred.

I'm sorry, he said.

I know you are.

I came all this way to tell you.

I knew you were coming, G. said.

You saw me plainly. I couldn't bear it. I wanted to hurt you, and I did.

G. said: It's all over now.

It is.

K. squinted at her, as if looking into radiance.

I see you've made your glass into a sword.

And you've made yours into a door.

A tempering all your life, then. A tempering and a war. As I have lived openings and closings. As I have yielded and withstood.

So you and I have been made of use.

We have, K. said. We have indeed.

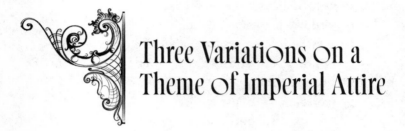

Three Variations on a Theme of Imperial Attire

THEY NEVER TELL THE STORY RIGHT. THE DANISH MUST HAVE their heavens and happy endings, and Andersen's tales are meant for children. We, however—you and I—know that people are people, and every one of us capable of—

But the story.

Once there was a vain and foolish emperor, who made up for his foolishness by a kind of low cunning. As such rulers do, he drew to himself a retinue of like men and women, who told him he was wise and humble, gracious and good. The emperor would smile at their flattery, which in his wisdom he knew to be the truth, and lavish gold and gems and deeds upon them. Thus was everyone contented within the palace walls. And those outside got on as well as they could.

Eventually, with narrative inevitability, two men with knapsacks and pockets full of thread came knocking at the palace gates.

"We are tailors," the first one said, "wise but humble tailors, who seek to offer our boutique services to men of might, such as yourself."

"Here is a list of our bona fides," said the second man. "Sterling references, one and all."

"The very best, I'm sure," the emperor said, looking at the ruby buttons on their vests of gilt brocade.

"What we'd like to offer you is an exclusive deal—"

"—the latest in fashion, which no one else owns—"

"—designed in collaboration with a distant country's military-industrial complex—"

"—top secret and cutting-edge—"

"—the Loyalty Distinguisher line of couture."

"What a mouthful," the emperor said, looking askance. "Call it something I can pronounce."

"What a brilliant suggestion! The Thresher, how's that? Since it sorts the wheat from the worthless chaff."

"Powerful," the emperor said. "I like it."

"Now, the key selling point of the Thresher line—what a wonderful name!—is that it'll let you sort at a glance your loyal, meritorious, and worthy subjects from—well, the useless ones."

"At a glance, eh?"

"Indeed! When we dress you in Thresher fabric, cut to the height of style, those subjects of noble character will see you as you truly are, with all your hidden virtues displayed. They'll swoon at your intellect, marvel at your power, gape at your discernment and understanding. You'll know them by their raptures and fits of joy. Then you can place them in positions of authority. Judging village disputes and distributing grain, for example. Or tax collecting."

"Good," the emperor said, rubbing his chin. "And the rest?"

"The Thresher fabric will reflect their true ugliness. They will pale and shrink back and avert their eyes."

"They will scream and faint."

"They will whimper at the sight of their deepest selves."

"And thus you will know your traitorous subjects."

"Hard labor would be too good for them."

"Make me this suit at once!" the emperor said. And his court, whispering amongst themselves, wondered how the marvel would be managed.

Well, you know how. The tailors placed loud orders on the phone for Italian leather and French wool, Japanese silks and bulletproof thread; had conspicuously large boxes airlifted to their quarters; and all day and all night they cut and sewed the air with an industry that was inspiring to see.

The appointed day came, red and hot. Crows rattled in the palace trees. In the emperor's chamber, before his cheval glass, the tailors presented their work with pride.

"Our finest piece."

"A triumph."

"A breakthrough in fashion."

"But let us see what it looks like on you. Habeas corpus is the haberdasher's true test."

The emperor looked at their empty hands—swallowed—scowled—thought—and said, "Bravo!"

"Is the jacket not to your liking?"

"Hm, yes, the pants are a little long."

"I'll fix that in a minute, never you worry. There."

"How's that?"

"Perfect," the emperor said, gazing at his reflection.

"Now you must show it to your subjects. Your courtiers have assembled and are waiting."

When the emperor strode into his court, a ruby-buttoned tailor at each elbow, his courtiers stared. Then one, then another hastily applauded, and the stamping and cheering shook the walls. A little color came back into the emperor's cheeks, and he whuffed through his blond whiskers in relief, though what terrible worry he had been relieved of, no one watching could say.

"You chose your court wisely," the tailors said. "Now ride throughout your kingdom and sift the wicked from the good."

And the emperor, glancing dubiously at the saddle, mounted his horse and rode through the city streets. His stomach billowed with every bounce. Before him rode his courtiers, shouting the people forth to praise the craftsmanship and glory of these new clothes, which would divide the loyal from the perfidious.

The people, who had not survived six decades of imperial whims and sudden prohibitions on various fruits, fats, and hats without acquiring a certain degree of sense, observed the wind's direction and vociferously admired the blinding gleam of the cloth-of-gold, the shimmer of silks, the cut and fit of everything.

Children, however, who through lack of life experience have not yet learned the salubrious lessons of unjust pain, while quite disposed to lie to avoid immediate punishment, are also inclined to speak inconvenient truths at the most inconvenient times.

"Ma, the emperor is naked."

"No, he's not. He's wearing the finest suit that I ever did see."

"Ma, I can see his *dick*."

At this the goodwife clapped her aproned hand over her son's mouth, but it was too late. The emperor had heard. He turned a pitying eye upon them, as their neighbors immediately began to point and hiss. Why, they'd always known—an absent father—single motherhood stirred up evil, that's what they'd always said—but the emperor's getup was magnificent—truly unparalleled—only a stupid blind woman couldn't see that—

The emperor nudged his horse with his knees and serenely continued upon his way.

In the morning the boy and his mother were gone. Their little stone-and-thatch cottage had burned to the ground. Their neighbors and their houses had vanished as well. Only a few cracked teeth and a fistful of phalanges were found.

The emperor retained the tailors on an exclusive contract at astronomical rates and took to riding out among his people on a weekly basis, since it was now clear that there was treachery in the land. People fell over themselves to report their parents, in-laws, rivals, classmates, colleagues, never failing to praise the newest suit of clothes themselves, until the streets turned black with blood and soot.

When the emperor was finally stricken with a fatal case of pneumonia—which happened far later than one might imagine, because he was a corpulent and well-insulated man—his former subjects, one after the other, dazed by the news, picked up the phone by habit to denounce their friends, and heard, on the other end, the dusty silence of a dead line.

UNNECESSARILY GRIM, YOU say? Unrealistic? Scenes this bloody no longer occur in the civilized world? I agree with all your criticisms, most erudite of readers. There's nothing for it but to try again.

Here then is a more charming tale, one that will better suit your taste.

Once there was a body politic that, through happy geographic accident, had avoided any number of devastating wars, and was thus left the most powerful government in the world. On the basis of that evidence, it thought itself the most enlightened body politic that the world had ever seen. It kept its citizens under surveillance, arresting or ejecting those who did not agree, and as a result enjoyed unanimous approbation.

One day, two men, sons of a vast clothing empire, who had recently been elected to the body, presented a sheaf of invisible bills.

"See how stylishly we've cut, trimmed, and hemmed taxes! How popular you'll be with the tastemakers of this realm—how perceptive and attractive you'll seem—if you pass them!"

"See how they funnel the vast majority of money to the military, which is always fashionable. How powerful you'll look to your enemies!"

"Look how your children will benefit, leapfrogging into elite universities, flourishing in the compost of your trusts and estates!"

"All honorable members of this body politic will see the good, glorious vision these bills represent. All citizens of discernment shall agree. The others? Well, they are not citizens, or they are fake citizens, voting without proper identification, and we should divert a portion of our security budget to uncovering these traitors and deporting or imprisoning them, as our fathers did in their day."

The platforms and proposals were trotted before the country with pleasing pomp and ceremony. The true citizens applauded them so loudly you couldn't think, and trained in militias to hunt down the fake citizens, and rammed cars into the bodies of fake citizens, and phoned in denunciations of their neighbors, ex-lovers, grandchildren, pets—and before too long the streets ran black and red with—

Ah.

That didn't go very well, did it? Heavy-handed, on the nose . . . it's hardly even a story. The artistic error was choosing a plurality as a subject. It's difficult to create complexity of character, complete with inner conflicts and landscapes and unique worldviews, when one's protagonist is an amorphous group. Especially when the members are as slippery as politicians. I understand now why Andersen chose to write about an emperor rather than, say, the Rigsdag. Artistically, that is, never mind that the first Rigsdag convened twelve years after his fairy tale was published. That detail will be conveniently left out of my forthcoming treatise on art. It is a treatise written for a very select few, and will be scorned by the unenlightened masses. Only a humble and wise reader such as yourself, magnanimous and perfect in character, will understand the secrets I disclose therein.

So a character study is what's needed, it seems.

Once there were two tailors—

You know what? You're right. We don't need both of them. They're hardly distinguishable as it is. Andersen might have wished to signify the multitudinousness of such men, or illustrate how well they work together, once they recognize each other, but we can take that for granted as something the reader already knows.

Once there was a man who called himself whatever was suitable to his purposes at the time. If it profited him to say he was a soldier, then he was a soldier who had served with distinction. If it furthered his aims to call himself beloved, then someone's sweetheart he was. By speaking the words that another person wished to hear, whether those words were flattery or promises or blame, he could insinuate himself into most others' trust.

He had few talents besides this one, and a loathing for honest work besides, but this one talent proved enough to feed and clothe him until such time that the trick was plain. By then, of course, the man was long gone.

He fed at first on the labor of farmers, progressing at length to literate merchants and clerks. Over and over his living proved to him the moral by which he compassed his world: that the slow and stupid existed to be ruled and robbed by cleverer and better men than they.

But the smell of damp wool and the low burr of laborers came to displease him; the damp, wormy odors of ancient books soon bored him; in short, there are only so many times a bright man of tremendous worth can fleece the same kind of idiot. The reward is small, the dupery tedious. One must establish trust, perform small favors, establish rapport and commonalities, and so on and so forth, and that routine grows repetitive. The man longed to leave a mark on the face of history, deeper than a bruise, and more lasting.

And to do that, one must be proximate to greatness.

So the man who would call himself anything stashed away the profits of his cleverness until he could move to the valley of kings and queens, where starry fortunes were built upon a vastness of sand. Like pharaohs these men and women lived, erecting monuments and pressing whole hosts into hard labor; and word of their power and wealth had come to his ears.

The man bid farewell to the women who all thought themselves his one and only love, with haste and without many tears, since he did not expect to see them again. He did not kiss the infant boy that one held, with his own dark hair and dimpled cheeks.

Time and space did not chain our storyteller, for the stories he told disregarded both as soon as they became inconvenient. And so by steamer and coach, Greyhound and plane, the man made his way to the valley of sand.

And where money flows and ebbs in deep tides like the sea, shifting mountains, crashing, storming, drowning, the humblest barnacle is sufficiently wetted if it only clings to a firm surface. So the man lived, studying the landscape, until he heard the clack of dice in every two shells rolled along by the sea. With adjustments to his former patterns, he crabbed small fortunes with the wire cage of his smile and landed wish-granting carp with his tongue for bait.

A little empire he eked out, nestling against the greater fortunes and powers that ironed the land flat, effacing a neighborhood there, shredding communities there. From the kings of that land he learned to spin his silken webs to catch not one fly but a thousand. Once stuck in his flatteries, they squirmed to be sucked, pleading to be wrapped in his glorious silks. And he, like a spider, was glad to oblige.

Dining on every rare delicacy, traveling to white-dusted parties by limo and helicopter, he was contented for a time.

Then, as he listened, as he grew familiar with that land, he learned that these kings were clever but lesser, that an emperor ruled over them, and that this emperor was a fool. The kings simpered and groveled when they came before the emperor, just as this man did before them.

Bit by bit, the glitter of the valley of kings faded. The man grew restless and hungry once more. Late at night, he spun plans to weave himself into the imperial court and staff. Favors were asked here, a rumor murmured there. A few careers had to be ended to clear the way, but what of it? Soon an invitation on cream-thick paper made its way into his hand.

All was ready, the story staged, waiting only for the curtain and the lights.

On the morning the man walked out of his old apartment for the last time, a plane ticket clutched in one hand, he found a boy no older than fifteen, dressed in the clothes of another era, standing in the building's entryway.

"Excuse me," the man said, stepping around the boy.

"You're my father," the boy said.

"I don't have a son."

"Here's a picture of us. I was three at the time."

"That could be anyone."

"It's you. I didn't come to bother you. I only wanted to ask—"

"You're making me late."

"—why you left. Why we weren't enough for you."

"Nothing personal. Nothing to do with you. But look at your mother. Was I supposed to grow old—with that? In that small, ratty house? In that backwater of a time and place? No, I am meant for greater things."

"She said you were a tailor."

"I do stitch, weave, and spin."

"Will you teach me to be a tailor too?"

"In ten minutes, I'm going to miss my flight, which will cause me to miss a very important appointment. See, I'm on a tight schedule. Call me another time."

"But," the boy said, looking after him, "I don't have your number . . ."

"So sorry, your imperial grandiloquence," the man said, several hours later. "Encountered an unavoidable delay. But now that I'm here, my various skills as a tailor are at your praise-worthy self's disposal. I can sew you an outfit, invisible, that all your subjects must nonetheless kiss the hems of, and admire. Sew half-truths and falsehoods together, until a listener can't tell head from tail. Weave tales to turn brother against brother, snipping all bonds of loyalty except to you. These matters make my trade."

"Be welcome here," the emperor said. "I can tell that you are a gifted man."

And the emperor threw a fistful of peas at him.

"Quick, a suit that will make me irresistible. I need it in five minutes. The Queen of Sheba is coming."

"Immediately," the tailor said.

But when the tailor returned after four minutes, carrying a suit of exaggerations, the emperor was already pawing at the Queen, who resisted with an expression of deep distaste, extracted herself, and stormed off.

"Where were you?" the emperor said, mashing a handful of gravy into the tailor's hair. "I told you to be done in two minutes. You took ten."

The tailor said, "That's right, O golden sun of wisdom."

"I didn't get to fuck her because of you."

"To make amends for your disappointment, may I offer you this suit of Impregnable Armor?" And he held out again the invisible clothes that mere minutes before had been an Irresistible Suit.

"Don't be stupid. I can't get pregnant."

"Ah, but this suit protects you from all harm."

"Gimme," the emperor said, and was quickly dressed.

Even though his wares were intangible, producing enough of them to please the emperor and thus avoid the latest flung dish of baked beans proved exhausting for the soi-disant tailor.

He spun the Three-Piece of Plausible Denial, the Vest and Cravat of High Event Attendance, the Cufflinks of Venality. Each time, the emperor toyed with his work, tried it on, pronounced himself satisfied, and promptly forgot it existed.

"May I suggest," the depleted tailor said, "stripping the populace of their rights, so that no one has rights but the most righteous of all, which is to say you, your rightness, you who are never wrong."

"Why not?" the emperor said.

That was carried out, despite demonstrations and strikes and scathing newspaper columns, and then the tailor had to invent a new diversion.

"What about setting neighbor against neighbor and stranger against stranger? Tell the old story of the dark-skinned foreigner with his knife dripping blood. A little chaos does for power what warm horseshit does for weeds."

"Whatever you like," said the triply-clothed emperor. "Next."

And those foreign-born or born to foreigners or born to those born to foreigners were rounded up, accused of crimes, and variously punished.

"May I suggest plucking the flower of youth before it grows strong enough to revolt?"

"Let it be so," the emperor said.

Across the realm, children were mown down like green grass ahead of the mower's scythe. Even the onion-eyed kings in their silicon towers felt their quartz hearts crack and said, "No more." But they spoke it softly, so the emperor would not hear.

And while the tailor measured and spun and snipped, the murmur of the people rose to a roar. For there remained some of intelligence and clear thinking and good judgment among them, and these had gently taught the rest to put on new eyes and see.

On a day when the emperor was deliberating between the empty Suit of Universal Belovedness on the tailor's left arm and the Trousers and Blazer of Religious Authority draped over his right, a herald ran in with the report that a mob had smashed through the palace gates and was headed toward the emperor's palace.

Indeed, through the window they could see a dark storm of humanity swelling on the horizon. All that stood between that flood and the doors was a line of police with loaded rifles. Most of the mob was children, with some old women mixed in, and some young, as well as a few brave men, and they stepped over the bodies of those who were shot and pressed forward to the palace, inevitable as death.

The tailor, with the instinct of a hare, twitched and backed toward the exit.

The emperor said, "Sit."

And the tailor sat.

At a snap of the emperor's fingers, servants tugged the curtains shut, so that they could no longer see the cresting wave. The lights were switched off. They waited in darkness.

"Bring me a bottle," the emperor said, and poured two fingers of sixty-year-old liquor into two glasses. One he drank. One he emptied over the tailor.

"That suit," the emperor said, "that prevents all harm—I'm wearing it now. But what will you do, clever tailor, when they come through these doors?"

Distantly, over the gunfire, they could hear the children singing, and the song rose sweet and clear on the wind. Soon there began, at the palace doors, a heavy and fateful thudding, like that of a heart under terrible strain. All the world, it seemed, kind and cruel alike, had come to beat down the palace doors.

If you'll excuse me, I am now going to join them.

Heaven help the children.

Heaven help us all.

The Cat's Tale

THE WHITE CAT SITTING BY THE SIDE OF THE PATH IN unseamed boots and battered hat grinned a huckster's grin. I tightened my grip on Bitsy's rope and tried to hurry us past the potions and knickknacks on the cat's calico cloth. It was daffodil weather, which means mischief, and the wind smelled of earthworms and new hay.

"Where are you going so quickly?" the cat said, its teeth as white as milk.

"To sell this cow," I said, tugging on the knotted lead. Bitsy had stopped to nose the potions and now looked brown reproach at me.

"Beans," the cat said. "You'll get beans for her. It's a bull market, lass. Not for milch cows and heifers. They'll eat you alive, bones and all—fo fum."

"So you'll do me the favor of taking her off my hands," I said. "For a pittance. Is that right?"

"No, no, I speak from pure altruism. I wouldn't like to see a pretty young maid like you get caught up with beanstalking, breaking, and entering. Jackie's no good for giant killing."

"Not interested in killing anyone of any size, thanks."

"But a potion—might you be interested in that?"

The cat swished a red glass bottle at me.

I shook my head. "Colored sugar water."

"Madame!"

"You'll tell me it's a love potion."

"Au contraire. A lady as lovely as you must have whole battalions falling at her feet. This is full of giant-killing vitamins. Giganticizing vitamins. See and dee."

"Not interested."

"Then this—" The cat waggled a bulbous bottle of smoke. "A domesticated genie to do all your chores."

"If you want Bitsy," I said, "try silver. Not tobacco smoke and colored water. Silver is what our landlord wants. Not beans, not potions, not genies nor giants."

"I'm not interested in your cow," the cat said. "Go ahead and sell her for a shilling to the butcher, for all I care. But *you*—" The cat circled me, tail lashing, eyes bright. "*You*, I'd like to hire. Pays silver. Starts now."

"I'll have Bitsy step on you," I said, cheeks hot.

"Mais non, you misunderstand! I am in need of a lad *or* lass with opposable thumbs, of a certain height, with a sharp wit. Not all treasure is cat-height. Bring the cow if you like—she shall be our Rocinante. Here's your first week's pay."

The cat produced, from its pheasant-feathered hat, a leather pouch that clinked dully when I caught it in my hand. The coins were a hundred years out of date, but good silver, unclipped. I bit one to be sure. Even rang them against Bitsy's iron bell, to check for fey glamour on leafmold and twigs.

"That should satisfy your landlord," the cat said, and I had to admit it would.

"Tell me," I said, "with this much silver in your hat, why are your boots agape? Why the nest of a hat?"

"I'm a cat with a pack of wonders," the cat-peddler said. "Small, harmless, and slow. You know something about that. Why take chances?"

"I'll to Ma with this," I said, swinging the pouch from its string. "See what she says. Then maybe I'll be back."

"You'll be back," the cat said. "You're a clever lass."

We scrapped, my Ma and I, the words *honor* and *scoundrel* flung like stones at the walls. But in the end, the heap of silver sat on the table, inarguable. Ma put the haft of her boning knife into my hand. It was a wicked blade that silked goose-meat from furcula in a blink.

"No daughter of mine—"

"I'm sure the cat only means to make me a thief," said I.

Ma covered her face with her apron and burst into tears.

I RETURNED TO the place where I'd met the cat. It was halfway up a tree, hissing. Several dough-faced boys dug through its curios.

"Be off," I said, and the louts cursed at me. I clucked, and Bitsy ambled into their midst, scattering bottles—the cat yowled—and stepping flat on one unsandaled foot before she tossed a boy on her crumpled horns.

They snatched up painted toys and knobs and fled toward the market, hooting.

"Gibbons," the cat said, fatly furred.

"Excuse me," I said.

"Present company excepted. Look at this mess!"

"At least the genie bottle's intact."

"That's the one they should have broken. I'd like to have seen—".

"What, exactly?" I said, all innocence.

"Never mind. What matters is that you're back—and useful. Put on these gloves. Clean this up. Then we'll be on our way."

Much broken glass and wrung-out calico later, the cat sat atop its bundle on Bitsy's back, directing us both with a reed in its paw. Up there the cat looked like a king, never mind the broken boots and hat.

"I figured you a scoundrel," I said. "Will you teach me to steal?"

"Something better than that," said the cat.

"Where are we going?" I asked.

"To an ogre's fief."

"I said no killing."

"You shall snap the neck of nothing larger than a rat."

"I can kill a rat," I conceded, and touched the haft of Ma's boning knife.

Once the cat was sure of my wayfinding, it would nap atop Bitsy for hours at a time. I listened with amusement to its small, soft snores.

We stopped in towns and villages, selling charms, marbles, tricks, and mummies' teeth for enough coin to buy me a cot for the night, as well as fodder for Bitsy and a trout for the cat. When there wasn't a town, or it wasn't to our liking, we camped under the trees. I milked Bitsy for us and ate the ears of wheat I picked while walking, roasted upon a small fire, and the cat ate the creatures that scurried in the wheat fields.

Soon the fields we passed grew rich and lush, the grain shining like silk, the cows fatter than sows. Sheep like puffs of cloud roamed over green grass.

But the people we saw were thin and subdued, their clothes patched and gray with washing and wear.

"Ho!" the cat called to a laborer in the fields. "Whose land is this?"

"Lord Walter's," came the dismal reply. "May he live in health and happiness." And the farmer spat into the dirt.

In an emerald paddock, fine horses paced under the eye of a ragged groom.

"Whose horses are these?" the cat called to him.

"Lord Walter's," the groom said, and looked aside and spat.

We passed vineyards heavy with sea-dark grapes, bursting with liqueur and busy with bees. A boy swept the bees from the grapes with a whisk.

"Whose vines are these?" the cat asked the boy.

"Lord Walter's," the boy said, yawning, his eyes red and blear.

"Cat," I said, "do you know this Lord Walter?"

"Well do I know him," the cat said without joy. "His first wife was my mistress."

"*Was.*"

"A grim ogre of a man," the cat said. "You'll hear more of him."

We came to a town as grim and gaunt as the land's inhabitants, the houses' foreheads louring toward each other. The innkeeper was surprised to have lodgers on his step, and left us outside to take a broom to the upstairs. The key he eventually presented to me was swollen with rust.

"Do you have hay for my cow?" I said, and was given wisps of something musty and gray. Bitsy, wise cow, tossed her head and would not eat.

"Come," the cat said, pulling a coin from my ear. "Buy a drink. Sit down. When the townsfolk enter, say—"

"Why in all this rich good land are the folk so thin?" I said into my sour beer.

"These are Lord Walter's lands," came the reply.

"And what does that mean?" I asked.

"Water in the ale. Two of three barrels of grain to his stores."

"Ever-changing laws."

"Our prettiest daughters."

"Health and long life to him."

"Health and prosperity to him."

"Have you considered what he'd do without you?" I said. "If you laid down your plows and stopped tending the wheat?"

"He has soldiers," the freckled barmaid said. "They'll shed blood soon as sneeze."

"But if you all refused," I said. "Could he kill you all?"

"He might."

"He had a wife, see. Kind and wise and good."

I said, "Where is she now?"

"He has another wife."

I sipped my beer.

"There's a kind of evil," said a shepherd, the sheep-muck still on him, "gets bored of kindness and goodness. Wonders what'll happen if he tortures her. Wonders when she'll break, and how."

The cat, who had been quietly curled in my lap, dug needle claws into my legs. I made no protest. I said, "Did she break?"

A silence. Then:

"He has another wife now."

"Health and long life to them."

I could hear Bitsy lowing from her damp stone stable.

"Listen," I said. "I have a magic cow, whose milk is courage.

And I have money for you, if you'll do as I say. If you desire to govern yourselves and have no lord."

I dropped the cat's purse of copper coins onto the inn's scarred table. It made a satisfying sound.

Their faces furrowed. They leaned forward.

"For your families," I said. "For your future."

Then I peeled off my gloves to show the garnet ring the cat had given me, simply done in silver and graven with a *G*.

"For the Lady Griselde."

They sucked in their breaths when they saw.

"For the Lady Griselde," the barmaid said.

"For my daughters," the shepherd said.

"For the whipping he gave me," a farmer said.

"Tell us what to do," they said.

They were ill-fed and hungry, and the inn's bread, as I found when I took my boning knife to it, contained equal measures of sawdust and flour.

"This won't do," I said. "Boy, bring us grapes from the vine. Shepherd, a fat sheep for the spit. Do not fret your hearts over whippings and the like. It is all paid for," I said, lifting and dropping the purse. "Barmaid, you shall milk my cow."

The forbidden things were done, and a little later there was a fire blazing in the hearth, fat hissing as it dripped from the sheep into the flames.

"That is better," I said. "One must not decide on matters of state—and overthrowing a lord and usurping his fiefdom is most certainly a matter of state—upon an empty stomach."

And indeed there was more color in their cheeks once they had eaten and drunk.

"The difficult thing is the children," I said. "He will threaten your children and elders and all who are too weak to fight. He will kill them if you disobey. Or he will beat you in front of them, and shame you thereby."

Around me came stiff nods. Hands curled into fists.

"So we shall hide them," I said, popping a grape into my mouth. "Just as the deathless enchanter hid his heart in a needle in an egg in a duck in a tree. And no one shall touch them."

"But—*how*?" the shepherd asked.

"Isn't there a hill between the pastures and the vineyards, a hill that has no crops or paddock or houses on it?"

"Aye."

"And don't the children hear music from that hill at midsummer?"

"That is true."

"And didn't the Lady Griselde bring a bowl of cream to the hill on that night, to honor those that live in the hill? And didn't she shake her stick at the cats that might drink from it?"

"Now how do you know that?" the barmaid said, her eyes sharp.

I stroked the cat and felt it purr. "I wear her ring," I said. "Is it so surprising that I know her business as well?"

"But what does the hill have to do with our children?" the shepherd asked.

"We shall hide them in the hill," I said, speaking the cat's words with the cat's great confidence. I had none of my own. Fairies and a genie and children in a hill! If this was a caper and a con, it was a cruel one.

"How, exactly?" the barmaid said.

"I have a German flute of bone," I said. "It plays a tune fit to break a heart, or split a hill, or trot a mouse on. On my word, I shall lead the children there and safely home once your lord is gone."

"There is still the matter of the soldiers," the farmer said.

"That's if we believe you about the hill," the barmaid said.

"You shall see and believe," I said with a smile. "As for the soldiers—give them no reason to harm you. You are ill. You shall cough. Get green slime from the brook to smear on your skin. Mix madder and cherry juice and pox yourselves. Stink so vilely that they will not come near but cross themselves against the plague. And dig burial plots for your children and elders. Say they are buried there. Weep.

"The soldiers shall retreat to the castle," I said. "Wail and mourn from day to night, while you eat and drink what is yours to eat and drink. And this shall go well, so long as all swear to it."

"I swear," the shepherd said.

"I swear," the farmer said.

The barmaid said, "If you open the hill for my son and the other children, I'll swear too, but not until then."

"Wisely said," I told her. "All of you, go home to bed, but bring your children and elders to that hill in the purple hour before dawn."

I accepted a rushlight from the barmaid and went up to my room on the upper floor. When I wrestled the door open with the bloated key, rust fell like scales. There was no locking it after that. I wedged it closed. The room smelled mildewed.

"I've half a mind to skin you, cat," I said.

"Whyever for?"

"If we're here to fleece these folk and flee in the night, leaving them to the mercy of their unmerciful lord—"

"Have some faith," the cat grumbled. "And get some sleep. It's five hours until dawn."

"I don't even know how to play the flute!"

"It plays itself," the cat said. "The trouble is getting it to shut up. Like you, sometimes. Now, sleep."

I tried, and eventually I did.

The sensation of very sharp claws pressed lightly against my nose awoke me. The sky was the plum color of a new bruise. A long, thin object was pressed into my palm, smooth but for a series of holes: the aforementioned flute.

"Get up," the cat said. "We haven't any time to waste." It poured a long list of instructions into my ear, which it made me repeat until I had them by heart.

The barmaid, looking as rumpled and sleepless as I felt, was waiting for us downstairs, her yawning son in hand. She gave a grim nod when she saw us.

We walked in near silence to what the cat claimed was a fairy hill, the long grass whispering against our clothes. The townspeople had gathered there with their old and young. The herdsman held his daughters' hands. They shivered in the dewy cold.

"It is good you came," I said. "Have the children and the aged ones stand close to the hill."

This done, I lifted the flute to my mouth and blew. And it did not matter where I placed my clumsy fingers, for the flute made its own music, as the cat said it would.

"*Woe to my sister, fair Ellen—*"

"Not that one!" I said, for *that* story I knew, and I wiped the flute on my tunic and tried again. And this time the flute played a song without words.

A dull gleam spread across the hill, brightest in a bisecting line. The children murmured.

In the predawn gloom, it was hard to see clearly, but it seemed to me that the green sward opened like wings, like a mother hen gathering in her chicks. I blew on the flute, and the flute played them in. Young and the old walked into the soft, silvery light at the heart of the hill. I thought I heard an answering fiddle and a drum.

Then the grass knit up, and the hill was as it had been. The flute fell silent in my hands.

"Well, that's taken care of," I said, as if I opened and closed fairy hills regularly. Around me, men and women shook themselves, with the air of those emerging from a dream. The sky had lightened to the color of storm clouds, with a gray glimmer beginning upon the horizon. "Now, listen to me. This is what you must do—"

By noon the next day, men and women were fainting in the fields, or shivering and weeping in their beds. Lord Walter's soldiers went through the town and the fields and kicked them here and there, and roughly shook one or the other, but the rashes and greenish pallor of those they touched unnerved them.

The soldiers gathered in the town square and conferred, and then they marched down the winding path to Lord Walter's castle.

Once they were gone, the cat and I emerged from our room and led Bitsy to pasture. She was glad for the good green grass, and expressed her gladness with lowing. The townspeople continued to moan most pitifully in the fields, though where fruit or fat green grain was within reach, it was surreptitiously eaten, and here and there a poxy body moved itself to a shadier spot.

As the day grew long, and the soldiers did not return, some rose and put their shoulder to the false gravedigging that needed to be done, and others quietly gathered enough for a good meal. In their homes that night, they ate and rested and refreshed the dyes on their skin.

In the morning, three soldiers rode out from the castle and found a dozen of the townsfolk wracked with chills in the square, even more miserable than they had been the previous day.

"Water!" the farmer croaked, grasping at their ankles with his red-stippled hands. "Mercy!"

The soldiers returned to Lord Walter with alacrity. The cat was sure they would report the fresh graves along the road. As we expected, no one emerged from the castle for the rest of the day.

On this day, the townspeople arose from their pantomime a little earlier, and harvested and cooked supper a little more freely. Though one or two looked longingly in the direction of the fairy hill, their hearts were brave now, for they could see the structure of the play.

On the third day, I led Bitsy to the castle with the cat upon her back.

Bitsy was a peaceful, placid creature, and we did not make much speed. Her bell clanked as she went.

"Ho!" I called to the two soldiers we met on the road. "What rich and beautiful land is this, that has no people in it?"

"No people?" said one soldier. "Did you not come through that town there?"

"I did pass through on my way here, and thought to stop," I said. "But the doors are barred, and all is silent as the grave. Indeed, I saw many fresh graves there. Is there a plague? Have the townsfolk fled to your castle? If any live, they must have come this way."

The two soldiers looked at each other, then wheeled about.

"Nay, slow down and answer me! If you do not know of this plague, then none from your castle has visited the town lately, and I will be safe if I shelter with you—"

But they did not stop and answer me.

"Well done," the cat said.

We came to the castle's reeking moat and the soldiers who were posted there, halberds in their hands.

"Long may you live!" I said to them. "Whose lands are these, that have been stricken with so deathly a pestilence?"

"These are Lord Walter's lands," one of the soldiers said. "Is the pestilence deathly, then?"

"I counted many new graves along the road. I did not enter the town for fear of disease, but some of the townsfolk are hitching carts to mules, that they may come to this castle for succor and respite. So they called out to me."

"They are coming here?" the soldier said.

"By and by. The sickness makes them dizzy, and they may be some time. Please let me speak with your lord before they arrive and overwhelm him with their petitions, for I bear news from abroad as well as matters pertaining more closely to his estate."

"Enter," the other soldier said, and we crossed the moat and passed through the bailey. Glancing backward over my shoulder, the cat informed me that the pair had laid down their heavy arms and deserted their posts.

"They'll ransack the stores and slip away," the cat said. "Just as every other soldier is doing or plotting now."

Indeed, Lord Walter's guard seemed thin on the ground as we progressed. Only one deigned to speak with us, and that reluctantly, his eyes darting this way and that like a bird's.

"Tell me, where may I find your lord? And has this castle enough stores for the ill and ailing folk from town? They are coming this way in carts as I speak."

"He sits in the great hall of his keep," the soldier said, and took his leave of us with unbecoming haste.

"Sit here for a minute with me," the cat said, and I set us both down on a stone bench by a pond. Red and silver fish swam in its murky depths.

"Why are we dawdling?" I said. "There is much to be done."

"Give the soldiers a few minutes to gather their goods and gear. Let them gossip to the servants, and let the servants slip away as well. Soon Lord Walter shall have none to serve him. Besides, my lady liked this pond," the cat added, its whiskers twitching at the fish. "The water used to be clear as glass, and she sat here for hours to watch them. Permit me a moment of mal du pays."

"It is a great pity your lady is gone."

"He shall surely answer for it," the cat said.

We watched the fish swim back and forth in their muddy demesne. All about us was a furtive rush and bustle, as each one in Lord Walter's household sought to steal and desert without any other knowing.

Soon it was almost quiet enough to hear the watery thoughts of the fish.

"Let us go," the cat said, leaping down from the bench.

It led the way into the keep and to the great hall, where Lord Walter sat in an ancient chair of dark and heavy wood, his face sallow and sour, his eyes like embers. Only two soldiers remained, one on either side of his chair, though they seemed ill at ease. The last servants were fleeing from the hall as we entered—on the pretext of fetching food or fresh rushes for the floor, I presumed, for relief flashed on their faces as they passed.

The lord's second wife, little more than a child, perched on the arm of Lord Walter's chair. She was dressed like a doll in heavy silks and rubies, and her feet swung in space. She stared at us with wide eyes.

The cat took no notice of her.

It strode down the hall toward the ogre, fur on end, tail a

bottlebrush, fine and fearless in its fury, reciting poetry as it went.

> *The sclaundre of Walter ofte and wyde spradde,*
> *That of a cruel herte he wikkedly,*
> *For he a povre womman wedded hadde,*
> *Hath mordred bothe his children prively.*
> *Swich murmur was among hem comunly.*
> *No wonder is, for to the peples ere*
> *Ther cam no word but that they mordred were!*

> *For which, whereas his peple there-bifore*
> *Had loved him wel, the sclaundre of his diffame*
> *Made hem that they him hatede therfore;*
> *To been a mordrer is an hateful name.*
> *But natheles, for ernest ne for game*
> *He of his cruel purpos nolde stente;*
> *To tempte his wyf was set al his entente!*

"I charge you with the murders of your own daughter and son!" the white cat cried. "I hold you to account for my Lady Griselde!"

Lord Walter stirred upon his dark chair.

"Now that is a name not often heard these days," he said. And he reached down and seized the cat by its scruff. With his other hand he drew a hunting knife from his belt, and before I could move, he had cut off the head of the cat.

"Nor do I wish to hear that name again," he said, and tossed the pieces of the cat to the rush-covered flags. "You'll remember that, won't you, little Pearl?"

"I shall," the girl said, her face very still.

I stood speechless, as if bespelled to stone, or I would have shrieked. The cat's plan, whispered into my ear, had not included a hunting knife or a beheading. Then my legs turned to water, and I wished to run.

But before I could do so, the limp, bleeding body of the white cat changed size and became the body of a handsome woman, strong and proud, with white hair and a well-traveled sorrow about her.

Lord Walter's soldiers stared at her, astonished.

She stood before Lord Walter and said again, "I charge you with the murders of your own daughter and son, and with the attempted murder of the Lady Griselde."

"They're alive," Lord Walter mumbled. "Both of them. I sent them to the Pope, to live in honor and wealth. This was all a test. You have passed the test. Finally, you are worthy to be my wife."

"You lie."

"What if I do? I shall kill you as many times as I must—"

He lunged with his bloody knife in hand. But she raised her arm to point at him, and he froze, transfixed, as if enchanted. Then she laughed, a laugh so rich and clear the whole hall rang with it. Lord Walter snarled at her, his eyes afire. And his snarl rose in pitch to a squeak.

For as she laughed, holding her sides now, red with mirth, Lord Walter shrank to the size and shape of a black rat. His second wife stretched out her hand for him, but he leapt off the chair and scuttled into the thick shadows beneath it.

Now I knew what I was to do. I took out the bone flute and set it to my lips.

The flute played a joyous jig that made my own bones itch to dance. From every corner of the keep, from storehouse and kitchen, the rats swarmed out. Out came the black rat from beneath the chair.

They twined and curvetted, pranced and minced. I led them out of the keep, across the courtyard, and through the bailey gate, all of them dancing as they went. And then I stood on the bridge above the moat and played the rats into the foul water. They poured off the bridge in a wriggling stream. First they swam, and then they began stepping on each other, struggling to find purchase on the sheer rock to either side.

I lowered the flute and left them there.

"I think this is yours," I said to the Lady Griselde, holding out the white cat's garnet ring.

"Thank you," she said, "but you may keep it, if you will remain in my service. You have been clever, faithful, trustworthy, and brave, and I would have none other for my seneschal."

She turned to the one that Lord Walter had called Pearl.

"I have no quarrel with you. You are welcome to stay here, and you shall never lack for anything, but I think you might prefer to return to your father's house."

The girl nodded.

"Then you may go with all the silks and jewels that you wear, and a sack of gold besides, with these soldiers to escort you. They are blackhearted ruffians, but they shall have a purse of gold each for their pains. And should they say or do aught to harm or distress you," Lady Griselde added, "open the bottle that I shall give you, with Solomon's own seal upon it, and a genie shall tear them limb from limb."

Both the soldiers flinched. The lady arched her brow.

"Do not think I cannot know your secret thoughts," she said. "With all the arts I have studied over the years of my enchantment, you are as present and breakable to me as a hair of my own head. And I shall break you, however far you flee, if you so much as scratch this Pearl.

"As for you," she said to me, "I think the flute has one more song to play."

I went as she bid to the fairy mound, calling the townspeople to come with me. There I played the melody that opened the hill. How it was done, I could not see clearly, but where there had been only grass before, now there was a tumble of young and old, every one of them wearing a flower crown, giggling and tripping and sleek and well fed.

When the town's children and elders had been claimed and kissed, there remained two small children who had come out of the hill with the rest. No one in the town knew whose they were.

I thought I knew.

It DID THE heart good to see the Lady Griselde when her two lost children ran to her. She swayed like one stunned, then knelt, held them tightly, and wept into their hair. She remarked that they smelled like honeysuckle and blackberries, and listened as they whispered the mysteries of the hill to her, one at each ear.

Then she addressed the townspeople, who had gathered in the square.

"Hear me! No longer shall you have a lord and master. I shall judge disputes among you for three years, and then you shall choose a judge of your own every three years thereafter. One tenth of your grain and dried meat shall be stored at the keep against famine and fire, to be shared among all should either occur, and if not, in three years the old stores shall be exchanged for new."

She could have told them she was confiscating their wine and requisitioning their sheep and they still would have cheered her, I thought, so glad were they to see their beloved lady again.

"I do ask you one favor, if you will grant it," she said. "I ask for your help in building a cottage and preparing a plot for my seneschal's mother, that she may join us here and live at ease, without payment of rent. If my seneschal thinks her mother will approve." Here she looked at me.

"I think she will," I said, my cheeks burning.

"I shall lay the foundation myself," the farmer said.

"And I shall build the walls," the shepherd said.

"I shall thatch it," the boy from the vineyard said.

"Everything that your mother might need, I will acquire," the barmaid said.

Then the others vied to outdo one another in making promises.

It was too late by then for me to ride forth, so I dined that night with Lady Griselde at the keep. She had ransacked the castle stores for the village, that they might eat well this night and thereafter, but the two of us shared a more modest meal, of trout and bread and wine from a cask, as we had done many a time on the road. Her children had fallen asleep early, worn out from the excitement of their return.

"My lady, are you an enchantress now?" I asked. "Powerful enough to change the shapes of men?"

"Would that I were," she sighed. "Let them think it. But in truth, there was only the one spell—that kept me as a cat, and turned me to a woman, and my lord to a rat. And it was not by my starry weaving, but the fairies'."

"How came you to be caught in that net?"

"I think it was the only thing they could catch me in. He pushed me out of a window, you see. And a cat can fall from a height that a woman cannot."

"I see. I think. But when he cut off your head—"

"It is an old precept of magic, decreed by Madame d'Aulnoy herself, that a woman transformed into a cat must have her head severed to return to her form. As to my husband's transformation, I think there was a little magic left, and I understand that a law of physics requires matter to be conserved, so a cat growing to the stature of a woman requires the diminution of another. Or so I theorize," she said.

"How came the fairies by your children?"

"Not long after each child was born, Lord Walter had them thrown from a high tower. Until today, I did not know that the fairies had saved them as well."

"Surely he was the wickedest of ogres ever born," I said.

"It is by their own choice, and not by birth, that men become ogres," she said. "But enough of all this dour talk. I shall send you home on the fleetest of horses, that you may come back just as quickly. And if you don't mind, while you are gone, it's Bitsy's milk that I'll give the fairies. I shall see to her care."

"Greater honor hath no cow than this," I said, and the Lady Griselde spit out her wine.

In the morning, which was clear, blue, and faintly bitter with the beginning of fall, I set off on a fine horse with a bone flute, a pocket full of silver, and a couple of many-colored bottles that Lady Griselde said would stand me in good stead. I wore the lady's garnet ring on my finger and Ma's knife by my side. Whatever adventure came to me on the road would be well met.

I passed through town and the fields around it, stopping only at the fairy mound. There I set down a silver bowl and poured cream into it.

"Thank you for minding the children," I said. "Weave me, if it please you, a net to catch me in, of starlight and story, as you once caught the Lady Griselde."

As I rode down the ribboning road, all the world before me, rich and strange, I thought I heard, from the hill behind me, the sound of fairy fiddles and bells and pipes.

The Valley of Wounded Deer

ONCE THERE WAS A PRINCE OF RUYASTAN WHO WAS BORN IN secret and hidden behind a false wall with a nurse to hush her and soothe and give suck. The prince and her nurse lived in narrowness for ten years, reading and watching the world through a crack no bigger than a needle. During those years, the dowager queen hunted down and killed, for jealousy, every one of the prince's half-brothers and cousins, carelessly begotten in cities and villages and forgotten apart from notes in the royal genealogies.

But the prince's mother had died in giving birth, and the crabbed old genealogists who pried and listened never learned of it. So the prince's name was never written, and she survived.

After a decade of the Queen's hunt, the cities and villages of Ruyastan cried out over the blood spilled, blood of farmhands, shoemakers, and councilors who never dreamed of their noble parentage. A mob rattled the palace gates with cannon and scythes until metal bent and mortar cracked.

But the Queen knew the mazes of power better than the taste of her own teeth. Clad in ashes and cloth-of-gold, she emerged on the palace balcony.

Spreading her hands, she proclaimed amnesty and pardon for those guilty of descent from her dead sons. Cozened by her honeyed words, the crowd subsided and dispersed.

This was all the Queen desired, though she was careful not to laugh, for sweet words aside, death could not be undone.

But one year and one day after the Queen's proclamation, the prince's nurse gave the prince clothes without patches to wear, pinched her chin for courage, and led her out of hiding. They walked across the city, the prince open-mouthed and speechless, turning her head this way and that.

At the palace gates, the last coins in the nurse's pockets, applied to the proper palms, brought them into the presence of the Queen.

Before the amber throne, in whose depths floated husks of ancient insects, the nurse recounted the night that the Queen's youngest son had spent with the provincial governor's daughter. She presented a ring and a letter as proof.

But these were hardly needed, for the prince's eyebrows, drawn like bows, were the same as her father's, and his father's, and his.

The royal smile soured. The prince stood blinking at the brilliance of the still, silent court.

Then the Queen arose from the throne and clapped her hands, and all the court, thawing, acclaimed the long-lost prince.

She owed the nurse great thanks, the Queen said. From this day forward the court would have the care of the child, to raise her as a proper prince of Ruyastan, for she, the Queen, repented of her thoughtless war with blood and brood. Family was family; blood was blood.

Thus was the prince immured in the palace, a larger yet more stifling prison than her hidden room. She was given tutors and hawks and lily-white hounds and horses as yellow as beaten gold. The nurse had raised her wisely, with sighs and truth, and so the prince knew to expect death in every cup, in every dish, and every night, after she blew out the lamp and cried herself to sleep.

Sometimes the Queen showed her the condescension one shows to dogs, and sometimes the Queen gibed at her clothing, or her countenance, or her character, as one kicks a dog lying in the way.

The prince's only solace was in hunting, when she could ride out fleeter and faster than the servants who followed her, and with the strength of her arm bring down a brace of ducks or rabbits for the palace cooks. She would ride as far as she dared, whistling down her hawks, until the palace looked as small as a stone set in the white crown of the royal city, and the woods closed dimly around her, loud with birdsong.

By law, since the Queen was a dowager and not of blood, the prince was to succeed to the throne on her sixteenth birthday.

That date approached more swiftly than anyone wished.

Four days before she turned sixteen, the prince brought three fat pheasants to the kitchens. The oldest cook stopped her with a floury hand and said, her voice breaking, "The Queen has commanded me to make halwa for your birthday dinner. Just enough for you, and just as you like it, with pistachios and cream." Then she covered her face with her apron and burst into tears.

The prince kissed the part in the cook's iron-gray hair and said, "I thank you for it—I would rather no one else."

In the morning the prince arose and saddled her favorite horse, who was pale as butter and swift as sunlight, and rode until the horse's flanks were feathered with foam. Then she lay in the shade of a sycamore to eat the mulberries in her bag.

"Here, you, give me some!" said a voice in the tree.

An old man sat on a branch above her, swinging his legs and twisting his beard. The prince tossed him the bag of mulberries, and he caught it and ate handful after handful, spitting the stems into her hair.

After a courteous silence, the prince inquired, "How did you wind up in this tree?"

"I climbed," the old man said, around a mouthful of mulberries. "Here I fish for the carp of vengeance, which swims through these waters every twenty-five years. Those who've seen it say its scales flash red."

The prince spied a fishing rod balanced among the branches, an unbaited hook dangling from its line.

She said, "I wish you luck with your fishing."

"And who are you to wish me luck, O Prince Who Weeps? You have none to give away."

"You may know I am a prince," she said, "but who calls me the Prince Who Weeps?"

"Your hawks hear you," the old man said, "and hawks talk, and pigeons gossip, and finally a sparrow tells it outside my door."

"It is true," she said, "although I am sorry it is widely known. Then again, it will not matter much in three days."

"What happens in three days?"

"If I live, I turn sixteen. When I am sixteen, I may claim the throne. But on the eve of my birthday I am to be poisoned with a dish of halwa."

"You have good reason to weep," the old man said. "I must admit that I myself occasionally indulge."

"And who do you weep for, good father?"

"A wife and children."

"You've lost more than kingdoms."

"I have. But there are better remedies than weeping. Fishing is one, and so I fish. Riding is another. So you must ride."

"Where shall I ride?"

"Half a day farther," the old man said, pointing with his fishing rod, "to where the earth cleaves in two. That is the Valley of Wounded Deer, which is a wonder worth seeing before you die. Here is a pill that will uncover to you the language of animals for an hour. Use it well."

He tossed the bag down to her, and in it the prince found a round black pill that reeked of bitter herbs.

"Thank you, kind father," she said. "May all my luck, little as it is, go with you and your fishing."

She rode onward through the dimming forest, until her horse tossed and shied at the brambles braided black before them. Then the prince dismounted, hobbled her horse, and proceeded on foot, pushing the thorns back with bare hands and dagger.

After hours of struggling through thicket and thorn, the trees seemed to suddenly part before her, their interstices filling with stars. The prince had but a moment to notice the starlight before her footing gave way, for in her weariness she had not attended to where she was going, and she tumbled down a steep slope on a billow of scree.

At the bottom of the slope she unfurled into a heap, groaning. Then other cries of pain rose out of the darkness.

"Who's there?" the prince said.

No one answered.

In the dusty starlight she perceived great shapes among the trees, shifting and sighing, and her blood ran quick and cold within her. But as the stars turned, and no wild beast stalked her, and no teeth tore, her heart settled and slowed, and finally, exhausted, the prince slept.

When she awoke, bruised but whole, the sunlight that broke through the trees showed her a small valley rich with moss and brown bones.

Three deer dark as leaves in winter lay grievously wounded beneath the trees. Their breaths came forth in soft white clouds. One had bloody gashes along its side that scabbed and cracked and opened to show bone. One had seven arrows buried in its flanks. And one had a golden collar around its neck and a marvelous tree of silver and gold, finely wrought with fruits and flowers, set between its antlers. The weight of it pinned the deer's head to the earth.

The prince stared, then recalled the old man's gift. The black pill's taste was loam and silence, and its odor filled her nose and mouth.

The bleeding doe raised its head as she approached.

"What kind of place is this?" the prince asked the doe.

Its voice cloudy and confused, the doe said, "This is the Valley of Wounded Deer, where we whose deaths are unfinished come to die. No one enters without a wound, and by the bones you see, no one departs in the same form. Only as seeds and birds and songs do we pass from this place. But you are not a deer."

"I am weary and hunted like a deer," the prince said. "This valley is lovely and would be a fine place to die."

"But you are not a deer," the doe said again.

"I am a prince and can judge for myself," the prince said. "You are badly wounded—how came you by this harm?"

"Men," the doe said. "Hunters like yourself, with dogs. They were slow and stupid, but not slow and stupid enough." Its eyes were deep as wells and gleamed with sorrow. "Princeling, hear me. The ways of wolves are kinder than the ways of men."

It turned to lick its ribboned flanks, as well as it could, and spoke no further.

The prince came to the deer transfixed by arrows.

"From whose quiver did these come?" she said.

"Hunters like yourself," the hind said. "Their aim was poor, but not poor enough. So you see me now. Listen, princeling. The ways of ravens are better than the ways of men."

And the hind said no more, but looked at the prince with reproach.

The prince walked on, thinking on what she had heard, until she reached the buck that wore a golden tree.

"Beautiful one," she said, "how came you to this place?"

The buck could not move its head, though the muscles of its neck strained and shivered, and tears pearled in its eyes.

"I lived in a king's parkland, and it was his pleasure to capture and ornament me thus."

"Then you know the injustices of kings and queens," the prince said.

"That I do."

"Like the others, you have suffered through no choice of your own."

"On the contrary," the buck said. "I could have hooked the king's eyes on my horns and torn them out. I could have fled farther than men could reach, rather than dwell in his demesne. But I bent my head to him, because the ways of men and the ways of wolves and the ways of ravens are cruel, but the ways of God are perfect and beyond our understanding."

"Does a creature like yourself know God?" the prince said. "I have had tutors and mullahs and before them the simple faith of my nurse, which was more persuasive to me than all of these, but even now I am not certain that I know God."

"In every mouthful of green, in every drink of cool water, in the velvet of our antlers and in our deaths is the name of God inscribed."

"Well," the prince said. "God or no God, all I want is a peaceful and private death, far from the jeers of my enemies."

"You will not find your desire here. God gave this valley to the harmless things. It is not meant for you."

"Then what is meant for me?" the prince said.

But the buck only gazed at her, dumbly and without comprehension, for the hour of language had come and gone.

Amazed, the prince picked her way out of the valley. She found her horse grazing among the trees. For a long moment, holding the bridle, she looked back.

"I could strike the Queen first, with my dagger concealed on my thigh," the prince said. "Some of her courtiers would come to my aid, for their hearts are full of hate. I could take the throne by force. And that is the way of wolves.

"Or I could flee as far as this good horse could carry me, and wait for her people to revolt. Then we would return in triumph to trample her bones. And that is the way of ravens.

"But what is the way of deer?"

The prince considered the matter, her heart as heavy as chased gold. Then she mounted her horse and spurred it toward home.

No tears wetted her face, but with a cold cheer she rode through the wood and through the city. All who marked her passage thought her brave, and they grieved in their hearts, for they knew their Queen.

It was evening when she reached the palace, where all the lights burned hectic with final preparations.

"How good of you to come back for your birthday," the Queen said, her eyes cold. The prince saw that the Queen had hoped and feared that she would flee—hoped, for then the throne would be hers without question, and feared, for then the prince might someday return.

The prince bowed silently and went to her chamber, where she did not sleep but knelt all night in prayer. And in the morning there was lightness as well as sorrow in her heart.

She walked in the garden and admired the flowers as if she had never seen them before, bid a pleasant morning to the cooks at their fires, and fed and made much of her horse and hawks and dogs.

"There is beauty in this place," the prince said to herself. "But it was never meant for me. God gave it to the great and powerful, and I am neither of those things."

Soon, too soon, the appointed hour arrived. The prince bathed and dressed and was escorted with fanfare to her birthday banquet. Every kind of dish that the realm could produce was spread before the court: rice studded with sultanas and jewels of meat, spitted larks and stuffed nightingales, fish in cream and fish in wine, skewered goat and boiled geese, ox and venison and lamb.

"All of this is in your honor," the Queen said, waving her ringed fingers over the repast. "Tomorrow you shall be crowned, but today you are still a prince. So tonight I have the privilege of spoiling you." She tore off a leg of swan and drained her cup, then gestured toward the prince. "Go on, eat—eat!"

The prince took a moon of bread and ate a dry morsel.

"What, you won't eat?" the Queen said. "So fastidious. So kingly. But I see that we lack your favorite dish. That must be remedied at once!" She clapped her hands, and the servants brought forth a single bowl of halwa.

The Queen smiled.

"My beloved prince, dearest of grandchildren, say that you'll taste what we've prepared for you!"

Up and down the table, courtiers flicked glances at each other, lips twisting with knowledge, amusement, and pity.

The prince looked at the Queen, bowed, and ate until the bowl was clean.

"If you will forgive me," the prince said to the Queen, who was rubbing her hands together and chuckling, "it has been a long day, and I will withdraw. But do not let my absence trouble you or lessen these festivities."

"Graciously said!" the courtiers cried. And they carried on feasting and roistering as if the prince had never been.

The prince returned to her chamber and stretched out upon her bed, waiting for death to creep over her. His touch would be cold, she thought, and painful, and then she would feel nothing at all.

IN THE MORNING, to her astonishment, the prince awoke.

She looked out the window at the sunlit city, then walked through the empty palace to the banqueting pavilions. The silk tents fluttered like flowers in the morning air. When the prince saw what was beneath, she was for many minutes unable to speak.

The Queen and her court sprawled among the broken meats, their tongues swollen and lolling. Half-eaten fruits softened and browned. Where wine had dried as black as blood, flies clustered and combed their claws.

"What's this?" the prince said. "How could this be?"

The old cook rushed in and flung herself down.

"It was my doing," she cried. "Kill me, and me alone!"

Behind her came the other cooks, shuffling and whispering, eyes round. At last one of the scullions said, "She rallied us
all. A shame and a pity to help murder the last prince, she said,
and a waste of good food, too. And which of us has not felt the
Queen's heavy hand? So we sauced everything with poison and
put the cure in the halwa. If you kill her, you must kill all of us.
And even that will be fine, because you will be King."

"We've already baked the pastries for your coronation," the
old cook said, still flat on her face. "Only we told the Queen they
were funeral cakes. So our deaths will not be an inconvenience."

"Enough," the prince said, pulling the cook to her feet.
"Hasn't Death had his portion, and more? None of you will die.
But neither will I be King."

"And why not?" the cook demanded.

"Because you would be a better King than I," the prince said.
"Because I have no heart to rule over anyone, not even a beetle.
And because the ways of God are better than the ways of men,
better than the ways of wolves or ravens—indeed, they are the
best of all."

She clasped the cook's cracked hand. "You've prepared the
cakes for your own coronation. I will see you crowned, and then
I shall take bread and mulberries and go out into the world."

"But where will you go?"

"Where God grants to me to go."

"And what will you do?"

"What God gives me to do."

Then the prince said no more, but bowed to her King.

The Queen and her courtiers were buried swiftly, with lavish
honors and a minimum of grieving. By evening the cook sat
upon the amber throne.

The prince in the meantime dressed in the cook's castoffs
and set out on foot. She walked, light as a deer, through city and

country, only stopping once, where an old man tended three graves by the road.

"Did you catch your carp, good father?" she inquired.

"I most certainly did. It was a feast fit—begging your pardon— for a King. Here, you can have your luck back."

"It seems I do not need it."

"Then I'll keep it. The luck of a prince is not given every day. Go in peace."

"May peace find you as well."

He looked down the line of graves, over which the ferns were beginning to grow. "Perhaps it will," he said.

Onwards the prince went. Time unbraided its stars, and the earth spun, and she was all but forgotten. But every few years, word came to the Cook-King of a beggar whose joy blazed like a meteor, or an itinerant teacher whose words fruited in the mind, or a stranger who went gleaning and singing through the fields, and the King, who had few secrets, allowed herself a secret smile.

Many years later, in a nut-sweet autumn, there came halting into the Valley of Wounded Deer a hart hoar with age, muddied and scarred by living, its antlers pointed like a crown. The hart couched low on the yellowing grass and sang a soft, consoling note. Had you understood the language of deer, you might have heard it say: "The ways of deer are better than the ways of men, but the ways of God are perfect."

Then the hart closed its eyes, and the only breath in that valley was the wind's.

The View from the Top of the Stair

UPON HEARING OF THE DEATH OF MY FATHER AT SIXTY-SEVEN to a slippery lentil of a clot in his brain, my first thought was that my mother would have laughed, and my second thought, I am sorry to say, was that at long last I could gratify my passion for stairs.

They were my first love and my truest. I adore a snappily spiraled stringer, volutes smooth as abalone, the twist of sunlight along a copper banister. On my minimalist salary as assistant to the art director of a well-known fashion magazine, the one indulgence I could afford was a slowly growing stack of architects' portfolios and builders' catalogues, which I special-ordered over the phone. These firms were the sort that issued business cards blank but for the tidy black serifs of their names, bearing nothing so vulgar as a number or address. I was never disappointed.

Each photo spread was a masterpiece. Here were no poured concrete stoops or factory-sawed treads, no pine or softwood, none of your suburban rickrack tacked with furry polyester runners. The stairs splashed over double pages were poems of bird's-eye maple and marble and chrome, tastefully composed, carefully lit, thick with varnish and money. I carried the catalogues in my bag and flicked through them at work. I ran my fingers over the coated pages before laying them on the bedside table. I tromped up and down the ugly cement steps, pricked all over with bubbles, that led through a square stairwell to my apartment, while I dreamed of owning a melted-chocolate Esteves, a twining Momo, a floating and impractical Lang and Baumann.

It is strange how electrifying the sudden arrival of a small fortune can be. My father, born into famine in another country, had saved the laces from unsalvageable shoes and eaten every fleck of food in his bowl. He left me a comfortable savings account and an insurance policy to be paid out over two decades. I went over his accounts three times to be certain. But there it was, a cold sum fanged with two commas. I could quit my job. I could build my stairs.

This is not to say that I did not grieve for my father. At the time he died, I had not seen him in two years. He had ensconced himself in retirement in a cabin in the Alaskan wilds, enjoying the elastic days and nights. Once every few months he would call me to describe the midnight explosions of color in the sky and the mosquitoes as big as cats.

I said, every call, "Have you seen a doctor?"

He said, every call, "You're turning into your mother."

My mother had been after him to see a doctor for as long as I can remember. She made appointments, and he canceled them. She warned him of lupus, hepatitis, diabetes, Alzheimer's, cancer. He laughed and shook his head at her. She had died too early, her hands roughened from cooking and keeping house for the three of us, the humor long since rubbed out of her laugh, which was like pebbles shaken in a cup. Apart from our ritual exchange, by mutual agreement, my father and I did not speak of her.

A week after my father's funeral, after the reek of lilies had left my nostrils, I called the art director and informed her that I would not be returning to work.

"A natural reaction, given the circumstances," the director said. She had smoked incessantly while cigarettes had been in vogue, and her voice always managed to convey impressions of hellfire and opulence. "Wouldn't you like another few weeks to think it over? Take your time. Take all the leave you want. It'll be unpaid, but—"

No, I said, giddy with freedom. Thank you, but no, I am in fact moving, here is my forwarding address.

By then I had selected, after a brief but methodical search, an old barn that had stood vacant for fifteen years after the death of its owner. It was out in the countryside and excitingly distant from neighbors, surrounded by ten acres of fallow farmland. I exchanged my pinching black pumps for boots and drove out in a spotless white rental for a look.

The gravel path to the barn was thickly overgrown, and the owner's son and I swam through waist-deep grass. What I saw was unprepossessing. The ancient red and white of the barn's sidings was peeling to gray. Over the door hung the brown circle of a hex, rusted and discolored beyond recognition.

The owner's son unhitched a padlock and chain and shouldered the door open, then showed me into the dim interior, dusty with down and mold. Despite the owl pellets and droppings whitening the floor, and the gloomy shape luffing its wings upon a crossbeam, several generations of mice roistered beneath the floorboards. Turning to me, the owner's son gestured helplessly at the dilapidation, as if to say, what could we do?

From the moment I walked in, I knew I wanted the barn. I knew what I would do. It was as if my vague, unsatisfied desires, cloudy in the colloid of privation, had at the first contact with money precipitated into a crystal lattice I could inspect from all sides, acquainting myself with the angles and edges of my hunger.

I packed half my belongings, disposed of the other half, and moved into the barn before it was fit for habitation. For nights on end the moonlight spilled through holes in the roof. I could look up and see Cassiopeia and Cygnus picked out in melee diamonds, except when the shadow of the owl briefly blotted them out.

It was summer, and warm. I suffered only small galaxies of insect bites and a few hours of damp and steaming clothes when a thunderstorm rumbled through. None of that mattered.

As soon as the telephone was connected, I punched in several phone numbers so familiar that I did not need to peel apart the sodden pages of my address book, and explained what I wanted.

"We can send you a proposal and preliminary contract," the woman on the other end said, her voice curving with doubt. She recognized my name if not my voice: the importunate caller who begged for catalogues year after year, her checks hardly worth the postage. She named a figure that iced my blood before I remembered that I was wealthy. "Twenty percent of the estimate is due as a deposit before any design work is begun."

My cheeks warmed and tingled. "That will not be a problem," I said. "I am writing the check right now. Listen. I am putting it in an envelope. I am licking the flap. What address shall I write?"

So it went at every firm. I waited a week, allowing four days for the postal system and three days for the banks. Meanwhile the local contractors I had hired, morose types in spattered overalls, continued to patch up the barn. They scooped out rotten

wood and ripped off moldering shingles, muttering at my super-
vision. At every opportunity, they shucked their work gloves and
lounged in the barn's shade until I chivvied them back to their
crowbars. Once I heard them remark on the audacity of a single
woman, particularly one with my face and eyes, in occupying
the abandoned Sutton farm in the middle of a vast whiteness,
and their faces grew ugly with something I recognized from subways and buses and shops, on corners and in offices, and I went
and hid in the woods until they had left for the day.

When I phoned the firms again, the men and women who
spoke to me were variously deferential, obliging, anxious, and
subdued. I understood well, having spent twelve years in their
place.

"When can you begin?" I said.

"The partners will have to visit the site—unless you have
blueprints—"

"Will tomorrow do?"

A silence of sucked breath, then effusive apologies. I was not
worried. I could wait. Soon the barn was restored to a state that,
though far from luxurious, no ordinary person would have been
ashamed to inhabit. I was scrubbed and steamed, and my ward-
robe was replenished, by the time the architects arrived.

Crisply sleeved, hair slicked, their noses shining from the
summer heat, they came and went with pursed lips and gridded
notebooks. I trailed them, clutching brochures gone wavy and
crackling with rain.

"What do you think?" I said and said again. Some of them
brushed me aside. Some were lost in contemplation and never
heard the question. One or two sat down and sketched for me, as
if for a child, the strange and lovely shapes in their minds.

"It has reached our attention," the starchiest of the recep-
tionists said over the phone one day, "that you have solicited

competing bids from at least two other firms. I thought I would take the opportunity to remind you that the deposit is not refundable."

"They're not competing," I said.

"I beg your—"

"I want all of them."

"I'm sorry?"

"Reed will build his design, and Ling and Martin will build theirs, and Jewett will build hers. I will pay you all in full. Please tell Mr. Reed that I am enchanted by his suggestion of automatic hourglass balusters. In addition, I would like to propose a pair of Galileo thermometers for the newel posts."

"But how many staircases can one person use?"

"All of them, Ms. Singh."

The egg-blue phone remained my solitary connection to the city. I used it rarely, but when I did I usually spoke to Sophia Z., who taught elementary school, and about whom there drifted an ineluctable odor of crayons. Just as I loved stairs, she adored doors, in her quiet way, never seeking them out on her own, but always appreciative of the ones she encountered in the course of her day. Many doors had been shut in her face over the years, which gives one time to admire the finer details of stile and rail.

"It's not finished, but you should come see it," I told her. "I've never been prouder."

"Proud? You?" she said. "That's a first."

"Doesn't run in my family."

"In that case, I'll have to. But the kids, the timing—I can't get them out of my hair—"

"I'll pay for a babysitter."

"That's too much."

"Please let me. Anthony's busy, I take it?"

Here the connection weakened, or else Sophia mumbled, but in the end we fixed the date of a visit.

She drove two hours from the city to my barn, which was still crumbly with sawdust and bustling with workmen. She had brought a bag of zongzi as a housewarming gift, and I plopped two in a pot and set it on the hot plate to boil.

"They've been all right," she said, when I asked about her children. She had named them Toronto, Manila, and San Diego, primarily as a geography lesson, but also in hopes of imparting a sense of spatial freedom that she herself lacked. Diego had caught every cold that cropped up at school; Nila was emptying tissue boxes over boys; and Toronto was acing her exams and bored out of her skull.

We ate on the upper landing of the first staircase I had commissioned, a graceful iron spiral not quite reaching the roof. The bars were worked with ivy and honeysuckle. The treads contained varying amounts of iron and were tuned to play, when struck in ascending order, the first notes of Handel's Water Music. We deposited the strings and bamboo leaves in a sticky pile beside us.

Sophia leaned over the edge and looked down. "What are you planning here?"

"A proper home," I said. "A space I can stretch out in."

"What will it look like?" She indicated the small platform we occupied, supported by the staircase on one side, on the other by a frame suspended from the roof. "Are you building a second floor?"

"Not really. Over there? That corner was part of the hayloft. The rest collapsed. It'll be cleaned and reinforced. I'll put a mattress there, and a flight of stairs up to it. That's all I need."

"How many stairs, in total?"

"As many as I can afford."

She sighed with the faintest tinge of envy. "I could never."

"Even something less extravagant? What about replacing your front door?"

"Anthony would never let me. It's solid core, triple locked and deadbolted. Hideous but safe. I'd want an arch—we'd have to redo the wall. And we don't have the money for that. Not with the kids."

"When they're done with school?"

"Maybe," Sophia said. Her eyes said: no.

Three weeks after her visit, I found myself the proud possessor of twelve sets of stairs. Each of the long walls boasted three straight flights in parallel, spaced far enough apart that the underside of one did not loom over the next. The long wall on the north side of the barn had, from left to right, one floating stair constructed of blunt silver blades; one extended undulation cut from a single slab of teak; and one staircase of white resin and lacquer molded into the shapes of wings and impressed with feathers. Across the barn, the southern wall had the Reed hourglass stair; a ribbon of steel painted yellow and blue that looped upon itself, alternating colors; and, last in line, a series of four bronze trees whose limbs bent into treads.

The short walls were only fitted with one staircase each, but these were sprawling and magnificent. On the east wall I installed an imperial staircase of Carrara marble with a handsome brass rail, topped with two brass sphinxes and ending in brass lion's paws. The western stair was pieced together from jigsawed rosewood, mahogany, ebony, and oak, and the pattern of woods pulled the gaze upward.

On the open floor, my musical iron spiral formed one point of a diamond, the other three vertices of which were also clockwise spirals. One, a child's stair, really, which I could not climb myself, was fashioned from polished bone and tapered like a narwhal horn. One was a square coil of aluminum pleated into steps. One had an illuminated newel controlled by a switch, and at night its warm yellow light fanned the shadows of the other stairs into lace.

This last spiral struck the ceiling and emerged onto the roof through a trapdoor. Several of the straight flights ended at high square windows. The hourglass stair abutted my sleeping platform, which I lined with matching glass balusters. The rest reached into emptiness and grasped nothing at all.

Looking at what I had made, I felt an unfamiliar contentment stealing over my heart. It was not finished, no; perhaps like certain emanations from the heart's most secret quarters, it never would be. There ought to be stairs on the exterior of the barn, for a start. Then I could excavate a cellar, or several, and perhaps add an attic, a tower, a retractable ladder.

But the trees edging the fields flamed crimson overnight, and geese dragged their brown chevrons across the sky. No work of the kind I imagined could be done in winter. I buried myself in quilts, with a pen and a wad of paper, and dreamed. As the snow fell outside, I covered pages back and front with zigzags, helices, crosshatches, scrolls, letting them drift to the floor.

Though I seldom visited town and barely knew my neighbors, when I began adding stairs along the outside of the barn in spring, people took note. A pest of a local reporter rang me three times and published lengthy speculations and several photos when I would not speak to him. Cars crunched down the dirt road leading to the barn, spitting out gawkers in the daytime and shining their headlights through my windows at night.

I resented the attention. I blocked up the original doorway and chopped and fitted a new entrance above the white winged stairs, accessible from without only by a transparent flight of glass. This discouraged a fair number of my visitors, but not all. On Friday nights, after pool or a movie, pock-faced high school students dared each other to climb the invisible steps. When I heard the whispering and giggling and the squeak of sneakers on glass, I pointed a flashlight out the window and shouted until they jumped down and ran.

In desperation I erected a fence, a gate, and signs that threatened bulldogs and shotguns, although I had neither, regretting the expense. The number of visitors presently declined. Some nights, a twig snapping outside was nothing more than a rummaging skunk.

Still, none of these things deterred the nut-brown man who came down the road in September. I watched his approach from an upper window. He wore jeans and a denim jacket. His hands were empty. He did not stop and stare when he saw the barn, but climbed the glass stair without hesitation and knocked.

"I don't mean to bother you," he said, his voice so soft I could barely understand him, "but I heard you collected stairs. I want to offer you one."

"Who are you?" I said.

"I make stairs," he said. "For those who appreciate them."

There was mud on his work boots, a silver buckle on his belt, and a pepper of white in his black ponytail. His face was clean but roughened and deepened by labor. I could tell nothing else about him. He had braved the signs, the chained and padlocked gate, the stairs that even now appeared to vanish beneath him, leaving him standing on air.

"I'll be honest with you," I said. "I've run out of money, beyond what I need to eat. I thought I could afford one more, one last stair to crown and complete my home, but I had to buy a fence instead. If you can build the kind of staircase I want, I can't pay you."

"All I want in way of payment is for you to climb the staircase that I build."

I stared at him. He studied the winder and switchback that led to the roof.

"Why would you build stairs for me if I can't pay you?"

"You can," he said patiently. "By climbing them."

"What would they look like, your stairs?"

"Cast iron, three foot radius, acanthus balusters, a stamp of birds on each tread."

"If I may ask, what is so wonderful about them? I can order what you describe from anyone."

"They are the highest stairs in the world," he said. "Higher than castles, taller than skyscrapers. They stretch up to the stars."

I paused. Who was I, with my house of seventeen stairs, to decide another person was delusional? He did not look the part. There was a soberness and solidity about him that put me in mind of granite.

"The stars?" I said.

"Or higher, maybe."

Odd as it sounded, I liked the idea. Already in my mind I owned a flight of stairs that like Jacob's Ladder raced into the celestial unknown. I did not care that what he described was impossible. I did not care if he built me a five-story factory-kit staircase that ended nowhere at all. I did not care if he never built anything. His beautiful dream had filled my head, and nothing could remove it.

"Build your stairs," I said. "I'll climb them."

"I'd like to start from the roof."

"All right."

"I'll need a support column underneath, for the weight."

"Send me the specifications and I'll have that done."

He began two weeks later, arriving at dawn and departing at dusk. His steps echoed on the roof. I could hear him whistling a tune I couldn't quite place, neither cheerful nor melancholy.

When I left the house I saw him measuring, scribbling, chewing the pencil he wore behind his ear. I did not speak to him. He did not knock again.

Then he vanished. I was disappointed but also relieved. I had wanted to believe in his impossible idea, but I had also been afraid of the consequences. What would the former plague of teenagers be, beside the crowd drawn by an iron needle threading the sky?

The steel support, featureless and cruelly asymmetrical among my spirals, filled me with hope and regret when I looked at it.

He returned at the end of October in a red pickup truck with a black tarp lashed down over the mound in its bed. I waved to him, he nodded, and that was all.

Throughout the day, the clang and shriek of metal upon metal echoed through the barn. I left water and covered plates of pasta and chicken on the stairs to the roof, and he returned the empty plates to my glass doorstep. He did not pack up and leave at dark, but worked more quietly, with a headlamp. I fell asleep listening to his footsteps and the hissing of sand in the hourglasses around me.

He worked steadfastly through six days and nights. The thump of his work boots overhead made the tuned spiral staircase hum in sympathy. If he rested, I did not know it. Sometimes I went outside to see the spindle rising over the barn. I did not wish to interfere, so I did not climb to the roof, though I longed to see my new staircase taking form. He only left my barn to replenish his mountain of parts, a task that took upwards of an hour. I might have gone up then, I might have looked and touched, but I thought that somehow he would know, and I could not bear him knowing.

I waited. This was harder than waiting for the repairs to the roof, harder than waiting for the architects' plans, far harder than waiting for the assembly of my other seventeen staircases. I lived in constant anticipation.

At last, one evening, there came a knock at the door. His hands were blackened with dirt and oil, his face streaked with the same. His eyes were still and quiet.

"Is it done?" I said.

"It's finished."

"May I see?"

"Please."

The sun was setting through the distant trees. The staircase ran higher than my eyes could follow, so high I grew dizzy looking at it. It might have ended after sixteen stories, or twenty, or thirty, and I would not have known. The black iron glowed copper and bronze in the slanting alchemical sunlight, though night crept up its length.

"When should I start climbing?" I asked.

"When you are ready."

"How long will that take?"

"As I said, when you are ready. Bring food and water, and a warm coat. Maybe blankets. It's getting cold."

"Blankets?"

"There are landings for you to sleep on. You can't see them from here."

I glanced up again, but it was growing dark, and any deviations from the regular spiral were invisible to me.

"Will I see you again?" I said, although I thought I already knew the answer.

He smiled.

The half moon brightened in the sky, spangling the stairs. His footsteps receded down the steps to the fallow earth. The truck stuttered and started. I turned my eyes from the fine filigreed structure in time to see the builder of stairs drive down the dirt road leading to elsewheres, the headlights of his truck flickering through the trees.

The reader of fairy tales will understand when I say that I did not hesitate or question the strange requirement, as one would ordinarily do, for at times there is a certain silver inevitability about our choices that no amount of reasoning can explain. It is an impulse to truth or rightness, felt in the marrow: feed the animals before eating, offer water to the crone.

I packed what food I already had: water, bread, tabbed cans of soup, apples, carrots, peanut butter, cheese. To these I added an armful of blankets and enough sweaters to swell me to the roundness of a drum.

I slept fitfully that night and set off at dawn. My stairs to the sky were conspicuous, and others would soon come to investigate. I did not want to explain myself to the dull and curious. I did not want to delay.

The air was cold and crisp, but I sweated under the layers of wool. After several hours I tugged off my hat and tossed it over the side, watching with pleasure as it tumbled, shrank, and disappeared. Its weight had been slight, but my heart lightened.

I climbed high above the lemniscates of birds, until the scattered houses below me appeared to be tokens from a game. There was no sound but the rushing wind and occasionally the rumble of a distant airplane. Otherwise, I was profoundly alone.

Night came without an end to the stairs, but I reached a curved landing I had not seen from my barn, just wide enough to curl up on. At that rarified altitude, the wind was bitterer than I expected. The iron was bitingly cold. I regretted the excess of spirits that led me to throw away my hat and abandon two blankets on the steps far below. I ate a can of soup and two slices of bread with chattering teeth, thinking that it would be better to eat during the day.

I passed the next seven days in this fashion. The air grew paler, the light thinner. I left my empty cans on the steps, weighed down with apple cores, and tied plastic wrappers around the balusters.

On the seventh day I finished the food I was carrying: the last apple, the last bite of cheese, the last sip of water. At that moment I looked down upon the contracting world and contemplated what I undertook to do. Sophia would miss me, but she would understand. Other than her, there was no one and nothing tying me to the earth.

In some ways this is what I have always wanted.

Soon, I think, I will pass the moon. Each time it swings by, it looks larger, closer, its scarred smile more delicate and more intimate. I wonder if I could have asked the builder of stairs to fix the end of my staircase in the moon. It looks like a friendly place. Too late, now.

I am a little thinner and lighter each day. Sometimes I feel so light that letting go of the balustrade would send me floating upwards, faster and faster, until everything is blue and infinite. But when I drop my hands to my sides, I do not rise. Not yet. So I climb, hour after hour, day after day, losing the clear thread of time in the unbroken repetition of tread and tread. They are stamped with robins, as he promised. The sun comes and goes. The moon waves. I climb.

I am climbing still.

Small Monsters

THE SMALL MONSTER, WHELPED, SLIPPED OUT OF ITS CAUL AND
onto the pebbly floor of the den.

Its emerald scales flexed. Its soft tail swept the earth. The
small monster stretched out its new limbs, shuddering. It
smelled raw white roots and mud and dried ichor.

The den was an egg-shaped void under a hill. A roof of rocks
and matted roots hid the small soft monster and its parent from
the moon's white gaze.

The small monster unstuck each gluey eye and saw the ruby
scales of its parent, whose side heaved with long and labored
breaths. The birthing of monsters is hungry work, a labor of a
week or more. And as the small monster looked upon the world,
still damp from birth, its parent lowered its great golden beak
and bit off a tender limb.

Humming with relief and satisfaction, the parent shifted its
gleaming bulk to the rear of the den and settled down to sleep.

The small monster bled, and bled, and wailed.

LIKE GECKO TAILS and starfish arms, the small monster's lost limb scabbed, healed, and regrew. Its parent left the den and returned with bloodied lumps of deer, bear, rabbit, and hawk. Over time, the small monster sprouted two rows of serried teeth; six hard, ridged horns; and stubby claws.

Occasionally the gold-beaked monster did not return to the den for days, finally dragging in a much-mauled haunch of deer.

Sometimes it returned without anything at all.

Those mornings, when the small monster felt its parent's footfalls through the packed earth, it fled cowering to the steep curved back of the den, though that was of course no hiding place at all. And by noon the small monster would be diminished by a leg or a tail or a bite from its side, too wise and afraid now, as its parent slept, to make a sound.

Though beak, fang, and claw speak more directly, monsters have their own harsh and sibilant language. Now and then the parent spoke, either to itself or in challenge to another monster whose shadow crossed the mouth of the den, and syllable by hiss, the small monster learned.

One morning, after they had devoured the remnants of a mountain lion, the small monster spoke.

Why do you eat me? it said.

Its parent lolled onto one side, spines bristling. Gobbets of meat warmed its belly and weighed it down, and it felt pleasant toward the world and its whelp. **Because I am hungry.**

But why not eat—the small monster took a breath—**your own leg?**

Silly. I am your parent. I birthed you. You are mine.

But it hurts.

It grows back.

And neither said a word more.

IN TIME THE parent waxed gibbous like the moon, growing too ponderous to hunt. It tore off and ate all four of the small monster's limbs over the course of a week, writhing and hissing as it did so, without the slightest sign of enjoyment.

At the end of the week, another, smaller monster was expelled in a pool of foul-smelling birth fluid, and the den rang with three cries of pain, snappishness, and distress.

After that, the small monster learned the trick of being farthest from the den's entrance when their parent returned unfed. It was not as helpless as the smallest monster, and so on most occasions, apart from ill-timed naps, the matter was decided in the small monster's favor.

The snapping, crunching, and sobbing were terrible to hear. The small monster quickly learned not to listen.

WHILE ITS PARENT hunted, the small monster played. In the evenings, starlight washed the opening of the den. The small monster rushed up to the brink of a world that smelled like wilderness and pine forest, from which the small and smallest monsters were both forbidden, then backed away.

When can I go out? the small monster had asked.

Never, came the reply. **You will remain here always. With me.**

While it was not brave enough to disobey, the small monster was clever enough to consider one claw within the den a perfect observance of the law.

Now a damp wind blew over the small monster, smelling of blackberries and yellow-pored boletes. Night birds hooted and sawed in the trees. Deep in the den, the smallest monster whimpered in its sleep.

Something slunk, lithe and stealthy, through the red-berried brush. It sounded larger than the foxes the small monster had seen, less twitchy than the rabbits the foxes hunted. The unseen thing paced back and forth, whuffing, and the small monster went as still as stone.

It was too late. A step, a spring, and then three slitted yellow eyes looked down upon the small monster.

Where the gold-beaked monster was clad in ruby scales, this monster was all tawny, wiry fur.

Poor thing, it said. **Who ate your leg?**

For the small monster had been unlucky not long ago, though the stump had scabbed.

Parent, said the small monster. **But it grows back.**

I remember being small, the tawny thing said. **Every month the tearing teeth.**

Every *week*, the small monster said.

If you came with me, the tawny thing said, **I would not bite you more than once a month. And only if I had to.**

This sounded like heaven to the small monster. It quivered its horns and clattered its scales. Then it paused.

I can't run as fast as you, it said. **With only three legs.**

No matter, the tawny thing said, lowering its head. It mouthed the small monster like a cat with a kitten. Then it tensed its muscles and bounded into the forest.

Its great paws struck the earth with such force that the small monster's teeth clicked against each other. Trees rushed past them, dark and blurred.

By the time they stopped, the stars had dimmed and sunk

into dawn. The forest was gone, and the world smelled new. They were a long way from the den beneath the hill where the smallest monster waited alone.

The tawny thing had scented something; its three yellow eyes grew black and wide. It dropped the small monster and hove into the wheatfields shivering around them, the long stalks pale under the rosy sky.

From the far side of the field came a stifled shout.

A few minutes later, the wheat parted, and the tawny thing dragged out the body of a man. His throat was open, wet, and red. His old, patched clothes ripped easily.

They ate, the steam from the man's entrails wreathing them. The small monster gnawed on knuckles and spat out the little finger bones. The tawny thing crunched the femurs for their marrow. They licked themselves clean of the blood, then went on.

Around them, plains billowed and shook loose their folds of gold. The tawny thing and the small monster did not converse. Their pace was leisurely at first, while the small monster hopped and hobbled on three legs. The tawny thing often carried it. After its fourth leg budded and regrew, though the limb was soft and tender for a time, the small monster kept up as well as it could.

The tawny thing was swift and lethal, and for a long time, as the moon filled and emptied and filled, the small monster kept all its limbs, and ate well. It learned to catch crickets while the tawny thing hunted.

Then one too many deer slipped the tawny thing's jaws. It did not particularly matter why. An old injury in one whip-muscled leg might have flared, or perhaps the canniness of all living beings in autumn had pricked the velvet ears of the deer. Whatever the reason, balked of its prey, the tawny thing bridled and gnashed its teeth. It returned to where the small monster was pouncing at insects.

When the small monster felt the earth shudder, it leapt up to flee, but too slowly.

A moment later, it was lying in its own green ichor, keening.

The tawny thing said, astonished, **You are _delicious_.**

The small monster moaned.

Bones cracked. Emerald scales dropped like leaves. The tawny thing swallowed what had been the small monster's foreleg, snuffled, and curled up to sleep.

You can still walk on three legs, the tawny thing said, yawning. Two of its yellow eyes shut. The third watched the small monster.

From then on, the tawny thing ate of the small monster regularly, finding itself partial to the taste. For fairness—even the small monster admitted this—it took care to leave the small monster with three legs to walk on, though not always a fine and lashing tail.

Bit by bite, though, even that changed.

The tawny thing hunted less frequently. More and more, its three eyes settled upon the small monster, who shrank from the hunger glowing there. Before long the eating was more than monthly.

There was nothing the small monster could do about it besides weeping and raging as the tawny thing slept. With two legs, it could go no distance at all.

No good, said a razor bird in the tree above them. It lashed its three barbed tails and craned its neck. **Better to eat you all at once. Less moaning. Less waste.**

Is that what you'll do? the small monster said, baring its teeth through its tears.

Only if you want, the razor bird said.

No, thank you, the small monster said.

Or, if you like, I could carry you away. For one of your legs and your talkative tongue. For you are heavy, the way is long, and my wings will tire.

You'll take me to your nest, to feed your own small monsters.

The razor bird laughed a red, raspy laugh. **A good idea! If I had them, I would. But I mean a fair bargain.**

Where would you take me?

There is a hollow tree in a distant wood where no monsters go, wormy with beetle grubs and wet with rain. I will leave you there. For a leg and a tongue.

They're yours, the small monster said, resigned.

Faster than thought, the razor bird stooped from the tree, and its claws closed on the small monster. The tawny thing slept mumbling on, even as the small monster's stumps spotted its pelt with ichor.

Have to do something about *that*, the razor bird said. It spread its wings wider than any eagle's, wide enough to blot out the moon.

They flew north until they reached a glacier-fed lake. There, the razor bird dropped the small monster in. Several times it snatched up and dropped the small monster, until the small monster was half drowned but no longer bleeding.

There, said the razor bird. **Let's see them track you now.**

Mountains passed beneath them, then rivers and woods. Stars glistened icily above them. A two-tailed comet shone in the sky.

But the small monster was too cold to notice, hanging mute and miserable from the razor bird's claws.

The wild flight ended with an angled descent through the canopy of an old beech wood. They landed upon a bare white snag.

There, the razor bird said, its crimson eyes bright. **Now open your mouth.**

Payment was settled with merciful swiftness. When that was finished, the razor bird lowered the small monster into the snag's hollow heart, which was barely big enough for its remaining limbs. The wood had gone spongy with insects and rot.

Mind you, the razor bird said, **I am what I am. I know where you are. If I hatch chicks, I'll look where I stashed you. Don't hide here too long.**

It flicked its three tails and soared away.

The snag was far from comfortable. When it rained, the monster licked at the trickles that ran down the wood and drank from the puddle that formed at its feet. For food, it had watery white wriggling grubs. On a day it remembered ever after with pleasure, it caught and ate an incautious squirrel. On that diet more fit for woodpeckers, the small monster's lost limbs returned with painful slowness. Its plump sides slumped, and its glossy scales dulled. But there were no severing teeth or beaks in the snag, apart from its own.

Bud by bone, claws and tail and all, the small monster grew into itself again.

When all its pieces were present, the small monster clambered out of the snag and fell snout-first into the grass.

When it had warmed itself in the sun awhile, motionless as moss, it caught a vole by surprise and devoured it, as well as the beetle the vole had been nibbling on. Then the razor bird's parting words came to mind. The small monster shuddered and headed in the direction of the snag's shadow. It snapped at grasshoppers as it went.

Now and then the small monster crouched behind a tree as something larger snorted and shuffled in the brush. Once, it froze under a whorl of ferns as the three-tailed shadow of a bird passed over. The small monster liked its legs and tail, and it wanted no more of monstrous bargains.

As it scrambled and slid down a slope of scree, the small monster chanced upon a gashed and broken thing. Deep gouges in its side showed the white of bone. Its pointed snout lolled in a pool of gore.

One scratched silver eye opened.

Please, the rat-nosed thing said. **Come closer.**

The small monster sat back on its haunches and sized up the battered bulk of the thing. Among the feathery grasses at the bottom of the slope, it caught a speckled frog, which it brought back and dropped near—but not too near—the creature's snout.

The rat-nosed thing licked up the frog and swallowed it, then shut its eyes. Its breathing was shallow.

In the meadows around them, the small monster searched for slithering, skittering creatures, garter snakes and earthworms, thrush eggs and wrens, to feed both itself and the broken monster.

Time trickled past, and the wounds on the rat-nosed thing scabbed. Its scarred eyes followed the small monster.

One day, as the small monster left a lizard by its snout, the rat-nosed thing lunged.

Why? the small monster cried, scrabbling backward, bleeding.

The rat-nosed thing made wet, happy noises. **Better than worms and slugs and grubs.**

Flinching with pain, the small monster fled. Behind it, claws scraped stone as the rat-nosed thing stood. It snuffed the ground and chuckled like boulders breaking. At this, the small monster turned and saw that its own dribbling ichor had painted a path.

Down that path, snout to earth, the rat-nosed thing hunted.

The small monster lashed its tail. Though the wound in its side was a white-hot knife, it scaled the nearest fir and crept out upon a bough. And as the rat-nosed thing came sniffling beneath, the small monster let go and fell.

Its claws clamped onto its pursuer's skull. And as the rat-nosed thing swung its head and shrilled, the small monster bit out one silver eye and slit the jelly of the other. Then it leapt down and tore at the taut, thin skin where the rat-nosed thing's wounds had barely healed. The small monster scratched until the tender flesh parted and showed again the stark white bones. It bit and squirmed into the rat-nosed thing, crawling inside the warm, plush cage of its ribs.

The small monster ate what it found there: bitter, bilious, savory, sweet.

When it had swallowed most of the rat-nosed thing, enough to push apart the ribs and emerge, there was a new sharpness to its face and a silver tinge to its scales.

It kicked a scatter of gravel over the raw red bones and prowled on, wary but unafraid.

A strange scent blew across the small monster's way, one it had never smelled before, and it turned and went into the wind. Days and nights it chased the scent, through forest and scrub, over salt marsh and fen, until the small monster stood at the edge of the sea.

Brown waves roared like dragons along the shore. The small monster lowered its head to drink and found that the water was bitter, and burned.

I see, the small monster said. **This is the end of the world.**

It crouched in the surf and stared at the sharp straight limit of the sea.

After a while, it noticed a little clawed creature beside it, no bigger than one of the small monster's teeth. Its tiny claws worked upon a shard of sea glass.

What are you doing? the small monster said.

Adding to you, the clawed creature said. **Not that you aren't already excellent. But anyone can be improved.**

Several flowery tufts sprouted from the creature's shell. Every now and then the creature tickled one of them and applied an invisibly slight secretion to the sea glass it was pressing against the small monster's scale.

At length it rested, sighing in satisfaction.

Ah, it said. **Art!**

Sorry?

Do forgive me. What I should ask is: Do you like what I've done?

The small monster studied the addition to its side.

You disapprove. I can remove it! the clawed creature said. It reached for the shard.

Don't.

Then will you let me add more?

If that's what you want, the small monster said.

The tide whisked in, rolling a fat seal onto the shore. The small monster took a few neat bites, then offered some to the laboring creature.

In a minute—in a minute—

By the time the tide whispered out, the small monster had been adorned with six chips of sea glass, blue and brown.

Now I have earned my supper, the clawed creature declared, extending its pincers to receive a morsel of seal. It ate with sounds of satisfaction. Every so often, it passed a crumb to the tufts on its back, which grasped hungrily at the flecks of food.

What are they? the small monster asked.

Anemones, the clawed creature said. **Some of the sea's more stinging critics. They keep me honest. And they produce a good glue.**

A seagull stooped at the seal carcass. The small monster broke its neck with a blow.

Wish I could do that, the clawed creature said.

Eat, the small monster said. **You'll be big enough, one day.**

When the small monster was thirsty, it went inland for water. When it was hungry, it dove for fish and seals. But most of the time it sat still and watched, puzzled, as the clawed creature embellished its scales.

Gradually, the small monster's gleaming green mail was encased in glass, agate, and mother-of-pearl.

Beautiful, the clawed creature said. Sunlight glowed in the small monster's new shell. **Exquisite. Exceptional. If I do say so myself.**

The anemones waved their fronds in lazy assent.

Are you done? the small monster said.

For a moment. Beauty must be appreciated. And then!

It's not over?

Never. Life is growth; art must follow. Why, I myself have shed two shells since I started this work! But for the present, I shall scuttle along the beach and search for my next stroke of inspiration.

The small monster did not understand much of what its companion said. Nevertheless, it escorted the clawed creature on its muttering constitutionals, waiting as a striped pebble or shapely stick held it rapt. Any seagull that swooped, thinking it had found an inattentive meal, died in a spray of bloody feathers. The clawed creature hardly noticed.

Sometimes it crept up the small monster's flank, perched upon a horn, and confessed its doubts.

What if it never comes, the next idea? What then? What if my great works lie behind me?

The small monster made reassuring noises, but did not know what else to do, for its life had been biting and bleeding, not art.

One night, the wind rose. The air prickled and itched. Lightning cracked the violet sky. In one sheeting flash, the small monster thought it saw a forest upon the sea.

I have it! the clawed creature shouted into the small monster's ear. **Quick, swim!**

The small monster plunged into the ocean. Though towering waves spun and flung them about, once they dove deep, the water gentled. Soon they reached the broad black hull of the ship, whose masts had looked like trees from the shore.

Wait, the clawed creature said, clinging to the small monster.

They did not wait long. A wave tossed the ship and smashed it down. The hull split neatly into halves. Small bodies tumbled out of it, as well as timbers and chests and drowning sheep. Here and there a broken chest poured a glittering of gold.

That, the clawed creature said. **I want *that*.**

The small monster surfaced, gasped, and dove again. It caught four coins in its claws and one in its teeth, marked where the rest sank into darkness, and swam back to shore.

Rain lanced down as the small monster hauled itself out of the water.

I hope they're worth it, the small monster said.

They will be, the clawed creature said. **You'll see.**

They huddled together under a dripping pine until the storm blew itself to shreds. A sickly dawn shone in the sky.

Pieces of the ship started drifting ashore, as did a fine banquet of brined sailor and sheep.

I suppose you want more of those round objects, the small monster said.

The clawed creature said, **If you don't mind.**

Day after day, by dint of much swimming, the small monster amassed a heap of gold.

What now? the small monster said.

Now, I work.

Though each golden coin was as large as its body, and so heavy it asked the small monster to hold them in place, the clawed creature labored without rest or food. Every so often, the small monster tried to coax it into eating.

The art is all! the clawed creature said, wrestling with its piece of gold.

Over the small monster's shell of glass and nacre, which had split and been mended as the small monster grew, the clawed creature affixed escudo and pistole. Sunlight danced on their faces and shook bright sequins across the sand.

There, the clawed creature said. **Magnificent. You're a treasure. Worth your weight in gold.**

Stretching, the small monster heard its golden scales clink.

Let them bite me now, it said.

Eh? Pass the fish.

After a day or two of dazzlement, in which the small monster flung sunlight every which way, briefly blinding a number of birds, it covered itself in seaweed at the clawed creature's insistence, until not a glint of its golden armor could be seen.

More prudent that way, the clawed creature said.

THE SMALL MONSTER ate, grew, fetched whatever shell or skull the clawed creature desired, and watched the ebb and flow of the tide. Despite gusts, gales, storms, and heaving waves, that stretch of seashore was the most peaceful place the small monster had known.

It mentioned as much to the clawed creature.

Nothing lasts, the clawed creature said, as it placed stones in a pleasing pattern on the sand. **Neither good nor bad. But one must always enjoy the good.**

THAT PEACE ENDED abruptly on a clear afternoon.

The wind was crisp and blowing off the sea. The sigh of the waves curling in and out hid for a time the sounds of approach. The clawed creature was carving a sand dollar into layers of lace, and the small monster, admiring, did not hear. Only when sand trickled in rivulets down the dune above them did the small monster lift its eyes and see.

Another monster crouched at the top of the dune. It also boasted a crown of horns, though its sides were stippled with ruby spots.

Uh-oh, the clawed creature said. **Excuse me.**

It tucked itself into its shell. The next wave that foamed in carried it off.

What do you want? the small monster asked.

You.

Do I know you? the small monster said. Then it shook itself from horns to tail in surprise, for it recognized the other monster.

As well as your own blood, the smallest monster said. **I've tracked you through mountains and forests and fields. And now I shall eat you.**

Why?

You owe me. The smallest monster dug its red, red claws into the soft white side of the dune.

Then it sprang.

The small monster turned sideways, and its sibling crashed into its seaweed-draped mail. Claws clacked on gold; a fang shattered. The smallest monster rolled and rose, snarling.

If you're hungry, the small monster said, **these waters have squid and dogfish in them.**

I'm not here for *fish*, its sibling said.

The small monster met the next charge with one glass-and-gold shoulder.

No.

Again its sibling found footing and lunged. Again the small monster knocked it aside.

The smallest monster howled. **Lie down and let me tear your throat out!**

No.

Let me bite you and drink your ichor!

No.

While they fought, shreds of kelp fell from the small monster, until it shone with uncovered gold. The smallest monster champed its needle teeth and struck, but it did no harm. As it reared to strike again, the small monster bowled its sibling onto its back.

The smallest monster writhed upon the sand. **I've given up so much for you!**

I'm sorry, the small monster said. **Go away.**

You think you're so *special*, its sibling said. **But I know you!**

The smallest monster splayed its horns, spat, and padded off. Its tail scribbled arabesques in the sand.

The small monster watched the smallest monster go, until it was too far to see.

After some time, it felt a slight itching on the side of its neck. This was the clawed creature, climbing to the small monster's horns. From that perch, it surveyed the aftermath.

You've lost some coins, the clawed creature said. **I'll fix them. Hold still.**

The small monster waited for it to cement the loosened coins back into place. Then, setting the clawed creature on its back, the small monster waded into deeper water and swam in the opposite direction from its sibling.

For hours it swam, long after the sky reddened and darkened, until a rising tide carried them ashore. The small monster rested its chin on the cold wet sand.

This should be far enough, the clawed creature said. **Sleep. I'll pinch if I hear anything.**

The small monster slept, dreaming of pursuit, and kicked the sand and the clawed creature in its sleep. Its tail flicked and twitched at the cry of a seal.

When it awoke, to screeching seabirds, it was hardly rested.

What is peace, after all, the clawed creature said, **if not a moment of repose. A breath between storms. Most importantly, an opportunity for art.**

The small monster sharpened its claws on a spar.

The clawed creature added, as an afterthought, **I've heard that bad news comes in threes.**

It was a strange, uncertain time. The small monster swam farther south every night, staying nowhere for long. Here and there it startled a family of seals, a cormorant drying its wings against the wind, or a solitary sea lion sunning itself. The small monster ate them carefully, digging up the bloody sand and giving the bones to the sea.

Unlike the small monster, the clawed creature evinced no anxiousness, though it acquired another two anemones. Five times now, the clawed creature had exchanged its home for sequentially larger shells. Each time, it cajoled its critics into relocating as well.

What do they say? the small monster asked. **About your art?**

Sometimes they say: Good enough.

Other times?

You're a hack who couldn't draw a straight line with a sea pen and swordfish.

Which one? the small monster said, eyeing the tufts on its shell. I'll eat it for you.

The anemones waved their stinging petals in threat.

Sometimes they're helpful. They'll say: It's crooked. Left corner's low.

Where did you find them?

Tidepools are full of them. These days, everyone's a critic. The clawed creature sighed. Hard to find ones with discernment, though. No one values an arts curriculum.

Have you gone far into the sea?

The clawed creature waved vaguely. A bit. Maybe. They're discussing the merits of formal education. . . .

Are there sea monsters?

The clawed creature did not respond, lost in reverie, or else an absorbing conversation. The small monster waited for a polite interval, then huffed its seal-smelling breath over the flowery shell. Indignant, the anemones snapped shut.

Ah, sea monsters. Deep down, yes. Deeper than you'll ever go, where the water presses with the weight of a mountain. I met vast and insatiable appetites there. Hungry lights in the dark. A bristling of teeth. I should have been a pair of ragged claws. . . .

The small monster said, You were not afraid of me.

The clawed creature patted the small monster.

I was inspired. I saw a canvas for my art!

So they will not hunt me from the sea.

Never, the clawed creature said. They live in the deepest waters.

Then I will watch the woods, the small monster said.

SINCE THE DAY the smallest monster had found them, one particular battle seemed inevitable. When at last a familiar form emerged from the trees, the small monster felt the tightness in its chest unspool, loop after loop unwinding into something loose and useful.

You should leave, it told the clawed creature. **To be safe.**

I won't go far, the clawed creature said.

That's what you think.

As delicately as it could, the small monster picked up the clawed creature in its teeth, then hurled it seaward.

At the dappled edge of the woods, where the sand began, the small monster's gold-beaked parent set its talons, frilled, and roared.

The small monster sat at the shifting verge of the sea, with an infinitude of unknown monsters at its back and one it knew well in front of it. The small monster took a breath of salt air. Then it roared in reply, and the waves roared with it.

You are _mine_, the gold-beaked monster said.

I am not.

Who fed you meat while you mewled? Who carved up lions and brought down falcons for you?

Who fed on me when the hunt went ill?

The parent's scale-sheathed shoulders trembled and chimed. It had grown lean and rangy in the small monster's absence. **Who birthed you? Who gave you life and breath?**

You, the small monster said. **Then you took.**

I've come for what belongs to me.

I am nobody's.

I was kind to you!

The gold-beaked monster loped across the sand.

Once more, the small monster turned to take the blow. Its parent's talons skidded over gold.

Tricks, it hissed. **You forget. I shelled turtles and sucked out the flesh for you.**

With its second blow, it sent a king's ransom flying.

With the third, it broke glass and scale and skin.

The small monster hunched down. It smelled ichor and roots and damp earth again.

Why?

I bore you to feed me when I am old.

The hooked beak dug into the small monster's side, ripping and swallowing. The small monster shrieked, as it had shrieked before, when it was helpless and wriggling in the den under the hill.

But the sound of its shriek was different now, deeper and louder than the sounds a small thing might make.

For the small monster was no longer small.

It felt its strength and cunning then, its size and power and cruelty. It whirled upon the gold-beaked monster.

No. I will not. Never again.

Talons flashing, the gold-beaked monster flew at the no-longer-small monster and was promptly tossed on its crown of horns. Foam and ichor flecked the parent's red sides as it rose.

They clashed, the wet sand churning beneath them, and the no-longer-small monster threw its parent a second time.

You're nothing, the gold-beaked monster said. **What good is your life? Give me it. It's mine.**

They circled each other on the tidal zone. The no-longer-small monster watched the sand sink under its parent's feet, and saw how each step began with a slight stumble. And when the gold-beaked monster struck, swift as an eel, it was hooked and flipped.

The no-longer-small monster fell upon the gold-beaked monster, gouging and goring. It tasted its parent's ichor and flesh.

Then the no-longer-small monster stepped back.

As the gold-beaked monster righted itself, ribboned skin trailing in the tide, ichor dropping like green rain, it keened and cringed.

It'll grow back, the no-longer-small monster said. **Now leave.**

The gold-beaked monster retreated, limping. When it reached the woods, it glared hunger and hatred over its shoulder. Then it was gone.

Fog rolled in like a dream, snagging in the bristled tops of the trees, smudging distance and detail.

The clawed creature said from the once-small monster's head: **Family can be difficult.**

Says someone who started as plankton.

Hey! My worst critics live upstairs.

The air was wet and white, and the monster's laughter stirred up eddies in it. They made a brave and merry island in the thick nothingness.

Then they heard the sound of some tremendous thing breaching and collapsing back into the sea.

O, wonder, the clawed creature said to itself.

Again came the fathomless, unfathomable sound.

The fog was too dense to see what moved in the dark and swirling waters offshore.

They listened in silence to the great thing leaping: a rush of water, a crash. Then there was a leap without end. They strained to hear the missing sound.

Out of the wisping fog swam a vastness. Its wings undulated in an invisible current. Its mouth, broad enough to swallow the once-small monster, sucked thirstily at the empty air. It steered itself in an arc with a whip of a tail.

As it drifted overhead, two large black eyes looked down, full of ancient indifference.

A very long time later—or so it seemed to the once-small monster, who had held its breath—they heard the distant boom of the vast winged thing returning to the sea.

Sea monster? the once-small monster said.

Sea monster, the clawed creature said, clasping its own claws.

The world is stranger than I thought.

It always is.

By the time the third trouble came sniffing about, the once-small monster was prepared. The clawed creature had layered it with glass and nacre, then with gold, and finally with bones plucked from a great fish that had washed up dead. The bones curved up the small monster's sides and made a double row of spines.

In those three layers of armor, the once-small monster cut an extraordinary figure. The wolfish, tawny thing that slunk between the trees did not recognize its quarry. It snapped its jaws, perplexed.

Then the sea wind brought the scent of the once-small monster to the woods. The tawny thing, whose hide was now peppered with gray, threw back its head and bayed in greeting.

Old friend, the tawny thing said. **It's been too long.**

You have terrible taste in friends, the clawed creature

said. It slipped from the once-small monster's shoulder into the sea.

This shore is mine, the once-small monster said. **You may not hunt here.**

For as long as this shore is yours, I'll not hunt here, the tawny thing agreed.

Are you passing through?

Following a trail, the tawny thing said, laughing softly, as if it had told a great joke. **Three trails, in fact. All running and jumbled together.**

Why do you laugh?

Because if the three had lived peaceably, in this place of plumpest bears and deer—if they offered battle with three sets of claws, beak, and teeth—I'd never have won.

Its purple tongue danced. There were green stains and spatters on the tawny fur.

Contrariwise, the tawny thing said, **even a bear could bring down a wounded and brokenhearted beast. For me, the matter was simpler still.**

You let me live, the once-small monster said. **When I was small.**

Small and obedient. I think you are neither now.

So you've come here to fight.

I came here to *finish*, the tawny thing said. **To eat a monster and its children whole, beak, bones, tendons, talons—it staggers the mind. Fat as pigeons, I'll be. I'll dig a den to overwinter, and in the spring I'll whelp my own pups.**

Am I the last?

You'd find their bones in the woods, if you looked. If I let you. But I won't.

The tawny thing danced before the once-small monster. Its eyes were fixed on the once-small monster's throat.

Run, it said. **Let me chase you, catch you, and drag you down.**

The once-small monster neither answered nor ran.

Stubborn, every one of you, the tawny thing sighed.

It seized one of the once-small monster's whalebones and shook it until the bone cracked from its carapace. The tawny thing cast it onto the sand.

Hissing, the once-small monster slashed at the tawny thing's ankles and came away with clumps of hair.

Better, the tawny thing said, breaking off another whalebone. **I remember when you had no fight at all. You'd lie in the dirt and cry. Poor little fool.**

Something like thunder rumbled in the once-small monster's chest. It met the tawny thing mid-leap. Then each fell away.

A gash in the tawny thing's neck beaded red and purulent gold.

The tawny thing purred approval. Then it launched itself again at the once-small monster. The two of them tumbled over and over, grappling. Gold coins scattered across the sand, followed by globs of sea glass and shell. Neat and quick as a gull cracking the valves of a clam, the tawny thing had the once-small monster stripped of its armor, panting and pinned under the heavy paws.

Laughing, its three eyes never looking away, the tawny thing bent its head and gnawed the once-small monster's leg. Clear to the bone its teeth tore and its tongue licked.

As delicious as I recall.

A wave swept in, salting the wound. The once-small monster bellowed and belled. As the sand beneath them liquified, the once-small monster kicked itself free. It stumbled backward into the water, falling, crawling, until each incoming swell broke over its head.

The tawny thing paddled after.

Don't go farther, it said. **Dragging your body ashore will be—well, a drag.**

Though it gasped and gagged with agony, the once-small monster swam on.

When the tawny thing neared, its countenance skull-like under wet fur—when not one of its deadly paws touched bottom—the once-small monster sucked in a breath, clamped its teeth into the tawny thing's neck, and sank.

The tawny thing sank with it.

A silver howl shook out of the tawny thing's mouth. It thrashed in the green water, slicing the small monster open. Everywhere it touched, it carved grievous wounds.

At long last, its limbs slackened.

The once-small monster released it. Its three eyes empty, its terrible jaws agape, the tawny thing drifted down to the seabed. Quick, ravenous shapes swam after it.

Afterward, the once-small monster could not recall how it reached the shore, whether the waves left it broken among driftwood and kelp, or whether it swam with three legs through the obliterating pain.

When the once-small monster opened its eyes, some time later, the clawed thing was scuttling back and forth on the sand. It waved a gold escudo like a shield. One after another, seagulls dove at the once-small monster, but their beaks pinged off of the interposed coin.

Graverobbers! the clawed creature shouted. **Vandals! Philistines! Desecrators of art! Vulgar, disrespectful fowl!**

The once-small monster stirred, groaning, and the seagulls screamed disappointment and fled.

About time, the clawed creature said. **I wasn't sure. . . . You present quite the conservation challenge.**

It'll grow back, the once-small monster said, its voice fainter than the echo in a shell.

If you say so.

For a long time, the once-small monster knew pain in all its colors and conjurings. First it was forked and lancing like lightning. Later it was brown and fogged.

Though the once-small monster was hardly a stranger to pain, this time it had a comforter. And so this pain was not as unbearable as the pain in the den, though it nevertheless was grim and obscene and lasted for an eternity.

Little by little, what had been lost turned soft and silver and regrew.

Eventually, the tawny thing washed ashore. Fish had dined on its eyes and the sea-rotted pulp of its body, and flies clustered and buzzed around the corpse.

The once-small monster retreated to the berried woods to escape the flies and the gaseous reek.

Gulls thronged upon the corpse in a noisy white shroud, tearing and shrieking. They dispersed, shrieking louder, as a three-tailed shadow swept across the sand. From a safe distance, they scolded the interloper, who sat and stripped the carcass clean.

The razor bird paused in the middle of its gorging. Its red gaze found the once-small monster where it rested on moss among the cinnamon ferns.

I think you've learned, the razor bird said.

What did I learn? the once-small monster said.

To be difficult to swallow.

Nothing was left on the bones when the razor bird finished. It cocked its eye at the once-small monster.

You were lucky. I was hungry.

You came looking for me.

And now I am fed. The razor bird shook its feathers, which rasped as they settled into place. **Be spiny and sharp, if you can't be quick.**

And it flew off.

THE SEASONS CHANGED, and changed again. The once-small monster, with the clawed creature's assistance, grew spiny, sharp, hard, and beautiful.

The clawed creature grew larger and older than any of its kind had a right to be, or so it informed the once-small monster. Defended from marauding gulls, it had increased in size and shell until its present house, dredged from the bottom of the sea, was approximately the size of the once-small monster's head. And one morning, as the clawed creature sorted agates, the once-small monster saw it clearly, in all its jointed and studded detail.

You're monstrous, like me, the once-small monster said, surprised.

Nonsense, the clawed creature said. **You're like *me*.**

The once-small monster snorted. **I've made nothing.**

A life is not nothing.

I've been bitten to the bone and hounded to the edge of the world. I've been dinner. I've been breakfast. An artist, never.

None of us can change what has happened to us, the clawed creature said. **But if we are lucky, we live. If we are lucky, we do not lose more than we can afford. Much regrows. Claws, tail, teeth, even the vaporous stuff the poets call soul. And bitter experience provides material for art. Ask a shipwreck. Ask an oyster.**

Even so . . .

Tell me, the clawed creature said. **What do you want to create?**

The once-small monster thought. It thought while the tide washed in and out, while the sun rose and set, while barnacles stuck out their pointed tongues and whispered in the absence of the tide.

At last the once-small monster said: **An island. With moss, trees, and small, scuttling things. With crevices and caves for the scuttling things.**

Then you shall create an island, the clawed creature said.

Despite having neither instruction nor prior knowledge, the once-small monster conceived of a plan. It wrested boulders from forest soil and sand and pushed them out to sea with the tide. Stone by stone it worked, slow and purposeful. Soon it had piled up enough rocks underwater that the current could no longer shift them singly away.

Between the boulders, the clawed creature sowed a garden of kelp, bladderwrack, barnacles, and mussels, until the hollow places were filled, and the rocks were knitted and cemented together.

The labor was long and strenuous, and also curiously satisfying.

Years passed before the stony stack was high enough that the highest wave did not douse its flattish top. The once-small monster rested on the stack's summit for a night and a day, watching the stars in their silver parade, then the clouds in their brightening and flaming. It felt the weariness of work well done.

The next morning, the once-small monster began to carry soil by the mouthful to the top of the stack. The clawed thing ferried pinecones, nuts, and dandelion clocks across the water on the monster's horns.

They did not stop when the first seeds put forth their plumules, but continued to lengthen, enlarge, and fortify the stack. In the course of their work, the once-small monster collected three heaps of bleached, bare, monstrous bones from the woods and shore and laid them in stones and roots and soil.

Fish of a thousand colors hid in the seaweed that waved at the base of the stack. Their glittering schools parted as the monster swam by.

One evening, as the two of them sat on the seashore, the clawed creature said: **What work shall we do tomorrow?**

The once-small monster gazed on their rich and cakelike sea stack. The soft green tips of a fifth year's growth were just visible at the tops of the spindly trees.

It is done, the once-small monster said.

Was it worthwhile?

Yes.

Will you rest?

One day and one night, the once-small monster said.

Then what will you do?

See how the waves break like flocked birds against our stack. Look at the water-light that flickers on the underside of the stones. I shall build another island, the once-small monster said. **And another. Until we have made a quietness between the wilds and the deep.**

Let me help, the clawed creature said, as the not-small, not-a-monster knew it would.

I could not do it otherwise.

Acknowledgments

Thanks as ever to my agent Markus Hoffmann, the wisest consigliere a writer could hope for.

Liz Gorinsky, whose courage and vision paved a way for me, first accepted this collection for Erewhon. Sarah Guan cut, shaped, and polished the book, and *Jewel Box* shines brighter for her care. Leah Marsh caught and corrected a hundred mistakes and filled the book's interior with beauty. With a magician's skill and thoughtfulness, Martin Cahill made it visible in the world. My thanks to the entire team at Erewhon for bringing the book to life.

I am grateful to the editors who first accepted many of these stories for their publications, especially Neil Clarke, Jonathan Strahan, and Brian Merchant and Claire L. Evans. Year after year their labor yields a rich and living garden of short fiction where one might have expected desert, and we are all better for it.

Workshop instructors in whose classrooms some of these stories were written, six of them teaching at Clarion West in 2013, include Ellen Datlow, Samuel R. Delaney, Neil Gaiman, Elizabeth Hand, Joe Hill, Valzhyna Mort Hutchinson, Margo Lanagan, and Colson Whitehead. My writing has benefited from their instruction.

Past and present friends, classmates, and acquaintances who read at least one of the included stories prior to publication include Maria Aristova, Anatoly Belilovsky, Ben Chang, Elizabeth Chen, Jennifer Dannals, Huw Evans, Derek Gideon, Allison Green, Caitlin Horrocks, Laura Lebow, Alma Garcia de Lilla, Polly Guo, Stacy Guo, Tod McCoy, Donna Miscolta, Jennifer D. Munro, Mari Ness, Jackson Popkin, Cat Rambo, Nisi Shawl, Rashida J. Smith, Rachel Sobel, Mary Margaret Stevens, and my fellow students at Clarion West, especially Helena Bell, Vince Haig, Nicole Idar, Usman T. Malik, Shannon Peavey, Nick Salestrom, and Neon Yang, who suffered first drafts from me long after the workshop was over.

People who each helped with specific research on a story include Karen Burnham, Aisha Onsando, Alisa Tao, and Ian Wong.

Finally, I thank Rick Wilber, Sheila Williams, Ken Liu, Richard K. Weems, Roberta Clipper Sethi, Cat Doty, Peter Murphy, and Diana Goetsch for the early and critical encouragement. I have not forgotten.

My records of the twelve-year span over which these stories appeared are appallingly disorganized. Any omissions above are accidental. Other people have extended kindnesses for stories not included in this collection; I hope to name them with thanks in a future volume.

Staff Credits

Thank you for reading this title from Erewhon Books, publishing books that embrace the liminal and unclassifiable and championing the unusual, the uncanny, and the hard-to-define.

We are proud of the team behind *Jewel Box: Stories* by E. Lily Yu.

Sarah Guan, Publisher
Diana Pho, Executive Editor
Viengsamai Fetters, Editorial Assistant

Martin Cahill, Marketing and Publicity Manager
Kasie Griffitts, Sales Associate

Cassandra Farrin, Director of Publishing and Production
Leah Marsh, Production Editor
Kelsy Thompson, Production Editor
Su-Yee Lin, Copyeditor
Rachel Kowal, Proofreader

Samira Iravani, Art Director
Christine Kim, Cover Artist

Learn more about Erewhon Books and our authors at erewhonbooks.com.

Twitter: @erewhonbooks
Instagram: @erewhonbooks
Facebook: @ErewhonBooks